He was a sure th

Ryan let out a nervous [...]
herself.

Cade raised an eyebrow. "What's the joke? All I said was that I take what I do seriously. I deal with people who have a certain set of needs and I come in and make sure they get satisfied. It seems pretty worthwhile to me."

"So you leave satisfied customers behind you?" She lost a beat watching him.

"I do my best. So what do you do, when you're not hanging around hotel lobbies?" he asked innocently.

"Oh, I spin yarns."

"Oh, yeah? Tell me a good story."

When Ryan was a child, her family vacationed near a lake in Maine every summer. In early June, the water was still icy cold and there were two ways to approach it: stepping in an inch at a time, or running and jumping in, taking the shock all at once. Ryan had always jumped.

"Let's go upstairs and I will."

"Whatever you say, darlin'." Cade rose and tugged her to her feet. "I'm all yours."

Dear Reader,

Being a romance writer has been a longtime dream for me. I'm thrilled that it's come true with the publication of *My Sexiest Mistake,* my first book for Harlequin's new Blaze line. I like my sex hot and my writing even hotter, so when I had gorgeous but stubborn Ryan meet her match in sexy hunk Cade, it was easy to steam up the pages. Let the two of them take you on a rollicking ride that starts with mistaken identity and turns into a red-hot love affair that's true-blue beneath.

Blaze is a line designed to appeal to women who demand more from their relationships and their reading—more steam, more tension, more romance. I'd love to hear what you think of Blaze, and of Ryan and Cade's tale. Write me at kristinhardy@earthlink.net, or visit www.kristinhardy.com for contests, e-mail chats between characters in *My Sexiest Mistake* and Blaze-ing excerpts from upcoming books.

Enjoy!

Kristin Hardy

P.S. Don't forget to check out tryblaze.com!

MY SEXIEST MISTAKE

Kristin Hardy

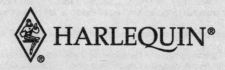

HARLEQUIN®

TORONTO • NEW YORK • LONDON
AMSTERDAM • PARIS • SYDNEY • HAMBURG
STOCKHOLM • ATHENS • TOKYO • MILAN • MADRID
PRAGUE • WARSAW • BUDAPEST • AUCKLAND

To my beloved Stephen
Te adoro, amor

ISBN 0-373-79048-1

MY SEXIEST MISTAKE

Visit us at www.eHarlequin.com

Printed in U.S.A.

1

"ARE THEY HAVING SEX YET?"

Ryan Donnelly jumped for the button that transferred the call from speakerphone to handset. In the stodgy offices of Beckman Markham Corporate Training, the last thing she needed was for her boss to hear a caller talking about sex. She blinked at the gravelly voice barking out of the phone. "Not even a hello today. You must be in a good mood, Helene."

"Well are they?" her agent persisted.

"You know the plot line calls for a love scene in chapter five." Ryan sounded evasive even to herself.

"Oh my god, you still haven't done it."

"I'm going to get to it." Ryan strove to seem placating rather than panicked.

"Get to it? Your final manuscript is due in exactly fifteen days. You'd postpone my trip to the E.R. for hypertension and heart failure if you could be a little more specific."

Ryan looked uneasily around her office. "Helene, I've got a class to teach in ten minutes. Can't we talk about this later?"

"Do I need to remind you what's at stake, here?" Ryan could picture the redhead sitting at her speakerphone, the cigarette in her hand sending a thin ribbon of smoke to the ceiling. "A legal contract. The other three books in the series. Your early retirement from corporate training. Your reputation. My reputation, and—not to be overlooked—my commission. You know I've had my eye on that hot tub."

"Helene, I'm trying."

"For heaven's sake, Ryan, the hard part is done. You've got most of the book written. All you have to do is get them between the sheets for a little nooky."

"A *lot* of nooky, Helene." Ten to fifteen pages, last time she'd checked. Ryan tried to stem the rising tide of anxiety. "The scene doesn't want to come out. I keep trying, but I just can't write it. Oh, why didn't you let me stay in sweets?" Her voice rose in a wail of frustration.

"Let you stay in sweets? I should be beaten for letting you stay in sweets as long as I did," Helene rasped, as a crack in the background signaled she was opening one of her ever-present Diet Cokes. "Eight of them, two awards. You're the best thing out there. You should be writing single-title books, but I can't get you there because everybody wants to see how you'll handle the sex. It was a miracle I managed to get them to consider a multibook deal," she grumbled.

For the past four years Ryan had been happily writing sweets in her spare time, short, snappy romances with nothing more provocative than a lip lock or two. Each time she sold a book she thought that this time, finally, she might be able to quit the day job she loathed and write full-time, but it never quite happened that way. She felt a distinct pang of longing for each of her eight books, lovely little tales that required nothing explicit, just some impure thoughts and a few kisses. Kissing she could do. Kissing she *had* done, with her own lips. At least, oh, well, half a dozen times, anyway. Sex was largely a black hole to her, enlivened by one memorably unfortunate outing.

Write what you know, she'd learned in her courses at Brown. Unfortunately, sex was something she didn't know. One fact was indisputable, though—the hook of the book she had sold was supposed to be hot sex between the hero and the heroine. All she had to do was finish the book, get the contract, and write full-time. If she screwed it up, though, there was no telling how long she'd be condemned to teach corporate management classes.

Helene heaved a long-suffering sigh down the phone. "Ryan, you have to do this. Now is not the time to get writer's block. Do you at least have a draft?"

Ryan thought of the miserable paragraph that she'd wrung out the night before. Normally, her prose galloped onto the screen. Okay, well, there were times it trotted and times it downright dragged its feet, but it at least came.

If only her characters could.

Helene decoded her noncommittal *humph* for the negative that it was. "Come on, kid, just pour yourself a glass of wine and think about the last time you had really hot, sweaty sex. You do remember sex, right?"

Ryan made a vague noise and Helene's voice sharpened. "How long has it been since you've slept with someone, anyway?"

"Oh, a while," she answered evasively, nervously straightening a stack of files on her desk.

"How long?"

"Um, eight years. Or so." Ryan's voice sounded thin even to her own ears.

"Eight years?" Helene's voice rose incredulously. "Since you were twenty-one? Eight *years?*"

"A little less," Ryan said defensively. "I've been busy..." her voice trailed off.

"Ryan. Honey. You're gorgeous. You're in the prime of your life. What are you waiting for?"

"I just haven't had too much luck in the dating department."

"You've been hiding away teaching Quark classes. No wonder you can't write about sex. You probably don't even remember what it's like. Sweetheart, we need to find you a man," Helene said decisively.

Ryan's eyes narrowed. ''Helene, you are not going to set me up with a sex partner.''

''Ryan, you're writing a Private Moments romance. You don't just need some Joe to have sex with, you need a sex *god.*''

''Helene, give me a break. It will be fine, really. I'm a novelist. Stephen King didn't need to have a demonically possessed car to write *Christine*. I don't need a sex god. I can handle it.''

''You need inspiration.''

''Helene!'' Ryan's voice vibrated with frustration. She took a deep breath. ''I have to go. I'm late for my class.''

''What are you teaching?''

''Conflict resolution for managers.''

''That won't help you with hot, sweaty—''

''Helene.'' The line went silent. ''Thank you. Now, I have to go to class,'' Ryan continued, enunciating carefully. ''I'll work on the scene this weekend and I'll call you next week.''

''I've already picked out the hot tub,'' Helene threw in. ''Just in case you're worried about me.''

''Goodbye, Helene.''

WRAPPING HER CHENILLE bathrobe around her, Ryan stared at the mercilessly blank screen of her computer in the fading light of evening. Candles winked around the room and Frank Sinatra crooned quietly in the background. Her silk camisole slid over her skin. A half finished glass of wine sat at her elbow, forgotten, and incense perfumed the air. ''Set the mood,'' she muttered, pushing her tumble of dark hair back over her shoulders. ''Fat lot of good that does me.''

Six years before, the plan had been clear—get a master's degree and teach English at some tony upstate prep school. Unfortunately, several hundred other Ivy Leaguers had had the same idea, she discovered on graduating. Her temporary—she thought—sojourn at Beckman Markham had rescued her from being an overqualified copy-shop clerk, but three years later it was clear that bigger and better things weren't going to materialize for her in academia. By now, though, she hardly cared. Since she'd discovered romance writing via a Sunday supplement article one day in grad school, she'd been writing sweets. Now her only goal was to turn writing into a full-time job and leave the purgatory that was Beckman Markham.

Finishing the first novel of the new series would open that door for her.

Finishing the book currently seemed like the last thing that was ever going to happen.

Heaving a sigh, she got up from the computer chair and wandered over to her silent TV to watch Dennis Quaid trap Ellen Barkin in a kiss in *The Big Easy*. Helene was right. That was what she needed, she thought, stretching out on the couch to sink into the film. Passion. True romance. A man who would sweep her off her feet.

Unfortunately, her life to date had been notably absent of feet-sweepers. Except for Ross, who had mostly swept the floor with her. Ryan sighed as the characters on the screen kissed. Sometimes she could almost feel a movie kiss, almost remember what it was like.

She untied her robe to feel the silk beneath. It wasn't her fault she never got involved with anyone. Guys just always seemed to look right through her. It wasn't that she didn't want someone to touch her the way Quaid was touching Barkin, she thought, absently stroking her fingers along her collarbone and sliding down the curve of her shoulder. She wanted to make love, she wanted to feel a man's hands on her. It just never seemed to happen.

She ran her fingertips down over her silk camisole and tap pants to stroke her thighs, then back up, softly, rhythmically. The feel of silk rubbing against her nipples made her shift restlessly. Just a man who could see her for what she was, instead of walking right past like she was invisible. So maybe she wasn't on the cover of *Cosmo,* but she'd inherited her mother's high cheekbones and her father's full mouth. Nobody quite knew where she got her green eyes, but they were her favorite feature. When she got dressed up, she thought she looked nice. Okay, to be honest she thought she looked hot, but somehow when she was around men she just seemed to disappear.

She could be sexy with the right guy, Ryan thought, slipping her fingers under the edge of her tap pants to tease the top of her thighs, stroking her breast with the other hand. It was just that somehow they never seemed to notice her.

She watched the characters on screen as her fingers slid up to feel the curls of hair between her legs. Maybe what she'd experienced sex-wise had been forgettable, but she knew just how good it could be from the way she could make herself feel. Her fingers slipped into wetness and she felt the surge of arousal as she stroked herself where she was most sensitive. On-screen, Barkin gasped in desire as Quaid slipped his hand up between her legs. Ryan closed her eyes and imagined the fingers of a lover driving her to the brink and beyond. What would it be like to have a man touching her there, to feel his naked flesh against hers? Would he know how to stroke, how to circle around in the way that made her hips jerk the way they were now?

She was on fire everywhere from her hips to her knees. She ached with tension. The rhythmic stroking took her higher and higher. She brought herself to the edge, caressing her breasts with her other hand, brushing and squeezing the nipples. She paused, letting the arousal ease off, knowing it would be even better at the end if she made herself wait.

She stroked her body, feeling her curves, then returned to the moist heat, finding herself again with a touch that made her catch her breath. She teased, circled, then she could feel it rushing in. Suddenly it was like a freight train, barreling along, no stopping now. Slick, hot, wet, her folds enveloped her stroking fingers. The flush of heat flowed over her like molten pleasure, then the orgasm slammed into her. Her body jolted as the glory of it surged from her center out to her fingers and toes in a flush of heat that flared, pulsed, and left a glow behind. Sighing, she lay back and closed her eyes.

She didn't go back to the computer.

"MA, YOU RUINED MY CAREER." Ryan clattered through her parents' back door and into her mother's kitchen.

Sonia Donnelly turned to smile at her dark-haired, leggy daughter, marveling as always at how she'd grown from the tiny, pink baby she remembered. "Morning, Glory. What brings you here?"

"I'm meeting Becka to go antiquing. She's up the street at her parents' house, helping make paper flowers or something for Nellie's wedding."

"Nellie's getting married?" Sonia blinked in shock. "I just bought Girl Scout cookies from her last week. She can't be more than fourteen."

"Ma, she just turned twenty-two." Ryan said gently. "I think you bought the cookies from Colleen's oldest."

"Colleen has a daughter old enough to be in Girl Scouts? Good god, where does the time go?" Sonia muttered, bending to pull a pan of cinnamon rolls out of the oven. "Anyway, what's all this about ruined careers? Are you in trouble at work?"

"I'm repressed, is what I am. I have two sex scenes to finish before the end of the month and nothing's coming out."

The wall of newspaper over at the kitchen table rattled.

"What are you two talking about over there?" a muffled voice said.

"Nothing, dear." Sonia flipped the sweet rolls out onto a plate and pulled them apart with forks.

"Hi Dad," Ryan called.

Her father's head appeared from behind the *Boston Globe* sports page. "Oh, hi honey. How's Cambridge?"

"Fine, but my life as a writer is over."

"That's because you do those girlie books. I keep telling you, detective novels are the way to go. You get a nice gory murder, a tough cop, a psycho villain. It'll sell a million and you can retire."

"Sure Dad, next book," she promised, tucking her tongue in her cheek.

"So you're having problems with your latest?" Sonia asked, setting the platter of cinnamon rolls on the table.

"It's my name," Ryan said morosely. "I have a boy's name. No wonder I can't feel enough like a woman to get a lover." She crossed to the cupboard and pulled out coffee mugs. "If I could remember how it felt to have sex, I could write about it," she said reflectively, carrying the mugs over to the table.

"You know why I had to name you Ryan," Sonia returned. "Your grandfather was on his deathbed. It was little enough to ask and we were just so sure you were going to be a boy. Anyway, you could have gone by your middle name."

"Gladys?"

"I couldn't help it," her mother said defensively. "I could hardly tell your father's mother no after giving you a name from my family."

"Don't bring me into it, I was just an innocent by-stander," said her father, rattling the sports page.

"You could have gone by a nickname," Sonia pointed out, carrying over the coffeepot.

Ryan sighed. "By the time I was aware enough to do that the damage had been already done." She picked at the sweet roll in front of her.

Her mother poured coffee into the mugs and set the pot on a trivet. "Sweetheart, you're a wonderful writer. Just watch a couple of Mel Gibson movies to get in the mood and imagine the rest."

"I tried that. Didn't work." She sipped the coffee, deciding not to tell her mother what else she'd done to try to get into the mood. Which had put her right smack in the mood for about five minutes. And to sleep for the rest of the night.

"Why don't you ask someone to set you up with a fellow? Mrs. Seberg across the street has a single grandson."

"It's a long way from a blind date to between the sheets, Ma. My deadline's in two weeks. What I need is a mental vision of a monumental lover."

"I guess stag movies wouldn't do it," Sonia said reflectively, slipping onto a chair.

"Mother!" Scandalized, Ryan stared at her mother, then burst into laughter. "I can't believe you just encouraged your daughter to go rent a dirty movie."

Her father peered around his paper with interest. "She never told me to go see one."

"Oh hush, you. You never needed one." Sonia stirred her coffee, unflappable. "I'm just trying to help salvage Ryan's career. Given that I ruined it to begin with."

"Well, it's a romance novel, not soft-core porn. I don't think those movies will do it." Ryan gulped the last of her coffee and leaned across the table to snag another roll. "Anyway, I have to get going. I just stopped in to lay the blame for my impending ruin at your door."

"Always happy to help, dear." Her mother followed her to the kitchen door. "Don't worry about it, sweetheart, you're such a wonderful writer, it will all be fine." She pulled her close in a hug. "You'll find the right fellow, too."

"When's that going to happen?" Ryan pulled back and looked at her soberly.

"When you stop running around looking so busy and overtaxed that any man who looks at you figures you have to be running to meet a date. When you make yourself available, you'll find him."

"But what if I don't? I'm tired of looking. It's easier to just forget about it." Suddenly all the joking was gone, and in its place, an ache of loneliness so familiar that Ryan had almost stopped noticing it. Almost.

Sonia looked at her levelly. "You don't really believe that or you wouldn't be writing romance novels as a second career."

"If I don't meet this deadline, my second career is going to go up in a puff of dust and I'll be forced to teach memo writing for the rest of my life," Ryan said dolefully.

"You'll do it, sweetheart, you'll see. Everything will be fine."

HOW COULD IT POSSIBLY be fine, Ryan wondered the next day as she sat in her office. She'd avoided thinking about her deadline for months, but now it was inescapable. For more than a decade, she'd dreamed of being a professional writer. Now, on the verge of making it a reality, she was going to blow it.

Her phone buzzed and she glanced at the display before picking up the receiver with resignation. "Hello, Helene."

"Have they done the deed?"

"Not yet, but I'm getting there."

"No worries, kid. I've got an answer for you." Helene was absolutely chuckling with good humor. This boded nothing good, Ryan thought.

"No blind dates, Helene, I told you."

"This isn't a blind date, honeybunch, at least not exactly. It's just what you need."

A stir of misgiving whirled in her stomach. "What, exactly, do I need?" Ryan asked carefully.

"Some quality sheet time with a guy who knows what he's doing and knows how to drive you crazy."

Ryan's brows drew together. "Helene, you are not going to set me up with a one-night stand."

"You're right, I'm going to do something better," said Helene, sounding far too pleased with herself for Ryan's comfort. "You need inspiration and I can deliver. A girlfriend of mine knows an agency that supplies guys she says will make you see God." She paused a moment. "In return for a token of your appreciation."

Ryan's jaw dropped "You're not suggesting..." Her voice trailed off. What was going *on* with people? First her mother suggesting she watch dirty movies, then Helene trying to line her up with a...a... "You're talking about a gigolo!" Her voice rose to a squeak on the last word.

"Not a gigolo, an escort." Helene corrected. "A class act. Come on, you loved it when the society lady went to one in those *Tales of the City* books."

Ryan closed her eyes and massaged her temples where a headache was rapidly forming.

"Think about it," Helene continued, her lighter snapping in the background. "A guy who's gonna focus only on making you feel good. You sit there, quiver in ecstasy all night long." Ryan could hear her drawing on her cigarette. "You make mental notes for when you go back to the computer, and you write it all down in the morning."

"I am *not* going to pay someone for sex," Ryan said in outrage.

"Well, right now, it doesn't seem like you're going to get it any other way, kid, and until you do, this book's not going to get written," Helene said tartly.

Was the whole world going nuts? Ryan groped for words, not even knowing where to start. "You do fine on your own, why isn't it okay for me?"

Helene's voice softened. "Ryan, I'm a dried-up old broad. I had my run, and it was a good one. H.L., God rest his soul, left me with a bundle of wonderful memories." She sighed a little. "But you, you're gorgeous, you're young. Enjoy it while you've got it. Get out and live a little."

"By sleeping with a gigolo?"

"An escort. Why not? Think of the great story it would make for your grandkids." Helene stopped. "When they're grown, anyway. Better yet, think about the manuscript deadline. This baby's gotta be good, Ryan." Her voice sharpened with intensity. "You've gotten the chance, but you've got to convince that editor Elaine that you've got the goods or you lose the other three books in the series. You'll be stuck in sweets, and you can't make a living doing those." She paused. "What you're doing isn't working. Why not try this?"

Ryan opened her mouth and nothing came out. She closed it slowly, considering. From nowhere, a rush of daring hit her. Why not try it, she thought, brushing a finger over her lips, shivering a little as the nerve endings woke up. What would it feel like to have a man kiss her? What would it feel like to have his naked body on top of hers, to have him inside her, thrusting in and out, his back muscles slippery with sweat beneath her fingers? To know what it was really like…

"…don't you think?" Helene's voice sounded in her ear.

"What did you say?" Ryan asked, shaking her head to dislodge the image.

"I said, it's worth a try, don't you think?"

What did she think?

She thought it was scandalous.

She thought it was outrageous.

And as a sudden surge of recklessness came over her, she thought it could be just what she needed.

"Yes." The word was out before she knew she was going to say it.

"Yes? Yes? You're going to do it?" Helene's voice rose in a whoop. "Yes! Now when? The sooner, the better to my mind." Her voice fell into her staccato deal-making cadence. Details and plans were her passion. "Got plans for tomorrow? Mavis says she meets her guy in the lobby bar of the Copley Plaza Hotel. See? Class all the way."

"I must be out of my mind to do this," Ryan moaned.

"Don't you dare back out," Helene ordered. "This is exactly what you need. We'll have to set you up with a room. I'll take care of it, and get the key delivered to your office. All you have to do is walk upstairs with him and into bliss."

"I should have my head examined."

"I don't know about examining your head," Helene said with a wicked lilt to her voice, "but we'll find you a guy who'll play doctor with you to your heart's content."

"GENTLEMEN, IT WAS A pleasure doing business with you." It was like a tribal ritual, Cade Douglas thought as he and his partner went around the conference table shaking hands with the members of the venture capital group that had just funded their start-up to the tune of $7 million. Even back in his days of wheeling and dealing at Shearson Lehman, in the end the deal came down to handshakes.

$7 million. He felt a surge of triumph. They had backers now, a group convinced that eTrain.com was more than a pipe dream. Backers who believed that they'd be a success, who believed enough to sink a small fortune into their ability to turn online education into money.

There was a whoop of jubilation somewhere down deep

in his throat, but he contented himself with a wide smile as he and his partner, Patrick Wallace, walked out into the hotel corridor.

$7 million.

"I still think we should have them to the office while they're here," Patrick muttered. "That dial-up connection was pathetic. They can't have any idea of what we're trying to do."

"Patrick, VC guys don't care about the technology," Cade said patiently. "They're in town for an Internet conference. They don't want to spend an hour driving out to Peabody. They just want the business plan."

"I still think…"

"Patrick. Did we or did we not get the money?"

"We got the money," Patrick said, a smile spreading across his face until it looked like it was going to crack. "Jesus, we just walked into a room and convinced five guys to give us seven million dollars." He whooped and punched his fist in the air. "Yes!"

Cade pushed the elevator call button, the heady glow of the deal rushing through his veins. Eventually, the weight of responsibility would descend, but right now, life was good. Reflexively, he pulled out his cell phone to check messages. An instant later, he gave a muffled curse.

Patrick shot a wary glance at him as the elevator doors opened. "No problems right now, buddy, I'm feeling too good."

"Nothing that you need to worry about," Cade said briefly, punching the button for the hotel lobby. "A message from the darling Alyssa. She apparently heard that we were pitching the VCs today and wanted to remind me that she still hasn't gotten the certificates on the stock options."

"Ah, Alyssa. Everybody's favorite ex-wife."

Cade snorted. "Yeah, right." Then he did a double take and his eyes narrowed. "I don't want to hear it, Patrick."

Patrick shook his head. "I just thought you'd want to know."

"Skip it, Patrick."

"She's getting married again," Patrick blurted.

Cade rolled his eyes. "Good for her. I don't care."

"It just bugs me, that's all. She guts you and comes out of it smelling like a rose."

"She didn't gut me. We both knew it wasn't right, practically on the honeymoon. Me getting off the Shearson Lehman gravy train to help start a dot-com just gave her the excuse she needed to make the break." He shrugged. "I'm not happy about the money part of it, but the rest doesn't matter."

"Is that why all you ever do is work?" Patrick's voice turned serious. "Don't get me wrong. As your partner, I'm not complaining, but as your friend I worry. Where's the guy of a thousand dates that I used to know? Hell, Cade, you don't even look at a woman anymore. Why don't you give yourself a break and at least get some kind of life going?"

Cade bit back temper. "Patrick, there are times I get home and even the people on the TV seem like they want too much from me. I don't have the time and energy for doing the dance, okay?" The elevator doors opened and they walked out into the brightly lit marble lobby. "Besides, chemistry doesn't last, that much I learned from Alyssa. Just give me a break."

"Cade, it's been four years since you guys divorced. I mean, forget about obligations, I'm just talking about a one night stand."

Cade snorted. "That sounds like the cry of a married man who wants to live vicariously."

"You're going to get hair on your palms and go blind if you keep this up too much longer, buddy. And that's going to turn the VC guys right off."

"Patrick."

"What about her?" he cocked his head as a curvaceous blonde in white passed them, then grinned to see Cade's eyes following her. "Well, I'm glad to see that your gonads aren't completely dead."

Too reminiscent of Alyssa's ice blond Beacon Hill debutante looks, Cade thought. The kind who would freeze you if you got too close. "Serve you right if I hauled you out on the town for a night of partying. See how much trouble I can get you in with Amy." They stopped in front of the lobby bar, talking over the whisper of the fountain burbling in the center.

"I wish I could stop for a drink to celebrate, but I've got to get home. Amy's got book club tonight. That shouldn't stop you, though," Patrick said, nodding toward a passing cocktail waitress carrying a tray laden with glasses.

Cade shook his head in mock remorse. "Tragic, what marriage does to a man."

Patrick smiled and patted him on the back. "Just because I'm peeling out doesn't mean you should. Hang around for a little while. Have a drink. Who knows, maybe in a couple minutes some gorgeous woman will show up out of the blue and come on to you." He leaned in closer. "And if she does, do me a favor, buddy. Don't question it, don't ask why. Just go with it and let whatever happens, happen."

Cade raised an eyebrow at him. "What the hell kind of advice is that?"

"Take it as a few words of wisdom from someone who knows a thing or two." Patrick grinned. "I gotta go. I'll see you tomorrow."

Cade waved him off and looked at the passing waitress. Maybe he would have a drink. After all the work he'd put in, he deserved it.

RYAN WALKED INTO THE Copley Plaza Hotel, teetering a bit on her heels as she spotted the lobby bar, her heart trip-hammering. The silk of her dress slithered against her as she walked, making her conscious of every brush of her thighs. She'd wanted to look good for tonight, but maybe dropping $250 on the peacock-blue mid-thigh number was overdoing it, considering it would be off in less than half an hour. *Oh my God.* Butterflies surged in her stomach at the thought. What in the world was she doing? She had to be out of her mind. Only the panic of facing her empty computer screen kept her from wheeling around and going right back to her car.

She glanced across the semi-crowded room. On one of the groupings of deep, soft couches, a group of noisy businessmen laughed at each other's jokes. From the looks of their rumpled suits and disheveled hair, she figured they'd been sucking down martinis for some time. On a nearby settee, an older woman with an air of faded elegance cast a disapproving glance at the group, leaning close to whisper to the young girl beside her. Up by the bar, a piano player was murdering an old Harry Nilsson tune. There ought to be a law, Ryan thought. And then she saw him, sitting on a couch, an empty glass at his elbow. He raised a beckoning hand.

Her knees turned to water.

Helene's friend hadn't exaggerated. Stunningly good-looking didn't come close to describing him. Thick, dark hair stopped just at his collar, a sheaf falling down over his forehead. His face was strong-boned, the eyes too shadowed under the slashes of dark brows for her to see the color. But his mouth…a fantasy blazed through her mind, her naked, on her back, looking down to see his mouth on her. And it was going to happen, everything she wanted, everything she could think of. *Oh my god.* She took a quick breath to fill lungs that felt robbed of oxygen. Then she breathed in again.

Okay. The thing to do was to be casual, classy, self-possessed *oh my god* just walk up, introduce herself, and go upstairs *oh my god, he's going to*—

Ryan reached the couch. Blue. His eyes were the deep blue of the Atlantic on a clear fall day. As he looked her up and down, she felt her cheeks heat. Casual, classy, self-possessed.

Oh my god.

He raised an eyebrow.

"Hello. I'm Ryan." She put her hand out.

He hesitated just a beat, then caught it up and brought it to his lips. "You're also lovely."

She was, simply, stunned. His lips sent a frisson of heat and electricity through her hand, which seemed to have instantly grown a thousand new nerve endings. She sank down on the couch because her knees wouldn't hold her.

Cade studied her in bemusement. Granted, he'd been out of the bar scene for a couple of years—okay, for six or seven if you wanted to get picky—but he was almost sure that gorgeous women didn't just fall into a guy's lap because he was sitting in a bar alone. At least not unless you were Russell Crowe, anyway. The waitress he'd waved at brought him another scotch. He passed her a bill and glanced at Ryan. "Would you like something?"

Nothing from the bar, thanks, a little voice in her mind answered back. *I'll just have you.* Cade and the waitress looked at her, waiting for her response. Her cheeks heated. Classy. What was a classy, sophisticated drink? "A martini," Ryan said quickly. "I'll have a martini."

"How do you want that?"

Great. How would a martini drinker answer? "Um, dry, please." Ryan breathed a sigh of relief as the waitress nodded and walked off. Then she pushed back her hair and turned to the man beside her.

She truly was something to look at, Cade thought, watching the blush slowly fade from her high cheekbones. Long and lovely in a narrow, electric blue dress that slipped up to show legs longer than any woman had a right to have. Glossy dark hair tumbled down her back. Her mouth was a deep, ripe red that sent his brain running down carnal pathways. He took a sip of his scotch. "So how are you this fine Wednesday evening?"

Nervous. Giddy. In heat. "Fine. How about you?"

"I'm good."

"So I hear." Ryan's eyes widened and she put a hand to her mouth. She'd said it out loud. It must have been that voice, vibrating her nerve cells and setting loose butterflies inside her. She forced a laugh that sounded fake and tinny even to her own ears. "Just, uh, joking. So, are you having a nice evening?" she asked brightly. *Jeez, Ryan, can you get any more pedestrian?* On the other hand, she thought, it didn't really matter if she was a fount of witty banter or not.

He was a sure thing.

She laughed again, this time for real.

Cade raised an eyebrow. "What's the joke?"

Ryan gave a small cough. "Sorry, I'm just in a good mood tonight. I don't usually go out on weeknights, so this is like a holiday for me."

"What's the occasion?"

Her mouth curved. "Oh, I think a chance to meet someone like you is occasion enough."

He glanced at her legs appreciatively. "I'd say the pleasure's all mine." He'd forgotten what it was like to sit in a bar and flirt with a sexy woman. Patrick was right, he did need to start getting out more.

"And do weeknights usually find you out and about?"

Cade shrugged and rested an elbow on the back of the couch. "Sometimes a special job makes it worthwhile. It was definitely worth it tonight, especially since now I'm sitting here in the company of a gorgeous woman." He eyed her over the rim of his glass. "You are gorgeous, you know."

He enjoyed watching her blush. She was luscious—dark, vivid, unconsciously lovely with none of the hard-edged gloss and sophistication that seemed to run through so many of the women he met. There was something addictive about the quick flash of her smile, something that compelled him to keep the conversation rolling. "Anyway, a buddy of mine was just lecturing me that I need to get out more."

"I suppose all work and no play makes life dull. Do you like your work?"

He paused to consider before answering. "Yeah, I do. It has its challenges, but boy, when it goes well I just feel like if I can do that, I can do anything."

Her pulse speeded up at the thought of just exactly what he might do to her. The waitress returned and Ryan reached out for her drink. This would be interesting, she thought, given that she'd never had a martini in her life. They always looked sophisticated, though, with that deep green olive glowing in the icy clear liquid. How bad could it be? "Here's to weeknights," she said, and clinked her glass against his. She took a sip and the cold, clean taste of the liquor flowed over her tongue. Then the heat slammed into her and she coughed fire.

"You okay?"

Eyes watering, Ryan nodded, giving up the pretense of sophistication. "My first martini." She coughed again. "I always thought they looked great but never had the nerve to try one before."

"And what's the verdict?"

She gave a rueful smile. "It's an eye-opener."

Cade ran his thumb lightly across her cheek. "So are you."

A shiver ran up her spine at his touch. Then the first flush of the liquor hit her. She couldn't tell whether the warmth she felt was from the drink or from the heat in his eyes. Her pulse jumped and she groped to organize her scattered thoughts. *Say something witty, Ryan.* "Do they give you guys a script or something?"

Cade blinked. "What are you talking about?"

"You say such pretty things it's like something out of a movie." She took another cautious sip of her drink and was pleased to find that it flowed down easily this time.

"Is that a polite way of saying 'stop feeding me lines'?"

She smiled. "No, it's nice. I like it. Guys just don't usually say things like that to me." And though she tried to tell herself it was part of his professional persona, she was charmed.

"You're obviously hanging around with the wrong guys. I guarantee any man in this room would be thrilled if you walked up and started talking with him." His eyes glimmered. "Unless his wife were sitting next to him, of course."

"Oh please."

"You don't believe me?" He surveyed the room. "There are about fifteen or twenty men sitting in this bar. We can take a poll." There was a burst of raucous laughter from the conventioneers. "Actually, I don't need to take a poll. Those guys over there? The only time they've been quiet the entire night was when you walked through the door. Aunt Cordelia and her charge at the next couch over were very grateful."

Ryan caught the glare the older woman gave the group. "I noticed when I walked in that she wasn't very happy. Why do you suppose she stays there instead of moving?"

Cade shrugged. "Boston Brahmin—she was there first, why should she move for a bunch of savages?"

Ryan's smile flashed again. "You seem to know the type well."

"I was married to a baby Brahmin for a couple of years. I learned to recognize entitlement from fifty paces."

"Where's the baby Brahmin now?"

Cade took another sip of his drink. "Getting remarried, last time I heard. Hopefully it'll stick for her this time."

It was Ryan's turn to raise her eyebrows. "You don't seem very bitter. Most people tend to be hostile after divorces."

He shrugged, his eyes dropping to where the blue silk dipped low over her breasts, then rising back up to meet her eyes. "No reason I should be. We just made a bad pair. It was best for both of us that we ended it."

"Was that how she felt about it?"

"More or less. I think her family was relieved. They lived off a one-hundred-and-fifty-year-old shipping fortune. Someone who worked like I did was an embarrassment to them."

She looked into his laughing eyes and found herself smiling at the thought of an unrepentant gigolo infiltrating an old-money Boston family. They must have been scandalized. "I take it you didn't agree?"

He tilted his head thoughtfully. "Not really. I dealt with people who had a certain set of needs and I came in and made sure they got satisfied. That seemed pretty worthwhile to me."

"So you leave satisfied customers behind you?" She took another sip of her martini and her eyes darkened as she licked a drop of vodka from her lip.

Cade lost a beat watching her. "I do my best. I think satisfaction is a pretty worthy goal." He hooked a finger in his tie to loosen it, then unbuttoned his collar.

Ryan suddenly had an image of pulling the tie off, unfastening the buttons one by one as he lay back on a bed. She shifted on the couch and her thighs brushed together, a tendril of heat starting to grow between them.

The bar had been gradually filling up with more patrons. Noticing the mood, the piano player switched from bad Harry Nilsson to bad Billy Joel. Ryan winced at the opening strains of "It's Still Rock and Roll to Me." "That's painful. I didn't think it could get any worse than the last tune."

"I think the quality of the material is irrelevant. He was murdering 'Love is the Drug' before you got here."

"I'm sorry I missed it," she said insincerely.

Cade grinned. "So let's see. You don't want the smooth talk, am I right?"

"Oh, I like it when you talk pretty. Just skip the stuff that sounds like a line. You've already got me." She took another sip of her drink and felt the warmth run through her.

"Let's see. Well, I could tell you that I've been sitting here thinking that your eyes are a very elusive color of green and I just realized that they match the olive in your drink. Now that's straight from the brain, no lines in sight."

Ryan winced. "I think I liked it better the other way."

She laughed and something flipped in his gut. Well that was new, he thought. Beyond her, he saw the blonde he'd noticed earlier. Against the swirl of vivid color that was Ryan, she only looked more icy pale than before.

Cade took another swallow of scotch, wanting to hear that soft, throaty laugh again. "So what do you do when you're not hanging around hotel lobbies with strange men?"

"Oh, I spin yarns," she said airily.

"Oh yeah? Tell me a good story."

When she'd been a child, her family would go to a lake in Maine in the summers. In early June, the water was still icy cold. There were two ways to approach it. You could start at the shore, stepping in an inch at a time, waiting for your body to acclimate until you got so chilled the water didn't feel cold anymore. Or you could run off the end of the dock and jump in, take the shock all at once. In for a penny, in for a pound.

Ryan had always jumped.

She took a deep breath and looked in his eyes. "Let's go upstairs and I will."

Cade blinked, and Patrick's words came back to him. *Maybe in a couple of minutes a gorgeous woman will show up out of the blue and come on to you. And if she does, do me a favor, buddy. Don't question it, don't ask why. Just go with it and let whatever happens, happen.*

Maybe Patrick was right.

"Whatever you say, darlin'." He rose and pulled her to her feet. "I'm all yours."

2

JUST WHAT HAD HE GOTTEN himself into, Cade wondered bemusedly as he listened to Ryan's heels click on the marble lobby tiles. He was pretty sure this was not the way pickups went in this day and age. But the scotch was singing in his blood, the flush of triumph was still flowing through him, and he couldn't stop wondering what it would feel like to touch her skin.

Ryan ran a hand through her hair, shaking it back. She'd thought she'd be more nervous, but somehow she was more at ease than she'd ever been with a man. Always before she'd wondered and analyzed, trying to figure out what he was thinking, how he felt.

Whether he wanted her.

This time, she didn't have to wonder. Everybody knew what was going to happen up front. The situation should have made her feel awkward, but it was strangely liberating. The deal was done, she could just ride with it.

And yet, somehow it didn't feel like a deal. She could swear she'd seen heat in his eyes when she'd approached him. Maybe he was just very good at his job, but it seemed too genuine to be an act. Helene's friend was right, it felt like a date. A perfect date who was going to put out. She laughed to herself.

"What's the joke?" Cade asked, those extraordinary eyes on her.

Ryan smiled. "This. I thought it would feel so strange, but it doesn't."

"Why should it?"

She shrugged. "I'm sure you hear this all the time, but I've never done this before. You know where it goes from here. It's all new to me."

"I have no idea where it goes from here," Cade spoke with perfect truth. "I thought we'd work it out as we go along."

A chime rang as the elevator doors opened and they stepped into the car. "Fourteenth floor," she said when he looked at her inquiringly. He punched a button and the car surged upward. Her stomach fluttered in a way that had nothing to do with the movement. Somehow their fingers were still entangled as though they'd fused together. The heat licked up her arm and a surge of pleasure washed over her. It felt so good to touch someone. Just to touch someone. Then his fingertips began tracing patterns over her palm, and she caught her breath.

The chime rang again, and the elevator doors opened on a plushly carpeted hall.

And the nerves hit. Ryan's hand shook as she dug in her purse for the room folio. "Fourteen twenty-seven. I think we're down here." One of her heels caught in the thick carpet and she wobbled before Cade caught her arm.

"Steady."

Steady? She'd never been less steady in her life. "No more martinis for me."

"They do pack a punch."

"So do you."

"Now who's talking like the movies?"

She laughed. "I'm the client. I'm allowed to do what I want."

"What?" Cade came to a stop, fortunately in front of the right door. What the hell was going on? The client? If she was the client, then who did she think he was? What was this all about? To buy himself time to think, he took the card from her hand and unlocked the door.

Ryan took a deep breath and stepped inside. Across the room, floor to ceiling windows looked out on the Boston skyline and a cool April night. Inside, warm light from a silk-shaded table lamp suffused the room. Ornate gold throw pillows accented a couch covered in soft, muted blues and an armchair pulled up nearby. She tried to ignore the acre of bed beyond.

On the low oak coffee table, a plate of cheese and grapes sat next to a bottle of cabernet and a pair of cut-glass goblets. "That Helene," Ryan said dryly, "she doesn't miss a trick."

Cade stepped up behind her to slide her wrap off, staring at her pale shoulders gleaming in the soft light. He wanted to curl his fingers around them and feel her skin against his palms, see if it was as silky soft as it looked. Fill his hands with the hair that flowed down her back, press it to his lips. Feel her move against him. God, it had been so long…

"Who's Helene?" he asked.

Ryan could feel the heat from his body as he stood behind her. Desire pulled at her and she swayed. Touch me touch me touch me drummed through her mind. Strive for sophisticated, she thought. "Helene's my agent. You have her to thank for the business, you know." Because her nerves were strained to the breaking point, she moved away and sank down on the soft blue cushions of the couch.

Business? Agents? Just who was she, Cade wondered, watching her reach toward the tray. She had the lush mouth of an actress, and a body dressed to drive a man wild. She'd talked about it being her first time, but then she'd mentioned spinning tales. Just relax, he thought to himself, ride along with it. "So you said you spin tales. Do you act?" He took the wine bottle and corkscrew that she handed to him.

Ryan gave a short laugh. "Hardly. I'm a writer. Part of the time, anyway."

"What do you write?"

His hands were long-fingered, capable, and she stared in fascination. "Oh, women's fiction," she answered vaguely, watching him twist the cork off of the corkscrew, then handing him a glass. "I've got a nasty case of writer's block and a deadline. My agent thought this would give me inspiration."

"Inspiration for what?" Cade asked, his brow creasing in puzzlement as he poured the wine into the cut crystal and handed her a glass. Pouring a glass for himself, he sat on the couch.

Ryan looked at him impishly. "To the power of inspiration." She clinked her glass against his.

"You still have to tell me what for," he reminded her, then drank, letting the dark flavor of the wine roll over his tongue.

"For my sex scenes, of course," she said.

Cade choked.

Ryan watched him cough, amused. "What, you don't think of yourself as an artistic muse?" she asked, watching as he walked over to the windows and back, catching his breath.

"If you're talking about what I think you're talking about then no, I don't," he said as he came back to the couch. He picked up the glass that he'd set on the table while he was busy coughing up a lung and took a long drink.

"Well I hope you live up to your billing. This has to be a very hot scene. Helene's friend said you had the hands and mouth of a god," Ryan said, and watched him choke again. "You came highly recommended," she said, then pounded him helpfully on the back. "Should I get you some water?"

"No, thank you." Cade cleared his throat and grabbed

his glass again. Christ, he definitely needed a drink while he worked out what to do here. All his instincts were telling him to go, not to get involved, but her scent wound around his brain. He started to drink, then lowered the glass. "Do me a favor. Don't say anything else dangerous while I drink this, okay?" He eyed her warily over the rim as he sipped, then he put it down.

Ryan popped a grape into her mouth, enjoying herself hugely. She felt desirable, gorgeous...sexy. Power surged through her. She crossed her legs slowly and leaned toward him, resting her arm on the back of the couch. "So what happens now?" Her pulse skittered over the deep, slow burn of arousal. She wanted to feel his hands on her, now. "Isn't this the part where you're supposed to start feeding me grapes and having your way with me?"

Her husky voice and the slow smile that went with the words hit him like a sucker punch. Didn't this one just beat all, he thought. He wanted her so badly he could feel it pulsing through him, but going along with this charade had the makings of a disaster. He owed it to her to tell her what was going on.

Yeah, but what did it matter really, asked a soft, persuasive voice in his head. That was the little head thinking for the big head, Cade thought grimly, but he stared at the shadows in the hollow of her neck and listened anyway. She thought she was sleeping with a gigolo. Really, she'd be better off sleeping with him. At least he'd be doing it because he wanted her, not because he wanted money. As far as complications went, well, it wasn't as though she could be expecting to have a relationship with a gigolo, so it could all begin and end here. He couldn't lead her on because the very nature of the situation meant that she wouldn't be expecting anything besides a one-time roll in the hay.

Besides, if he told her the truth now she'd strangle him.

Okay, here was the deal, he thought, shutting down the

voice. He'd go to the bathroom and figure out some kind of fake excuse, and then he'd go. He'd do the right thing and get up and go. Right then.

Except that just then he had a hard-on that would hammer nails.

Ryan was watching him closely. "What's wrong? You've got a really funny look on your face."

"I uh…I just remembered that I forgot to bring along any condoms," he said, and gave himself points. In today's world it was a pretty valid excuse.

"Oh." She fought down a quick surge of disappointment, then paused as she considered some of the alternatives. "And here I thought you were a professional," she said mockingly. "I guess you'll just have to think of something special to keep my mind off the fact that I'm not getting the full package, so to speak."

He should have known there'd be no easy outs here, Cade thought. He must be out of his mind trying to escape it. Any other single guy would be all over this one in a heartbeat. Any other guy would be all over *her* in a heartbeat. "Well, it's actually got me thinking. Based on what you said before, I just…I think you're doing this for the wrong reasons."

"The wrong reasons?" Ryan echoed in bewilderment, her euphoria dying away. "Because I'm paying you for sex for business reasons rather than for personal companionship? You've got to be kidding."

"I just don't want this to turn out to be a bad thing for you. We're having a good time. Why don't we just leave it at this?"

Suddenly it felt like every horrid date she'd ever had. Like the worst times with Ross, thinking he wanted her, finding out it was all entirely different than she'd imagined. "I thought we were supposed to have sex," she snapped. "I didn't realize that this was a pass/fail interview." She jumped up and stalked to the wall of windows, leaning against the handrail that ran across it and staring out into the night. "This is unbelievable. I must be the only person I know who can't make it with a guy even when I'm paying him."

"This has nothing to do with me not wanting you," Cade said sharply, rising to follow her. "But if we do this I think you're going to be sorry, and I don't want that. I like you. And I don't think you're thinking this through."

"You don't think I'm thinking this through?" Ryan spun to face him, sputtering in outrage. "What business is it of yours? Who set you up to decide what's best for me?" Two spots of color stained her cheeks. "Whatever happened to all your talk about satisfying needs? This is supposed to be about money, honey." The words dripped with sarcasm.

"This has nothing to do with money," he said quietly.

She refused to be mollified. "Oh come on. Money's why you're here."

"No it's not. It's you."

"I find that hard to believe," she said coldly.

"Why? Don't you see yourself when you look into the mirror?" His words came to her softly, and the low thrumming started again in her blood. "When I saw you walk in tonight it stopped me dead."

"Oh please." He wasn't going to play her for a fool, Ryan thought. And yet, when she looked into his eyes she could swear that he was telling her the absolute truth.

"I mean it." He stepped close to her and tilted up her chin, running his fingertips lightly down her throat. Smooth as cream, he thought. And he knew he was about to make a big mistake. "This has nothing to do with money." He brushed his lips over her jawline. "This only has to do with you and with me."

Then his mouth closed over hers and a roaring madness swept them away.

3

IT WAS NO SOFT, gentle kiss. There was no time to sample and savor. Urgent with the suppressed desire of the past hours, he took her, possessed her, his mouth driving her into a frenzy. The wanting, the desire drove them both.

This is what it's like, ran a refrain in her head. For years she had watched, yearned, tried to imagine what it felt like, the riot of sensation that was rushing through her body. Now there was no more need to imagine, just to feel. Ryan pushed his jacket off his shoulders, greedy to have him against her.

Cade tossed it impatiently on the floor, throwing his tie off after it. Running his hands down her sleek body, he pulled her to him, then spun her around to face the glass.

Ryan was dizzy, drunk with arousal, glorying in his urgency. After a seemingly endless drought of affection, she was suddenly in the arms of a man who wanted her so badly he trembled. It was intoxicating. More, was all she could think. She wanted more.

His hands curved down over her shoulders and his lips traced a line to follow. "When I was taking your shawl off earlier, all I wanted to do was touch you like this, just feel your skin under my hands," he murmured against her skin.

A slow, molten flow started deep in her belly.

Ryan groaned at the heat of his hands on her, at the feel of his body behind her, his arousal pushing hard and insistently against her. She turned her head, letting it fall back so she could kiss him. "And is that all you want now?" she murmured against his lips.

"Not by half." He spun her back around and pulled her against him. Then his mouth was on hers again, parting her lips to taste the dark flavors inside. Any thought of principles had been annihilated in the burning pulse of desire that consumed him. His hands slid down her sides and curved around in front to fill themselves with the soft fullness of her breasts and he caught his breath.

Ryan reveled in the riot of sensation, the textures, the flavors, the scents. How had she ever managed to live without this? How had she ever managed to do without this driving urgency, without the heat of a man's hands hard against her body? Without feeling him stiff against her and knowing without a doubt that he wanted her? All the nerves were gone, the second-guessing was a thing of the past. Certainty flowed through her. She didn't have to think about it—the way she touched him was inevitable, instinctive. She kissed as though she would inhale him, then broke off to nibble a frenzy of kisses down his cheek and neck, feeling fresh amazement at the smooth tight feel of his skin against her mouth.

His hands stroked down the smooth skin of her back until he found the zipper of the low-cut dress. She was alive in his arms and he wanted more. He tugged the zipper down and felt the fabric part beneath his fingers.

The cool air from the window brushed over her skin, making her shiver, but the heat of his lips made her shiver more. "The lights are on in here," she whispered. "People will be able to see in from the outside."

"We're fourteen floors up. Let 'em look if they want to." Forcing himself to go slowly, he slipped the dress from her shoulders and let it drop to the floor, holding her steady as she stepped out of it. And stared dry-mouthed at the low-cut black bra and garter belt that had been hidden underneath. Holding her arms out to the side, he stepped back and simply looked. "You're so sexy," he whispered huskily, then filled his hands with her breasts.

So long, it had been so long since he'd felt the yielding softness of a woman's body. And he wanted her more than any woman he'd known. He pressed her back against the glass, stroking his hands over the swell of flesh that rose above the black satin cups, then sliding his hands down her sides.

His tongue traced a line down her neck to linger at the tops of her breasts as he unsnapped the front clasp of her bra and peeled the cups back. Her breasts tumbled out, rounded and full. He whispered something and took one of her nipples in her mouth.

Ryan moaned, nearly delirious at the liquid warmth of his tongue against her. Part of her was utterly amazed that this was happening at all. This was the kind of passion she watched in movies, not the kind of thing that happened to her. Only now it was happening, and she gloried in every groan, every brush of skin against skin.

Twisting sinuously, she brought herself into closer contact with him, tangling her fingers in his hair. He sucked and stroked his tongue against her, dwelling on first one peak, then the next, driving her higher as the tension built deep inside.

Then he traced his tongue lower still, licking across the quivering skin of her belly as he dropped to his knees in front of her. Impatiently he unbuttoned his shirt, flinging it to one side, then wrapped his arms around her waist, pulling her to him to feel her against his bare flesh.

Ryan ran her hands over his shoulders, feeling the curve of hard muscle against her fingertips. She was greedy for everything she could feel, everything she could take, everything she could give. To know that she could make his breath come fast, make him shudder was intoxicating.

Knowing that they were only scratching the surface was more intoxicating still.

Cade heard her moan as he slid his hands down her back and over the curve of her buttocks, hooking his fingers in the sides of her black lace bikini. He smiled as he realized she'd put it on last when she dressed that evening. Then he stripped the silky thing down and she stood against the wide window in only her garters and stockings, looking like some delectable advertisement for sin. The smoothness of the gossamer hose against his palms as he ran them up and down her legs made him catch his breath. He pressed his lips against her hip, then journeyed lower, brushing against the first curls of hair, then lower still. Sliding his hands between her legs, he pushed them gently apart.

Ryan gasped and jolted as the wet warmth of his tongue slipped into the slick cleft between her legs, stroking the tight, hard bud of her sex. The slight roughness of his cheeks scraped the tender insides of her thighs as he caressed her with his tongue, swirling it in a way that made her lose control and move her hips mindlessly, crying out in breathy moans she wasn't even aware she was making. Touching herself had never been like this, she thought in shock. In her wildest dreams she couldn't have imagined anything could feel this good, that the wet, slick strokes could bring on such heat.

Feeling her response, Cade drove her higher, inflamed by her arousal. "This is what I wanted to do from the moment I saw you," he whispered, his mouth on her. "You walked in that room and I just wanted you naked, under me, against me. I wanted to know what you tasted like, how you moaned when you came." He ran a finger back and forth where she was most slippery, tormenting her with his touch, then plunged it inside her as he worked her with his mouth.

Ryan arched and cried out as the climax ripped through her in a rush of pleasure and light. Her body shuddered with the contractions and the flush of heat that rocketed out to her fingertips and toes. She surged to another peak and cried out again. The jolts lasted long after the flood of sensation had abated. Her legs turned to water and she swayed.

"Easy," Cade said softly. "I think we need to go over here." He guided her to the bed. Ryan laid back bonelessly against the sweet-smelling sheets, watching him strip off his shoes, trousers and briefs. God he had a gorgeous body, lean and muscled like a champion swimmer.

The mattress gave as he laid down next to her, turning on his side to watch her as he stroked a hand down her body. Ryan reached out to touch his face, then ran a fingertip down his body to his hip. He sucked in a breath and she felt a surge of triumph. Sitting up, she pushed him flat on his back. "I think its time you sit back and let me drive," she murmured. Before she had relaxed and taken. Now it was her turn to give, her turn to feel the power of desire.

On her hands and knees, she leaned down to kiss him slow and lingeringly, rubbing her lips against his, tracing a line down his neck with her tongue. Tasting the salt tang of sweat, she licked her way down his flat belly, letting her hair trail over his skin, then sank down to the mattress by his hip, staring at his pulsing erection in fascination. Slowly, she touched a finger to the drop of clear liquid that glistened on the tip, then spread it along the sensitive underside. Cade's body jolted and his breath hissed.

The last time she'd done this, she'd been a clumsy innocent groping in the dark with a man, a callow boy, really, who had been wishing she was someone else. This time, for just this hour, she knew Cade wanted her. After years of longing for contact, she was touching someone who desired her, feeling his response to her touch, watching his arousal leap and pulse in response to her teasing.

Heart hammering, she leaned over and ran the tip of her tongue where her fingertip had been. The sensation was incredible. He was hard yet silky soft against her lips as she rubbed them against him, running them up and down, first slowly, then faster, swirling her tongue around the rounded tip of him. She was rewarded with a strangled moan. More boldly now she grasped him with her hand and slipped him into her mouth.

Power. It surged through her as she heard him groan, as she felt his hips rock helplessly in response to her touch. To know that she could bring him to this level of intensity was intoxicating. She ran her head up and down in an intimate caress, feeling him get harder and harder against her mouth with every stroke. The skin was like silk stretched over marble.

"Ryan," Cade said in a strangled voice.

"Hmm?" she looked up but didn't slow her movements.

"If you keep doing that I'm going to—" he broke off and hauled her roughly up his body. Kissing her hard, he put her hand on him and stroked it once. A groan tore out of him and he surged against her, pulsing in her hand.

RYAN STRETCHED, FEELING relaxation settle over her slow and heavy. Cade pressed a long, lingering kiss on her lips. Ryan turned her head on the pillow and looked at him intently. "Thank you."

"Thank you?" he laughed. "What for?"

"For bringing me back," she said simply, and kissed him. "I haven't done this in a very long time, years." Her eyes were serious. "You probably don't know what it's like to be without sex that long, but you lose touch with the world. After a couple of years go by, you're afraid to touch anyone, afraid you'll hug a friend too hard or stare someone in the eyes too long because you've been so disconnected with the world that you don't know what it's like anymore, to be in touch with people."

She was describing his life for the past four years, Cade

thought. He'd been running hard and trying to ignore it, but he knew the feeling that she was talking about. Isolation, in a way that went deeper than being alone. He pulled her close, feeling the luxury of her naked body against his. ''I can't believe that you don't have guys coming on to you right and left.''

Ryan blushed. ''Well, I don't usually wander around dressed like I was tonight. I don't know, guys just don't ask me out.'' Suddenly self-conscious, she reached for the sheet.

Cade put a hand on hers. ''Uh-uh.'' He pulled the sheet back. ''I want to look.'' He ran the flat of his hand over the curve of her hip. ''I think you're amazing.''

''*This* is amazing.'' She shook her head. ''You don't know what it's like. It's as though you're living in the world but you're only a spectator to the life that everyone else is living.'' She kissed him again. ''You've brought me back from that. I feel like I'm part of the human race again.''

''Incredible,'' he murmured, rolling her over so that she lay on top of him. He ran his hands down her back, resting them on her hips. ''I don't know what those other guys you've known have been thinking. I'm glad to be the one you let inside.''

''Well, I didn't let you in everywhere,'' she said impishly, squirming against him. ''I can think of some places you haven't been, what with your forgetting items key to your profession.''

Cade winced at the reference, but his expression was lightly amused. ''Oh yeah?''

''Well, yes. And as a professional, what do you propose to do about that? After all, the scenes for my book do have to be complete in the particulars.''

He rolled her again so that she was half underneath him. ''Well, I pride myself on keeping my customers satisfied,'' he said between kisses. ''I suppose the fair thing would be to forgo payment until you receive the full treatment you were led to expect.'' He stroked the tender skin on her breast until she shivered, then slid his hand over the soft curve of her hip to linger at the tops of her thighs. ''What do you say you hold on to your payment and we meet again tomorrow night to close the deal?'' His clever fingers teased her, stroking her into arousal all over again. ''In the meantime, I think a demonstration of good faith is in order.''

Ryan's yes was a moan that he stopped with his mouth.

4

RYAN BOUNCED TOWARD HER office building, dancing on air. With only three hours of sleep under her belt, she should have been exhausted, but she walked down the pavement buoyed by a bubble of euphoria. The sun was shining, the streets gleamed from the previous night's rain. The whole world looked shiny and new, just like she felt.

She was no longer on the outside looking in. She was a part of it all. The elevator that boosted her to the tenth floor was no match for the buoyancy that had taken her over.

"'Morning, Mona," she called to the administrative assistant assigned to their group.

The plump blonde smiled to her as she walked past. "Morning, Ryan. Barry says he wants to see the viewgraphs for the Internet meeting by the end of the day."

Ryan rolled her eyes. "Barry always wants something." She heard her phone ringing before she even made it into her office. Swinging inside, she picked it up with a grin, stretching to close the door behind her. "Hello Helene."

"So what happened?" the gravelly voice demanded.

Ryan dropped into her chair and turned toward the window, stretching luxuriously. "God, Helene, it was amazing. Incredible. It was like nothing else that's ever happened to me before."

"Well, that's surprising considering that he never got near you. What'd you do, chicken out?"

"I was up until four in the morning writing the lo..." Ryan stopped short. "What did you say?" she asked slowly.

"I just got a call from a very irate person at the agency wondering why their high-priced best boy spent the evening cooling his heels at the Copley. They were demanding payment in full, I might add."

"Helene, I don't know what you're talking about. I met him at the Copley at eight," Ryan protested. "We spent most of the night together."

There was a short silence. "Oh really."

Ryan stared at the phone. "This is the part where you say ha ha, just kidding, Helene," she said. "Helene?"

"Ha ha, just kidding." The words were in a robotic monotone.

"Helene, tell me this is a joke," Ryan said with slowly dawning horror. "Tell me the man I was with last night was the guy from the agency."

The silence stretched out.

The blood began roaring in her ears.

"That son of a bitch," she said slowly. "That goddamned son of a bitch." Pure fury slammed through her so quickly it took her breath away.

He'd lied to her. He'd let her think he was the gigolo and as a result she'd taken a complete stranger into her bed. Admittedly, she had expected to take a complete stranger into her bed, but it was supposed to be a complete stranger with references. Instead, she'd been shanghaied by Cade Douglas, who was heaven only knew who.

Her imagination painted steadily more frightening pictures. He could have been anyone, she thought with a chill. She was lucky she hadn't been robbed or worse. Yet he'd turned down her money, so he wasn't some down-and-out hustler. He was doing it for kicks. It must have been quite the joke to him. She could just imagine him laughing inside the whole time he was scamming her.

She thought of him groaning as he came and the chill flamed back into fury. Oh no, he hadn't been laughing the whole time. He'd been getting off on it all, playing up his whole little charade. "You're doing this for the wrong reasons." "What do you say we meet tomorrow night to close the deal." Close the deal, indeed, she fumed. It wasn't enough that he'd played her once. He had the nerve to keep going. Sure, and why not? It was the ultimate male fantasy, sex with no commitment.

"Hey kid, are you okay?" Helene's voice broke into her thoughts.

She wanted to yell. She wanted to scream. She wanted to hit something, preferably Cade Douglas. No, hitting was too good for him, she thought dizzily. He should be horsewhipped. He should be roasted over a high flame.

"Talk to me, Ryan."

She unclenched her jaw and forced her face to move. "Sure. I'm fine," she said tonelessly. "Just surprised."

"Hey, at least you got some good material for the scene, right?"

"Helene, skip the bright-side stuff. I have to go now."

"Don't do anything drastic," Helene put in hastily.

"I won't. But if I wind up in jail, bail me out, okay?"

Ryan hung up, waiting for the roaring in her ears to go away. She fumbled in her purse until she found the phone number Cade had given her the night before, she started to dial the digits, then stopped. Her desk clock ticked the seconds away and she sprang up to pace. It wasn't enough. Reading him the riot act over the phone was not enough to pay him back for what he'd done. For this, she needed to see him in person.

She stopped and stared out the window, remembering the feel of his hands on her, the promise of his naked body. Anger and desire warred in her. Tonight they would be together. No matter who he was, no matter what game he was playing, she couldn't give up the chance to be with him one more time. If she told him off now, she'd be the loser. She'd gotten her lovers through much of the scene, but was missing the final climactic moments.

Which didn't matter nearly as much as the fact that *she'd* be missing the final climactic moments. After all these years without touching anyone, how could she really walk away from finally, completely knowing what it was like? From having him inside her? All she had to do was show up tonight and he would be kissing her, making love with her, taking her to the edge and beyond. Ryan rolled her forehead against the glass.

She had to feel his hands on her again, but how could she let him get away with what he'd done? The anger flowed back afresh and Ryan shook her head. He needed to learn a lesson about honesty and taking advantage of people. He needed to learn a lesson, but she needed to make love with him.

There had to be a way she could have both.

She stared out to the street and raked back her hair with her fingers. And then she blinked. Slowly, slowly a smile crept over her face as the beginnings of a plan took shape in her mind. Oh yes, she thought, there was definitely a way she could have both. Walking back to her desk, she signed her computer onto the Internet. It was time for a little research. This needed a personal touch.

By the time she talked with Cade an hour later, her plans were in place.

HE HAD TO COME CLEAN, that was all there was to it. Cade stared out the windows of his office for the hundredth time that day. Hearing her voice on his cell phone had brought the previous night back to him in Technicolor. He hadn't realized how sterile and empty his life had become until he'd held her against him. Now everything felt different. Now all he could think of was Ryan in his arms like a column of flame.

The current situation, though, was a disaster waiting to happen. If there was anything he'd learned in his life, it was that the truth was the only way to go. He'd seen where the lies got you.

He'd grown up in L.A. with a father who worshipped the art of the deal and beautiful women, pretty much in that order. Cade and his mother had come in a distant third. Unfortunately, Cade's father wasn't nearly as good at lying as he was at cutting deals to finance feature films or high-rise office buildings. By the time Cade was eleven, his parents were in the midst of an acrimonious divorce. One hadn't been enough for his father, though. With monotonous regularity, every four or five years the man got hooked enough on one or another of his mistresses to marry again. In a year, sometimes two, the shine would wear off and they'd divorce.

Infatuation didn't last. After seeing his father go through wives two through four, he should have known that. Some lessons, though, you couldn't learn by observation. Nope, Cade had had to find out himself with Alyssa. It was true love, he'd been sure of it. He was going to show his parents how a marriage was supposed to be. Except that when the flush of infatuation had faded, there'd been nothing left. "Chip off the old block," his father had said when Cade had told him about the divorce. Christ, he'd hated him for that. In a way, though, he'd been right. Some people were cut out for it and some people weren't.

Cade sighed. Maybe he wasn't set up for happily ever after, but he could do with some more of Ryan's company. The problem was how to salvage the situation. He'd botched things up the night before. He should just have told her the truth and tried to worm loose her phone number so he could see her later. Sleeping with her had been a big mistake. Unbidden, a smile stretched over his face. Huge mistake, and boy was he glad he'd made it.

So what now? Calling her up and telling her the truth wouldn't do it. The only thing to do was to show up and be honest with her. If he put his mind to it, he was pretty sure he could bring her around sooner or later. He had to come clean with her, though. He owed it to her.

He owed it to himself.

RYAN STARED OUT THE window of her room at the Beacon Hill Hotel, watching night fall. Stepping into the room was like stepping onto a movie set for a turn-of-the-century bordello. Cade Douglas had a few surprises coming to him, she thought as she rose to open the bottle of wine that sat on the impeccable cherry wood vanity table. Of course, she thought, pouring herself a glass, if all else failed she could just brain him with the antique porcelain ewer.

Moving around the room, she lit candles. Roses and mums perfumed the air. A tufted brocade chaise longue sat in front of the window, bearing an ornate, tasseled pillow perfect for cushioning milady's head. With sheer hangings draped over the canopy of the lace-covered, four-poster bed, it was a scene for romance and seduction.

Time for her to get in costume.

The knock on the door came as she was spritzing on perfume. She tried to ignore the quick surge of adrenaline, equal parts fury and desire, and walked over to the entry hall.

It was unfair that anyone should look that good, she thought, peering through the peephole. He stood there in a dove-gray suit, the indigo of his shirt bringing out the blue in his eyes. His hair looked black under the gas-lamp-style sconces in the hall. Taking a deep breath, she opened the door.

The words he'd planned to say died on his lips. She stood in a black lace merry widow, garters stretching down to silky hose, eyes challenging him to take her on. A red silk dressing gown swirled over the lace and matched the spike-heeled pumps she wore. Her dark hair tumbled down over her shoulders. Her mouth was an irresistible temptation. He stepped inside and she flowed into his arms.

She'd remember why she was furious with him in a minute, Ryan thought hazily as she sank into the kiss. Desire flowed around her thick and sweet, and she lost long minutes to the feel of his arms around her, the taste, the dark honey taste of his mouth. She barely heard the door swing shut behind them, enclosing them in the candlelit room.

Cade pressed his lips to her neck. "I've thought about this all day," he murmured, sampling her skin.

Ryan broke loose first, breathing hard. She looked at him, eyes heavy-lidded. "I wasn't sure if you'd forget again this time, so I planned ahead," she said, glancing at a handful of condoms on the bedside table.

"Wouldn't do to disappoint a lady." Swiftly, he pulled her to him, running his hands down her body, over the curves beneath the lace. "Or myself."

Ryan ran her fingers through his hair. It felt glorious, but it wouldn't do to forget why she was here. "Seems like one of us has too many clothes on, and it's not me."

He stroked the bare flesh above her stocking. "Oh no, darlin', what you've got on is exactly right." Cade stepped back and grinned, shrugging off his coat. "Guaranteed to give me good dreams tonight, assuming you ever let me sleep."

She watched him strip off his tie and stepped in to help unbutton his shirt. "Does being a gigolo always require such formal wear?"

"You know, all these career advancement seminars always talk about the importance of appearance." He leaned down to unlace his shoes. "There are even rules about how to undress."

"How to undress?" Ryan sank down on the bed to watch him, propping her head on her hand and casually flipping her dressing gown back to reveal lace and garters. Lazily, she stroked a hand up the inside of her thigh and circled out over her hip.

His eyes flashed hot with desire. Leaning over the bed, he kissed her until her breath came fast, then he stood back up. "Well, yes." Enjoying himself, he watched her intently. "For example, even the sexiest guy looks like a dork parading around in socks and jockey shorts. All the best gigolo manuals advise removing the shoes and socks before the pants come off." Sitting in the chair by the window, he demonstrated.

"Do tell. I'd always figured that natural talent counted most in your career. Clearly, I was misinformed." Ryan stroked the skin of her neck, fingertips sliding down to the swell of her breasts.

Cade's eyes were riveted on her hands. "Well, there's certainly something to be said for talent and enthusiasm," he said, standing up to drop his trousers, his "talent" jutting out from his boxers.

Then he stripped them off as well and her mouth went dry.

"Now who's got on too many clothes?" he asked, easing onto the bed beside her and sliding his hands down her silk gown. He kissed the smooth skin of her shoulders as he eased the silk down her arms.

"Cade," Ryan said as she felt his lips on her. "I was thinking about this all day today when I was at work." His response was muffled as he pushed her flat and began to kiss her breasts where they rose above the merry widow. Despite herself, she moaned. "I was thinking about what we could do tonight and what would really turn me on," she managed.

"And this isn't doing the trick?" he asked mischievously,

running his fingertips lightly up the bare skin of her inner thighs.

It felt wonderful, she thought, fighting not to writhe against him. She had to stay focused. "I wouldn't say that, but I thought your stock in trade was making fantasies come true." And this was her fantasy happening this instant, but he was playing her even now. Payback had to be on the agenda. But oh, it felt blissful.

His lips traveled back to hers. "What's your fantasy?" He pulled back and looked at her, his hand stroking the soft skin of her breasts, his eyes hot. "Tell me and we'll do it."

Ryan ran her hands down his torso to capture him hard in her hand, slipping her fingers up to the velvety tip of him, then back down. When he sucked in his breath, she smiled. "My fantasy has always been to drive a man crazy."

"You've got a good start on that right now, sweetheart," he said in a strained voice as she continued to move her hand.

Ryan shook her head. "Oh, I mean reeallly drive you crazy," she said, pushing him onto his back. She came up on her hands and knees to lean over him, nibbling her way down his torso. "Take you right to the edge until you're begging for more." She nuzzled his hard erection, then blew a warm breath over it. "And then give it to you." For a heady instant, she took him in her mouth, felt him pulse against her.

"Sounds like quite a fantasy to me," Cade said raggedly, reaching out reflexively as she pulled away.

Ryan leaned over to pull open a drawer at the side of the bed and pulled out a tasseled silk rope. "You haven't heard it all," she purred, running the silk tassel up and down his chest. "What would you say if I told you my fantasy included tying you up?"

Cade raised an eyebrow. "Bondage?"

She gave a short laugh. "Hardly. It's not as serious as all

that.'' Ryan teased his chest with the tassel, and followed its path with her tongue. Then, she moved up the bed to lie beside him, stroking him with the silk. ''I just think it would be kind of a turn on. Besides, it's not as though you haven't done this before. I imagine in your line of work you've seen this more than a few times.'' She leaned in to kiss him hard. ''Anyway, I thought your job was to do anything I asked.''

Against his will, he sank into the kiss she pressed on him. She felt so good and smelled so good that it was a struggle to stay focused. His choices were simple: fess up or get tied up. There didn't seem to be any other way out. If he stayed in character, getting tied up would be no big deal, familiar territory. It would be part of the job. The only way out would be to break character, in which case he'd be lucky to get out the door in one piece, let alone with his clothes. He'd lied to her and led her on. All his fine resolutions to tell the truth had evaporated when she'd opened the door. He'd deserve anything he got.

That didn't mean it would be pleasant, though. He wished that this tangle didn't exist and he was just here to be with her. At this point telling the truth would basically ensure that he never saw her again.

And that just wasn't an acceptable option right now.

Her fingers were on him again, sending a curl of heat through his body. She'd said her fantasy was to drive him crazy. The whole reason she was here was to find out what making love was really like. He felt her draped against him and thought of driving himself deep into her softness, of having her hot and tight around him. If he told her the truth and left, that was what he'd be walking out on. If he stayed, that was where they were sure to go. After that, maybe he could do some fast talking, work out a way to see her again for real.

''You're spending a lot of time thinking, Mr. Douglas,''

Ryan purred. "Are we going to do this, or will I have to call the agency and ask for someone else?"

In a flash he rolled and had her beneath him. "Over my dead body." His mouth was possessive on hers. Marking territory, Ryan thought through a haze of desire.

Cade rolled on his back and stretched one arm out lazily toward a bedpost. In the flickering candlelight his skin looked bronzed, as if from ancient Rome. "You want to tie me up, sugar, you go right ahead."

5

RYAN PULLED THE LAST silk rope tight around Cade's wrists and eased herself down to lie on the bed beside him. "What's it like being tied up? I've never done this before. Is it sexy?"

Strange, Cade thought uneasily. Definitely strange, and not something he'd be doing again any time soon. "You seem to have done an efficient job," he said, testing his bonds. "Were you a Girl Scout?"

"Yes." She traced patterns over his chest, brushing lightly over his nipples, then leaned over to nibble. "Were you a Boy Scout?"

Cade's body jolted at the contact. He nodded. "Resourcefulness is my middle name."

"What was the Boy Scout list of virtues, again?" Ryan began kissing her way down his body, pausing now and again to sample the flavors of his skin. "Cleanliness? Politeness?"

"A Boy Scout is loyal, helpful..." he broke off as she licked him, then let her hair brush over his chest until every nerve ending shivered at attention.

"Go on," she prompted, stroking her hands along his sides.

"Mmm, friendly...courteous..." She was driving him crazy, he thought, just as she'd wanted to. The soft, cool stroke of her hands, the warmth of her mouth, it was all pushing his control to the limit. "Kind...obedient..."

"Don't stop," she whispered, tracing his hip with the tip of her tongue.

"Cheerful...thrifty..." Cade took a shuddering breath as she drew closer to where the hard length of him trembled. "Uh, brave...clean..." he managed in a strangled voice as she put her mouth on him. "Reverent...trustworthy," he groaned. He started to reach for her and found his hands stopped by the rope. Then the heat of her mouth went away.

"Trustworthy. Honest. Yeah, that's the one I want." Ryan rose up suddenly and stepped off the bed. "You didn't learn that one so well, did you Mr. Douglas? Assuming that's your real name, of course. I already know this isn't your real career."

Busted. It flashed through him. Reflexively he tried to sit up, and was faced with the inescapable fact that he was trussed up like a Thanksgiving turkey. This was not good, he thought. Not good at all.

"I can explain." God, what a lame response, he thought disgustedly.

"Oh, I certainly hope so." Ryan pulled a chair up to the side of the bed. "I'm dying to hear this one. Wait," she stopped him when he started to talk. "Let me get my wine."

She took her time coming back to the chair. Cade knew it was to annoy him, and she succeeded. It infuriated him to be so helpless. It was even more irritating to know that he probably deserved whatever she could dish out to him. She draped herself over the chair, and it annoyed him even more that he still wanted her.

"You planned this, of course," he said calmly. "I wondered why the sudden change in location. The Copley Hotel doesn't have any four-posters. And you played the fantasy thing brilliantly. You tricked me and I walked right into it."

"Well, you tricked me into bed," she shot back at him. "I don't see the difference."

"You had a choice."

"So did you."

Cade shook his head. "I didn't know what was going on at first. It isn't every day that a gorgeous woman comes by to pick you up, even if it is an accident. It wasn't until we got upstairs that I realized what was really going on."

"You thought I was a pickup?" She'd thought she was angry before, but now she was livid.

"What did you expect? You walk up to me unexpectedly, you ask me upstairs. What am I supposed to think? You caught me in a mood to take a chance. I know it was stupid but I wanted to be with you." He blew a breath out in frustration. "I tried to get out of it when I realized what was going on. You wouldn't let me."

"You didn't try very hard."

"I wanted you. Is that a crime?" His eyes blazed at her. "You were ready to happily jump into bed with a guy who sleeps with people for money, but you're pissed off that I slept with you because I wanted you."

"No, I'm pissed off because you lied to me." She sprang up from the chair and paced across the carpet. "I liked you. I thought we clicked. It could have stayed that way if you'd been honest with me."

Cade snorted. "If I'd been honest with you, you'd have said goodbye and gone looking for your hustler and we would never have said another word to each other."

He was right, she thought. But he'd still been out of line. "It never occurred to you to try to set the record straight?"

"Of course it did," he said impatiently, then closed his eyes and shook his head. "From the minute I figured out what was going on I was trying to find a way out that would let me set things straight and still keep this going."

"'This' meaning the sex, of course," she said frostily.

"This meaning being with you. And yes, the sex—it's not like we've spent a lot of time talking politics or philosophy. But what we had together felt pretty damned good, and at the time I wanted it to keep going more than I wanted to come clean. I came over here tonight thinking I'd tell you everything. Until you answered the door looking like that.'' He stopped for a moment. ''I'm not proud of it, but there it is.''

She stared into his eyes, softening. She wanted to believe him. She wanted to be with him, to feel the way she had that morning. If only... Her breath huffed out in frustration. In all honesty she was as bad as he was, searching for a justification for keeping it going instead of recognizing it for what it was and letting it go.

Cade raised his head and looked at her. ''You've obviously been planning this ever since you found out today. So what happens now? Please, fill me in. I'm all tied up in knots over it,'' he finished sarcastically.

Ryan looked at him stretched out on the bed, his skin gleaming copper-colored in the candlelight. Heat flared in her blood, driven this time not by anger but by passion. ''Well, it looks to me like I have you at my mercy.'' She rose to lean over the bed and brush a palm over the smooth, hard lines of his belly. ''Your punishment is that I get to amuse myself with your body until I'm ready to let you go.''

Standing, she shrugged out of her dressing gown, letting it slide down her arms to pool on the floor. Then she kicked off her shoes and sank down on the bed beside him. ''You see, I've always been very curious about the male body. Outside of last night, I've never even seen a naked man up close before, at least not in the light. The only things I know are what I've read in *Cosmo*.'' She gave him a serious stare. ''I don't know what parts are sensitive or what will make you moan, or even how the equipment works.'' She kissed him hard, then drew back. ''Tonight, I get to experiment.''

''You're not seriously expecting me to cooperate with

this, are you?'' Irritation replaced the momentary empathy in his eyes. ''I'm not some lab monkey.''

''No, indeed, Mr. Douglas. I'd say you're all man.'' She smiled wickedly. ''And I hope you've been taking your vitamins. Tonight, you're going to need them.''

Hell of a position to be in, Cade thought. On the other hand, he could think of worse punishments than having someone play with his body and looking for what pleased him most.

That didn't mean he planned to enjoy this.

Ryan leaned over to the bedside table and came back with a feather. With excruciating slowness, she traced the soft tip over the lines of his face, stroking his brow and his cheeks, teasing his closed eyelids, tracing the line of his lips. Then she went lower, writing swirling patterns like cursive script over his arms, his palms, his chest. He stiffened as she dropped lower to trace over his torso, then his flat belly. He sucked in a breath as she drew down close to his hips, feeling the moist heat of her breath fanning over his skin as the feather tip trailed along. He steeled himself not to react as he felt her trace circles on the sensitive skin of his hips, but instead of going to the next obvious destination, she twirled it down over his legs and stroked the tender flesh of his instep in a surprisingly erotic caress.

He couldn't stop it any longer and was starting to react when the tip of the feather suddenly traced the hardening tip of him. He caught his breath.

Ryan tossed the feather aside and rose onto her hands and knees. Dropping her head, she let her hair spill down onto his chest. Slowly she dragged it down his torso so that just the ends stroked over his chest, his hips, and beyond. Swaying, she ran it down his legs then back up again, across his arms and back down his chest.

The silky brush of her hair brought his skin to a state of exquisite sensitivity. The anticipation was as much a part of the experience as the touch. When the soft spill of hair stroked over his most tender parts, he bit back a groan. This was something new, and he liked it more than he wanted to. The teasing touch was lighter than hand or mouth, and more tantalizing than either.

Then he felt her lips against his neck, trailing down over his shoulder then over to linger over his nipples, kissing the newly sensitized skin. Her lips traveled lower and he felt himself stir in anticipation. Instead of touching him, though, she stopped and straightened up.

"You know, this merry widow feels very sexy but it's starting to get hot." She straddled him and reached down to begin unfastening the long chain of hooks that wound down the front of the garment. Her breasts spilled out first, then a growing triangle of white skin appeared. Hook by hook, the triangle widened, exposing rosy nipples, soft white breasts, and her flat, smooth stomach. Finally she finished and tossed it away, sitting astride him gloriously naked. How he wanted to fill his hands with her breasts, feel their weight and softness. Instead, he pulled his hands impotently at the ropes.

"Now, now, don't get impatient," she chided him. "Everything in good time." She moved back down his body to stare at his hardening erection. There was no sense in pretending that he wasn't aroused. In fact, he wanted to drag her close and stop the teasing, erase this maddening need that was overtaking him.

Ryan traced her tongue down the hard heat of him, feeling the incredibly arousing contrast of the slippery skin against her lips. She took her time, stopping to dwell whenever she heard his breath come fast or felt his hips twitch. Finally, she slid him into her mouth, ripping a groan from his throat.

Then she stopped and leaned over to pluck a condom from the bedside table. "Let's just put one of these on you, shall we?'' She unwrapped it and rolled it down the length of his shaft. "I thought the slippery kind sounded best.''

She straddled him again until she was poised just above where his pulsing erection lay flat against his belly. Holding her breath, she lowered herself until she was pressed against his hot flesh. Her innermost folds closed around him. Then she moved her hips so that she slid against him to feel him hard and hot against the slick swollen bud of her sex. She was ready. With each motion of her hips she rubbed herself against him, teasing them both with the slick, intimate caress of skin against skin. Swiveling her hips slowly, she stroked herself and him, inflaming their increasing arousal. She stared down into Cade's face. His eyes were dark with desire, and she leaned in to take his mouth with hers.

He kissed her back hard, parting her lips, his tongue darting in to duel with hers before she pulled away. She knew the slow stroking of her softness against him was driving him mad. He pulled futilely against his bonds and ground his teeth.

Ryan felt her body start to shudder in climax as she swiveled her hips against Cade, then she was jolting and feeling the heat and glow surge through her. Before she was even done, she reached down and slid him swiftly into her. Their groans came in tandem as his heat speared deep inside.

It took her breath away. For a moment she was absolutely still, absorbing the feeling of having him fill her. It was excruciatingly exquisite, the hardness, the heat. Her one brief encounter had never felt like this, the slow, hot flow of arousal running through her body. Instead, she put her hands on his shoulders for balance and began to ride up and down on him. It was impossible to keep from moaning at the glorious friction as he slid in and out, as she felt him get harder and thicker with every stroke. Second by second, the intensity increased, her muscles tightened as she drove

herself to a higher and higher pitch of arousal. This was
what she'd been missing, this, this…this…

She looked into his face again, drawn tight with an ecstasy that looked like pain, and slid forward to kiss him.

"Oh honey, I can't hold back," he whispered raggedly.

It put her over the edge and her body bucked with a
second climax.

Feeling her soft heat convulse around him took him past
control and he spilled himself deep inside her.

THE PAST FEW HOURS HAD been hands down the most memorable of his life, Cade thought, but he was beginning to
wonder just when she planned to let him go. Her body was
a comforting warmth as she dozed against his chest, and
after everything, damned if he didn't want to put an arm
around her and pull her to him. Except that he was still tied
up.

He looked past the clutter of condom wrappers to where
the digital clock blinked to 2:00 a.m. "Ryan." He jiggled
a bit to wake her. "Ryan."

"Huh?" she asked groggily, then snuggled next to him
with a little purring noise.

"Ryan." He joggled her again until she muttered. "It's
two o'clock in the morning. You've had your fun, now wake
up. I've got meetings all day tomorrow…today," he corrected himself.

Ryan sat up and stretched, feeling an unaccustomed soreness throughout her body. Had her fun was an understatement. She blinked, coming back to awareness. It was done,
she thought, the slow realization giving her a sharp pang of
regret. Now the only thing left was for her to get away
safely and count herself lucky.

Except that she didn't feel lucky at all.

Slowly she got up off the bed and scooped her robe off
the floor, sliding her arms into the sleeves as she wandered

into the bathroom, yawning sleepily. Her body felt unfamiliar to her, as though it wasn't hers anymore. She could smell his scent on her skin and it pulled at her. It wasn't fair that he was wound so deeply into her brain. This was over, it was done with, she thought as she stripped in front of the mirror. She was going to walk out the door and that would be the end of it. She'd never see him again.

Ryan spun the knob on the shower and stepped into the hot gush of water, holding her hair up with one hand. The stream brought her back to some degree of alertness. Okay, so she had a strong, agile, and fairly ticked-off man tied to a bed. The question was, how did she set him loose and get out the door in one piece? She turned the temperature to cold and came fully awake.

Stepping out, she dried herself off with a soft, fluffy towel. Her face looked strange, she thought as she glanced in the mirror, her eyes heavy-lidded and somehow wiser. As she pulled on her street clothes her body felt almost too sensitive for the touch of anything.

Anything but Cade's skin.

She touched her forehead against the cool glass. It had to end, obviously, but it was so hard. It was like giving up air.

She turned back to the shower and spun the taps, flipping a lever to send water gushing into the claw-footed tub. Walking back out into the room, she picked up Cade's shirt and hooked a finger through a belt loop on his trousers.

"What are you doing?" he asked sharply.

Ryan shook her head at him. "Can't hear you over the water. I'll just be a minute." Steam billowed around her as she walked into the bathroom and dropped his clothes into the water.

"What in the hell did you just do?" he asked heatedly as she walked back into the room. Anger sharpened the lines of his face and he jerked at his bonds, making the bed creak. Ryan felt a quick thrill of fear.

"Well, I can't very well let you go and have you catch me," she said in a logical tone as she tossed her discarded lingerie and shoes in her overnight bag. "And it won't do to leave you tied up until the maids find you."

"Thanks so much for your thoughtfulness," he said sarcastically.

"So I have to find a way to leave you so that you can get yourself loose but you can't come after me in the hall." She reached into her purse and pulled out a twenty. "You'll pardon me if I don't pay you the full fee, but under the circumstances I think it's understandable." She laid the money on the bedside table, pushing the condom wrappers out of the way. "I believe this will cover your cleaning bill. Your clothes should dry out enough to wear in a while or so."

She bent over the silk rope tied around one of his wrists and loosened it. Before she could step back, his hand snaked out to grab her arm.

Ryan fought to calm the spurt of alarm. "As long as you're holding on to me, you can't untie yourself," she said calmly.

Cade pulled her within inches of his face. "This isn't over yet," he gritted out with eyes blazing. He released her so quickly she stumbled backward.

Ryan took a deep breath and picked up her overnight bag and purse and walked to the door. "Of course it is, Mr. Douglas. You haven't a clue where to find me." She opened the door and stepped out into the hall, slamming the door behind her with finality.

6

MORNING SUNSHINE SLANTED across the Charles River as Ryan pulled into the paved lot on the greenbelt adjoining the water, then parked. Half a mile beyond her, the old stone bridge arced across from the Boston side where she stood to Cambridge soil. Near the parking lot, volunteers had set up for one of Boston's innumerable outdoor festivals, erecting bright canvas booths and stringing electrical cord. Out on the river, wisps of mist still trailed over the surface of the water.

Like the fog she'd been in throughout the previous day, a fog that had nothing to do with it being Friday and everything to do with what had happened the night before. She'd thrown herself into alternately preparing notes for a new course she was designing and dodging calls from Helene, who'd left a string of increasingly peeved voice mails. Ryan didn't care. Maybe it was silly, but she just wasn't ready to talk about what had happened with Cade. She was as unsettled as she was angry, and still hadn't figured out exactly what she felt.

Sighing, she opened her door and swung her feet onto the asphalt to tighten her shoelaces.

"About time you showed up, sleepyhead." Ryan looked up to see a pixie with a short, ginger-colored shag.

"How can you possibly be perky at five after eight on a Saturday, Becka? You're sick." Ryan yawned, looking at her friend who crackled with energy. "I'd be on time if you didn't insist on running at the crack of dawn."

"You know what Ben Franklin said," Becka returned with a smirk. "Early to bed and early to rise."

"Ben Franklin was a sexually incontinent dirty old man," Ryan shot back, swinging her car door shut. She stooped to tuck the keys into a small pocket on the inside of her shorts. "Why should I believe what he said?"

"Better not let Mrs. McCormack hear you say that," Becka warned, raising the specter of their grade school teacher who'd worshiped the founding fathers.

Becka and Ryan didn't remember meeting each other. Perhaps it had happened in kindergarten, perhaps in the suburban Boston neighborhood where they'd toddled around in diapers. Either way, the bond that had been struck was deep and lasting, holding up through kindergarten and high school alike, prevailing even after they became adults pursuing their own careers. They were fixtures in each other's lives.

Ryan turned toward the running trail that twined along the bank of the water.

"Not so fast, slick. Time to stretch, first." A massage therapist who specialized in treating athletes, Becka took her workouts seriously. "I spent half the week massaging athletes straight out of spring training who didn't have enough sense to stretch out before they hit the field." Her head bobbed down by her knees as she spoke.

"If you're going to insist on working with weekend warriors, you get what you've got coming." Ryan reached behind her to bend her raised leg double, stretching her quads.

Becka shook her head, stepping on a cement bar marking a parking slot and sinking into calf pulls, her eyes glimmering with fun. "No, this doesn't have to do with the physicians' healthcare job, it's something totally different."

Swimming up out of her early morning haze, Ryan took a closer look at her friend. Becka bounced lightly on her toes, excitement fairly humming around her. "So what's going on? You look like you've got some hot news. Spill it, baby."

"Well, if you're going to force me into it…" Becka gave her an amused glance, unable to stretch it out any longer. "The team therapist for the local farm club was diagnosed with carpal tunnel syndrome. He's going to have to have surgery and rehab, and they expect him to be out all season. They called the physicians' health sports medicine department and asked Wally for a recommendation. He sent them to yours truly," she said airily.

Ryan stopped in her tracks and gave a whoop of surprise. "Becka, that's huge!" She grabbed her friend for a hug and did a little victory dance. "Oh my god, this is wonderful. I can't think of anyone who deserves it more."

Becka flushed with joy. "It is great, isn't it? I just got the offer yesterday. When I woke up this morning and remembered I was just over the moon." Her attempt at an offhand shrug didn't quite make it. "I'm not getting my hopes up too much, though. It could turn into something more but there's no guarantee. Maybe the team therapist will come back later in the season or maybe they won't need me next year."

Ryan rolled her eyes. "Or maybe he'll retire and work on his golf game, or maybe they'll find they need two massage therapists. Let yourself enjoy this," she said impatiently. "Deal with that stuff when and if it happens."

They started back into a slow jog. "So what does Scott think about it?" Ryan asked curiously, referring to Becka's sometime suitor.

Becka shrugged and sped up a notch. "Typical Scott. He doesn't like me being around all these young guys, he doesn't like the weekend and nighttime hours, he doesn't like me traveling with the team and not being home to give him rubdowns." A thin, brittle edge of anger colored her voice. "He's never once said congratulations. I don't know why I even waste time with him. He's in love with his image in the mirror, not with me." Scott was a bodybuilder with enormous biceps and an ego to match.

Ryan shook her head. "Men. Why do we even bother with them?"

Becka gave her a rueful grin. "You tell me, girlfriend."

"So how far are we going today?"

"Three miles."

"Three?" Ryan squeaked in horror. "Running season just started. Cut me some slack here, we don't all live in the gym during the winter." Ryan was sure that her voice sounded almost entirely unlike a whine.

"You can do it." Becka was barely winded from their current pace. "It's penance for canceling on Wednesday."

An image of standing naked in front of the windows with her fingers tangled in Cade's hair flashed into Ryan's mind. Her mouth went dry. Then she remembered the other half of the story and tightened her jaw.

"You're looking mighty grim. Don't tell me you're getting grief at work?"

"No, work's fine." It was the play that had her tied up in knots. "Barry's being a pain over some deal he's cooking up, but the rest of it's the same old same old."

Becka shot her a penetrating look. "Come on, Ryan, talk to me. We've been friends too long for you to pull this loner stuff."

Ryan ran in silence for a few more paces, working up her nerve. "The new book's almost done. It's a big deal. If they like it, I'm contracted for three more and Helene thinks she can close on another multibook package at a different publishing house. Basically, if I get this one right, I can afford to quit and write full-time."

"Quit teaching conflict resolution for kindergartners? How will you ever stand it?"

"You know how much I want this, Becka." Ryan hesitated. The next part was the hard bit. "The problem is, it's a lot more explicit than anything else I've written before and I'm having problems with the love scenes. I know I have to get this done and it's got to be good, but every time I've tried to sit down at the computer, nothing's come out. Helene told me I needed inspiration that was a little more concrete. So to speak."

"She set you up with a one-night stand?" Becka guessed.

"Not exactly." Ryan swallowed. "She set me up with a gigolo."

"What?" Becka came to a dead stop in the middle of the trail and stared at her, goggle eyed.

Ryan cringed. "Well, it seemed like a good idea at the time," she said weakly.

"Good? I think it was brilliant!" Becka clapped her on the back. "Honeybunch, you got laid! That's the best, good for you." She pulled Ryan back into a run. "Now tell me all about it, I want to hear everything."

Ryan felt a reluctant smile tug at the corners of her mouth and launched into her story, warming to the tale. Whether it was the endorphins and the metronomic thud of their footfalls or the release of telling the tale to another, Ryan felt her mood lightening. Hearing herself talk about meeting Cade, walking up to the room, feeling his hands on her for the first time, she was able to relish the sensations all over again. Then she got to Thursday morning and the moment it all changed.

"So I'm sitting in my office all giddy and mushy and just about to call him like we'd planned when I see Helene's on the line. She tells me the agency called her wondering what had happened because I hadn't shown, and they were demanding their money."

"What do you mean, you never showed? You were there."

"That's what I told her. They said I wasn't."

Becka stared at her, eyes widening in comprehension. "Oh my god..."

"Oh my god is right," Ryan gasped. "We've got to walk, Becka, I'm dying." Absorbed in their talk, they'd just kept running as one mile turned to three, then four, unnoticed. "How far have we gone?"

Becka glanced at her sports watch. "Probably about four and a half miles, but don't change the subject. You mean he..."

"Is a lying snake? Exactly. He wasn't the gigolo, he was just some guy waving to the waitress. My mistake. On the other hand, he didn't bother to straighten me out. He deliberately lied to me." Ryan felt the fury bubble up afresh. "God, it just fries me that I got taken in." They walked several minutes in silence and gradually their cars came back into sight.

"Well, how was it? Did you have fun?"

Just thinking of it still gave her flutters in the pit of her stomach. "Fun doesn't even come close. It was amazing." She blushed. "Not that I'm much of a judge, but it pretty much left all my previous experience in the dust."

Becka stopped to stretch. "Mmm." She bent until her forehead was against her knees. "Well all things considered, I'd say you came out of it pretty well."

Ryan stared at her. "Pretty well?" Her voice rose. "He lied to me. He jerked me around. He was a creep." And she'd walk over hot coals before she'd admit that she still wanted him.

"Well," Becka said thoughtfully, "how much of a creep is a person who'd sleep with you for money? And fake like he's enjoying it. At least this guy did it because he wanted you, not because he wanted the money." She stretched her quads, pulling her leg up behind her ballerina style. "If he was breathing hard, you know it was because he was turned on, not because it was part of the act. Besides, this is actually something that could have a future. Granted, it could also be a one-night stand, but it's not like a night with a gigolo is going to turn into true love, Richard Gere films to the contrary." Becka bent from the waist and blew all her breath out, then straightened back up. "Come on, let's walk over to the festival. I'll buy you breakfast."

Bright colored bunting trailed from booth to booth, and Bob Marley played over the loudspeakers. The aromas of food from ethnic restaurants all over the city weaved around them. Becka, predictably, gravitated to the sound of blenders at a health-food stand and picked up a pair of protein shakes.

"Can't you ever just order an egg sandwich like a normal person?" Ryan asked in exasperation.

"You'll clog your arteries eating that kind of stuff. It's poison."

"Oh, right, my body is a temple…"

Becka gave her a sidelong glance. "The way you eat, it might be more like the bleachers at Fenway Park after a game."

Ryan sipped from the frothy, peach-colored concoction. She'd have suffered torture before admitting that it was good. They ambled aimlessly through the rows of vendors selling everything from New Age crystals to CDs.

"So what happens now? You said he wanted to see you again."

"Well, yeah."

"So are you going to?"

"Am I going to what?"

Becka gave an impatient huff. "See him again."

"Oh, that. I already did." Against all odds, Ryan was enjoying herself. A table of brightly colored sunglasses caught her eye and she drifted to a stop. "We met at the Beacon Hill Hotel Thursday night."

"Everything's half off," said the woman behind the table. "All UV protected and scratch resistant, too."

"The Beacon Hill Hotel, no less. Don't you live the luxe life." Becka picked up a hand mirror to admire herself in a pair of black cat's-eye sunglasses with rhinestones. "I've heard the rooms in that place are filled with antiques."

"Not to mention four-poster beds, which comes in handy when you want to give someone a little talking to." Ryan said with relish.

"Four-poster be..." Becka gave a startled laugh. "Girlfriend, what did you do to that poor man?"

"I just wanted to be sure I had his full attention, so I made sure he couldn't get up and walk away...or move a whole lot," Ryan said innocently.

A siren sounded out on the street. "Oh my god," Becka said in a low voice. "You killed him and that's the cops coming to get you."

"Oh, no, I'm quite sure he was fine. I mean, he was groaning and panting a little while we were, um, talking, but I'm almost sure he was having a good time. I had him all undressed with nowhere to go. I figured I might as well get some use out of him." She gave a bawdy wink.

Becka pulled the glasses down on her nose and stared. "You tied up a man you hardly know in a hotel room and used him as a sex toy?" she burst out. The woman sitting behind the table choked on her coffee.

"Sorry," Ryan said hastily, setting Becka's glasses on the table and yanking her along. "Can you say it a little louder next time?" she hissed.

"I'm sorry, but I'm just trying to keep up here." Laughter burbled in Becka's voice. "You haven't slept with a guy since you were what, twenty-two, and now you're into bondage?"

"Hey, with my record who knows how long it'll be before I have sex again. I figured I'd already been jerked around. I might as well get something for my time."

"You're too much."

"Wait until you hear about the suit," Ryan said smugly. All in all, it made a pretty good story, she thought sometime later. She hadn't seen Becka laugh so hard that things came out her nose since they were in second grade, and that time it was milk, not frothy peach smoothie.

"Is your friend all right?" asked a passerby.

"She's fine, just a little overexcited," said Ryan, patting Becka on the back solicitously.

"Oh," Becka gasped, holding her stomach. "That poor guy, what he must have thought. Here's the Wicked Witch of the East on a tear and he's totally helpless." She giggled again as they wandered over to sit on a stone bench overlooking the river. "So I'm thinking that's the last we're going to see of Mr. Douglas. What about you, though. Are you okay? I mean, it's a great story but it must have been a pretty intense week for you."

"Well, I guess I'm…" To Ryan's horror, her voice broke. Becka rubbed her back sympathetically. "I don't know why I'm doing this," Ryan said, blinking back tears. "It's not like I was expecting anything from a gigolo."

"Oh Ryan, you're a romantic. You write sweetheart novels, for god's sake." Becka blew out a breath. "Helene was looking out for your best interests as a writer, but you were both out of your minds to think that you could sleep with a guy without getting emotionally involved. Especially when it's the first guy you've slept with in, what, seven years?"

"Eight," Ryan said weakly. Out on the river, a pair of sculls raced toward the Harvard bridge, oars skimming over the water, the cries of the coxswains floating across to the bank. "You know, the bad part is I really liked him. And he said the same thing about me. Though admittedly he was tied up and at my mercy at the time."

"I suppose that might make his comments just a teensy bit suspect," Becka allowed. "On the other hand, he could very well have meant them. You're good company, you know. And while you may not believe it, you're a babe when you want to be.''

"Oh yeah, that's me, fighting them off," Ryan said dryly. "Come on, Becka, you know guys look right through me."

"Because you tune them out. You dress in baggy clothes and you're always rushing around in a hurry." Becka tipped her head consideringly. "Let me guess, when you teach a class, you either skip out at lunch or you sit with the women students. And you leave as soon as possible after it's over."

"We're specifically not allowed to date students," Ryan said defensively. "It's Barry's number-one rule."

"The point is, you spend most of your time at work and the rest writing. It's not you, it's the way you've set up your life."

"I don't want to be standing around and waiting for someone who's not going to show up," Ryan burst out hotly.

"Isn't that what you're doing anyway? Avoiding them all and thinking that somehow Mr. Right is going to show up, cut you out of the pack and choose you for happily ever after? It's like you got totally derailed when Ross worked you over."

The words cut Ryan to the quick, cut to the heart of what had underlain every encounter with a man since she'd known him.

"He's not the standard for all men," Becka continued. "He was an immature little college boy who drank too much and gave you a tumble without thinking about it. He was a jerk, Ryan. If you'd ever dated anyone else you'd know that. He didn't deserve a minute of your time. The son of a bitch certainly didn't deserve to screw up the entire rest of your life." She pulled Ryan close for a hard hug then looked at her seriously. "It's time to go forward. You've been caught up in this too long. Getting back into the swing of things with this Cade guy was a start. Now we need to find you a man.'' Becka scanned around and pointed to a grizzled septuagenarian flipping ribs at the barbecue booth. ''Hmm, what about him?''

Ryan wiped her eyes, and this time the tears were from laughter. ''You always look out for what's best for me, Becka, that's why I love you.'' She rose and they began to walk back toward the bazaar.

''Well, I'd ask Scott to set you up with someone but I don't think you'd like anyone Scott picked. Come to think of it,'' she reflected, ''I'm having serious thoughts about Scott myself.''

The glimmer of gold at the next booth caught Ryan's eye and she stopped to look. Gold chains snaked across black velvet, earrings dangled from racks and danced in the light breeze.

''Do you think happily ever after is a pipe dream?'' Ryan held a pair of amethyst drop ball earrings next to her face, admiring the results in a hand mirror.

Becka shrugged. It was a question they'd often asked each other. ''I don't know. Look at your parents, still holding hands after thirty-three years. On the other hand, I think things were easier back when they met. Everyone knew what the rules were and what was expected. Now it's confusing. No one knows what to expect, not the guys, not us.'' She blew out a breath, surprising Ryan with her frustration. ''I think it can work if you meet the right man, but even then sometimes I think it's not worth the time. Of course, that could just be Scott burnout talking.''

''Don't give up on the gender, though,'' Ryan said. ''Speaking as someone who's had a long dry spell, there's something to be said for sex.''

''Can I take it that you're recovering from your experience with Cade?''

''If that's even his name, yes. I'm starting to put it into perspective anyway. Talking about it helped. Thanks. And you're right, it's not as though I'd have had a serious relationship with a gigolo. So all things considered, maybe he wasn't so evil." She sighed. "The frustrating part now is that it's over. God, playing with his body felt good. It's like I've just gotten my motor revved up after all this time off and there's nobody to fool around with."

"Like I said, we need to get you a man."

"First things first—I need to finish my book," said Ryan, starting to angle toward her car. "We going to run on Monday?"

"Wouldn't miss it for the world. Maybe you'll have another great story."

"Nope, I think this is one in a million," Ryan laughed.

"Good. I don't think my sinuses could handle any more peach smoothie."

DUSK SENT LONG SHADOWS through the bay windows of Ryan's second-floor Victorian flat as she worked at her computer. The weekend had slipped by while she sat at the keyboard in the grip of a creative tumult. She had to hand it to Helene, her idea had worked. The love scenes smoldered and leapt off the page. When Ryan reached a hot scene between the hero and heroine, like now, she had only to think of Cade's hands roaming over her body, hotly possessive, his mouth searing hers. The sensations roared back, slick, hot, hard, and wet, and she ran a fingertip rhythmically up and down her throat.

The phone clamored for attention. Ryan blinked, snapping out of her reverie. "Hello?"

"So what's with ducking my phone calls Friday?" The rough voice leapt out of the phone, obliterating Ryan's fantasy.

"Hi, Helene."

"So did you kill him?"

Ryan smiled. "Not quite. I made it a night he'll remember, though. It'll teach him not to tell lies."

"I'm almost afraid to ask, kid. Was he breathing when you left him?"

"Yes," Ryan said airily. "He was tied up, so it was hard to say how perky he was, but I'm almost sure he was breathing."

"When I told you that you needed to think about publicity, I didn't mean arrests for assault."

"He'd never do that, trust me. We just had a discussion about what happened." Ryan couldn't keep back a smile at the thought.

"So how's the book coming? You've only got to the end of this week, you know."

"You'll be happy to hear that I've finished it."

"Even the hot stuff?"

"Especially the hot stuff. It's filled with nothing but hot stuff. Want me to e-mail you some of it?"

"I trust your instincts. Just be sure the full package is on Elaine's desk first thing Friday morning. I don't want you to get a rep for missing deadlines."

Ryan saved the file she was reviewing and pressed the print button. "Hear that? That's my laser printer spitting out chapter eleven. I'm on my final polishing run. It'll be on time, Helene, I swear."

"Just remember, if this one goes, you're a professional writer for life, or as long you keep cranking out novels." Ryan could hear the grin in her voice. "Not to mention the fact that I'll get my hot tub."

"And you definitely deserve your hot tub for pulling my fat out of the fire, Helene. Don't think I don't appreciate it. You're the best." Ryan pulled the pages off her printer and shuffled them into order.

"Well, you can buy me a drink next time we get together.

Speaking of which, are you still coming to Manhattan for that conference?''

''Week after next. I've got you penciled in for dinner one of the nights I'm there, so don't forget.''

''I wouldn't dream of it. It'll give us a chance to catch up.'' Helene's voice softened. ''You're one of the good ones, kid. I want to see you do well.''

''Not to mention get your hot tub.''

''And get my hot tub.''

7

WRITING FULL-TIME, wouldn't it be bliss, Ryan thought a week and a half later. She scooped her briefing charts off her desk and headed to the on-site classroom for her morning course on public speaking. Four or five days like the previous weekend, followed by two or three days off to relax. Time spent worrying about pleasing her characters and her readers, not a neurotic, micromanaging boss.

Barry was currently calling her name as he hustled down the hall toward her.

Ryan sighed. "What do you need, Barry? I've got a class starting in five minutes."

"Your briefing charts, I just wanted to check over your briefing charts."

"They're identical to the ones you reviewed yesterday in the run-through." Ryan looked at her watch uneasily. "Barry, I've got to get in there or I'll be late to your meeting. Can we…"

Barry's chubby fingers smoothed the strands of hair that trailed over his nearly bald pate. "I just want to be sure we're all set. This deal could mean a lot to the company. It could completely change the way we do business."

"I'm sure it will be fine," Ryan said distractedly, fantasizing about the magic phone call from Helene. Anything to get her away from Barry's endless fussing. One would think that after four years of success, he'd have a bit more faith in her.

"Let's just review the schedule," he said inexorably.

"Barry, it's nine o'clock," Ryan said a little desperately. The morning went downhill from there.

FOUR HOURS LATER, Ryan hurried out of the classroom, looking at her watch. Barry would be furious that she wasn't already in the conference room ready to deliver, but since he'd been responsible for getting her off schedule to begin with, she wasn't feeling very sympathetic. Anyway, he was always working on something that was going to be the next great thing. It usually wasn't and she doubted that this would be any different.

Ryan snatched up her viewgraphs from her office, then made a beeline for the conference room.

"They're already in there," Mona whispered. "I brought in coffee just a little while ago and Doris was talking."

Ryan stopped outside the conference room, listening to the muted buzz of voices inside. Smoothing her hair, she took a deep breath and opened the door.

About eight people sat at the long oval conference table, staring at the far end of the room where one of Ryan's colleagues gestured at a vividly colored briefing chart displayed on a large screen. Ryan's heart sank. Even in the dimmed lights, she could see Barry looking daggers at her. She gave a helpless shrug, crossing quietly to the open chair left for her.

With one ear on Neil's presentation, she shuffled rapidly through her notes, doing a quick scan to ensure she remembered the salient points. She raised her head for a quick glance around the table.

And found herself eye to eye with Cade Douglas.

All the breath left her lungs in an instant. It couldn't be, she told herself. She had to be dreaming. This was one of those stress nightmares, like the ones she'd had in school where she showed up for a crucial exam an hour late and without her shirt.

Last time she'd seen Cade, she'd been missing more than her shirt.

Of all the conference rooms in all the companies in all the world, Ryan thought, stifling a hysterical giggle. She slowed her breathing with conscious effort, trying to calm her racing heart. It was too ridiculous to believe—the star of the biggest personal fiasco of her life, showing up here of all places. It was just her luck. Any normal person would have met the gigolo and had their fun. She had to stumble up to some ringer and take him upstairs for, okay, for what was pretty amazing sex. But then afterward…well, okay, after the second bout of excellent and amazing sex, and after the part about the bathtub, to have him show up here? Here, of all places?

So much for her bold words at the Beacon Hill Hotel. He knew where to find her now. The question was what was he going to do about it? Embarrassment wasn't the half of it. After all, this was her job, at least for the time being. What would this do to Barry's deal? Would Cade actually say something or change his mind? *Excuse me, Barry, the deal's off. Last time I met your curriculum manager she tied me up, used me for sex and threw my clothes in the bathtub.* Ryan felt another giggle rising up that felt dangerously close to screaming hysteria. Okay, stay calm, she told herself. She was probably safe on that count. He'd never go that far.

But how far *would* he go?

Neil wound up his presentation and flipped the lights on to take questions. She glanced up again and found Cade's eyes on her, glinting with the lazy amusement of a cat about to toy with a mouse.

God, he was gorgeous.

Behind her, Barry cleared his throat. "Thank you, Neil. Gentlemen, I'd like to introduce our curriculum manager, Ryan Donnelly. Ryan, meet Patrick Wallace and Cade Douglas from eTrain."

On your feet Ryan, she told herself. Make nice with the other kids. "Good afternoon. It's a pleasure to meet you. My apologies for arriving late," she said briskly, leaning over the table to hand her business card to the two men on the other side of the table: Patrick Wallace, who was slight and dark with a good-natured face that would have put her instantly at ease if her stomach hadn't been tied up in knots.

And Cade Douglas. She braced herself as she extended her hand, but the snap of static electricity caught her by surprise.

Cade raised an eyebrow. "Sorry. Staticky rug, I guess. We haven't met before, have we? You look so familiar." He made a show of reading her business card.

Ryan narrowed her eyes at him fractionally. "Not to my knowledge, Mr. Douglas."

Stepping up to the front of the room, she paused. Get it together, Ryan, she told herself grimly as she loaded up her presentation in the computer. Earlier in the week she'd been ready to murder Barry when he insisted that they run through the presentations a third time, but now she could have kissed him. Well, not quite kissed him, but it was a relief that she'd practiced the talk so many times she could go on autopilot, because she wasn't going to be doing a lot of thinking on her feet this particular day.

Ryan took a deep breath before beginning her presentation, just as she taught that morning in her public speaking course. She couldn't remember teaching anything about speaking to a group that included a former one-night stand, though. Or two-night stand, if you wanted to get picky. She began and her voice took on a smooth tone as she got into the flow and focused on the presentation. The only problem was that she saw him every time she looked up, and every time it sent her pulse thudding.

FATE WAS CERTAINLY having some fun with him these days, Cade thought, watching her. Her face was serious, her voice sober, her dark hair pinned back decorously, not flowing wildly over her shoulders as it had been the last time he'd seen her. Her boxy, wine-colored suit gave only the slightest indication of the luscious body hidden inside.

He wondered what kind of lingerie she wore underneath.

A couple of weeks ago he'd been ready to wring her pretty neck. Unfortunately, he couldn't find it to wring. Directory service hadn't had a listing for her anywhere around the area. She'd used cash and a fake name at the Beacon Hill Hotel. At the Copley Plaza Hotel, he'd met a blank wall and not even bribes got him the information he'd sought. It appeared that it was, indeed, over, just as she'd said.

He couldn't get her out of his mind, though. That was the worst of it. Despite the whole fiasco with the four-poster bed, he couldn't stop thinking about the quick flash of her smile, her throaty laughter, the feel of her bare skin against him. Being with her had felt right from the first moment she'd sat down to talk with him in the bar. He hadn't felt that quick snap of connection in years, maybe never, and despite everything, he couldn't stop wanting her.

And now here she was, delivered to him on a platter. What he was going to do with her he wasn't sure. His initial anger had faded in time with the soreness in his muscles. Clichés about playing with fire and getting burned kept dancing through his head as he sat in his health club sauna trying to work the kinks out. Still, he was a man who liked to be in control. As he'd told her in the room that night, he wasn't done with her, not by half. He'd be the one to decide when they were through.

He looked at her in her prim little suit. The flush on her cheeks was probably only a small indication of the snit she was in, he'd have bet his first million on it—if he hadn't already sunk it into eTrain. He watched her mouth move and remembered the feel of it on his skin, remembered having her naked and trembling against him. Oh yes, the game pieces had been reset, and if she thought it was ended as of the other night, she was very much mistaken.

First, he wanted to make her squirm a little, just in payback.

Then, he just wanted her, period. The fact that they'd be working together might complicate things, but it didn't make it impossible.

When he set his mind on something, he usually got it.

As Ryan reached her summary slide, Cade glanced over at Patrick and raised an eyebrow. Patrick gave him a fractional nod. Beckman Markham had the content that they needed to make eTrain a success, and that was the most important part. Getting a chance to equalize things with the lovely Ms. Donnelly was going to be the icing on the cake.

"THANK YOU FOR YOUR attention, gentlemen. Any questions?"

Cade gave her a lazy glance out of those startlingly blue eyes. "I assume you can e-mail us a copy of your course lists?"

"As long as Barry gives the okay, you have free access to any information I can provide."

"Anything you need from Ryan, just ask for it," Barry put in.

"I'll be sure to remember that," Cade said, looking directly at Ryan. Then he slightly pushed back from the table. "Well, I'm very impressed with what I've seen here today, Barry. I think Patrick and I can count ourselves lucky to team up with Beckman Markham as the content provider for eTrain."

A little chorus of happy noises went around the room, complete with backslapping and handshakes. The man was a master, Ryan thought sourly. He had them all sitting up and begging, as happy for his attention as a row of eager puppies. Well, she'd come through for Barry, which ought to have netted her some brownie points. Now if she could just stay away from this project, she'd be a happy woman.

"WE SHOULD PROBABLY put a few organizational steps into place," Cade continued, ticking off a list of action items. He leaned back in his chair a bit and crossed his leg over his knee. He was going to enjoy this next bit. "Given the importance of this project, I'm going to be point man for content and content planning. Ryan, that means you and I will be working together closely. I want to be very hands-on here." He wondered if anyone in the room but him had noticed her stiffen. "Let's coordinate schedules before I leave here today so we can set up a planning meeting for sometime in the next couple of days. I'm looking forward to it."

"I'm not entirely sure how soon we'll be able to arrange a meeting, Cade. I'm pretty booked over the next two weeks with classes."

"We can get one of the other instructors to fill in for you if necessary," Barry put in with a warning glance at her.

"Great," she said without enthusiasm. "In that case, do you have an administrative assistant I can call to coordinate the meeting?" She flicked her gaze toward him. "I don't want to tie you up at an inconvenient time."

Cade's jaw tightened at the crack.

"Why don't I stop by your office before I leave so we can touch base, Ryan," he said. "We've got a long way to go with this before we're done."

The meeting broke up, leaving only Barry and the eTrain contingent to finalize paperwork. Before they could start, though, Mona walked into the room. "Barry, you've got a call from Mr. Rickman."

"Oh, excuse me a moment guys, this is a call I've got to

take. Stay here and I'll be right with you in a couple of minutes. Mona can get you coffee, if you want.'' He hurried off.

As soon as they were alone, Patrick leaned over to Cade. ''Want to tell me what that was all about?'' he asked quietly.

Cade turned to look at him. ''What?''

''Point man for content? Where's that coming from? Every other time we've had this discussion you wanted no part of anything but the wheeling and dealing.''

''I've just been thinking, that's all.''

''Thinking about the company or thinking about our little friend in the purple suit?'' At Cade's startled glance, Patrick nodded. ''I thought so. I mean, don't get me wrong, I'm happy you're back to noticing the female of the species. I just don't want you to confuse work with playtime, because we cannot afford to mess this up, buddy o' mine.''

Cade pushed back a surge of irritation. Patrick had every right to voice his concern. The business was half his, as was the risk. ''Business takes center stage with me, Patrick, you know that. I just think I need to take more of a hand in the product side of things. Business development is quiet for the time being. I need to find another place to contribute or else I'm just taking up space.'' He closed the binder in front of him. ''We've been looking for a content manager for three months without finding someone who suits us. If I can step in here and take care of some of the initial content negotiations until we hire someone, then great.'' And if he could take care of some unfinished business at the same time, so much the better.

''Just as long as you're sure of what you're doing here.'' Patrick eyed him warily.

''It's going to be fine,'' Cade assured him.

IT WAS GOING TO BE A nightmare, Ryan thought, walking through the door of her office to throw her files down on the desk. Too wired to sit, she paced the patch of carpet in front of the window, looking out over the Boston streets. That was all she needed, to work with a man who reminded her of her most ridiculous mistake every time she looked at him. Of course, the fact that it was her sexiest mistake and made her heart race every time she thought of it only added to her frustration.

Cade had her neatly cornered. There was no way Barry was going to let her off the project, not when the new clients wanted her in. She was completely under his thumb and he was reveling in it. "We've got a long way to go" indeed. How ever much she might have wanted out from under his control, remaining employed was unfortunately going to mean dealing with Cade. He'd get tired of that game sooner or later.

She hoped.

In the meantime, they had to set some ground rules. There was a knock on the door. "Come in," Ryan snapped. It was Mona, she saw, and felt immediately contrite.

"Jeez, Ryan, you having a bad day or something? I just wanted to give you your course feedback from this morning."

"Probably sucked, considering all the problems we had." Ryan took the proffered file and sank into her chair as she leafed through the sheets, looking without seeing.

"Not even. You walked on water, as usual." Mona lingered to chat. "So, I guess the meeting with those eTrain guys went well, huh? Boy, the tall one sure is good looking."

"Pretty is as pretty does, my mama always says," Ryan muttered.

"Yeah, well, he can do me any time."

Ryan was surprised at the bolt of possessiveness that went through her. "Down, girl."

Mona blushed. "Sorry. I've gotta get a personal life. I know it's bad when I start drooling over the clients." She sighed. "He sure is fine to look at. I wouldn't mind if he showed up for a few more meetings." She glanced at her watch, then ducked out the door. Almost immediately there was a thump and a quick murmur of voices. Ryan craned around to catch the source of the commotion, just in time to see Cade Douglas step around the door, apologizing handsomely to Mona. Hard for him to do it any other way with that face, she reflected sourly. Mona, of course, was beet red and tongue-tied as she backed away down the hall.

Cade tapped lightly on the door. "Got a minute?"

"Would it matter?" It irritated her beyond belief that he affected her the way he did. "Come in, sit down." She didn't bother to get up, but sat at her desk and did her best to look like she had more important things to do. Hastily, she brought up her calendar on-screen and scrolled through it to check her schedule. It blinked at her, telling her there was an afternoon Word class she hadn't remembered and wasn't prepared for.

Cade closed the door and walked around her desk, glancing at her computer screen. "You're looking at your appointments for May of 2001," he pointed out helpfully.

Ryan paused and looked at him, she hoped coolly. "Do you want something or did you just come in here to bother me?"

"That's a fine way to welcome your new business partner," he said mildly, dropping into the chair across from her.

"You're not a partner, you're the customer. That's the only reason I'm being civil to you, in case you're under any misconceptions." Cool and classy, she thought, fighting off the urge to snarl as she saw the smirk flirting with the corners of his mouth. The man was so good looking that even his expressions flirted with him. "Of course, I'd fawn all over you if you'd back off and let me out of the project."

"Oh no, I don't believe I will." He gave her an assessing look, watching the pulse beat at her throat. The high color that had come into her cheeks suited her, he decided, pulling out her business card and flipping it over in his fingers idly.

"You're enjoying yourself," she said flatly, watching him sprawl in the chair and glance out her window to admire the view.

"Immensely."

His eyes came back to hers and despite herself she felt the jolt of heat. It made her snappish. "Great. So all right, you win, you're king of the hill. Is that enough for you?"

"Not by half." Anger flared in his eyes for an instant. "My shoulders were sore for a week after that stunt you pulled, you know. And you may very well have succeeded in ruining half of an Armani suit."

"I left you money for the dry cleaning." They were only trousers, after all.

"According to my dry cleaner Luigi, a very excitable man, such fine cashmere wool blend trousers should never be exposed to water and all of his considerable expertise may not be enough to right the insult to such exceptional fabric."

Ridiculous to feel guilty over it, she thought, pushing down a twinge of conscience. "That's what you get for lying to people."

"That's what you get for jumping to conclusions," he countered. Restlessly he got up to stare out the window, then turned back to face her.

"You could have set me straight at any time," she said hotly. "It wouldn't have been that hard."

It was Cade's turn for a pang on conscience, but the memory of his aching shoulders was an effective antidote. "Oh yes, but it was so delightful letting you go on being confused. And while we're at it, let's talk about this lying thing. I believe you said you were a writer? Odd that your card says curriculum manager. What was the Copley, a little fantasy role playing?''

Ryan flushed. "I am a writer, in my spare time. I do this to pay the bills.''

"Not to mention your stud fees.''

"I told you I'd never done that before.''

His eyes taunted her. "Sure seemed to me like you knew what you were doing.''

She couldn't block the memory of his mouth burning into her breasts, his hands touching her everywhere. Ryan felt herself reddening. "This is not going to work, I'll tell you right now.''

His expression closed as the dealmaker came back into sharp focus. "That's not an option—we've got a contract. We need what you know to make this project work.''

"Fine,'' Ryan snapped. "All right, then, here's your option. You want to work together, we'll work together. I've got this thing for staying employed.'' She took a deep breath to calm herself. "It's going to work one way, and one way only, and that's if we're both professionals about it. That means we set some ground rules.''

"We?''

"Me. You're the one insisting we work together. That means I get to make the rules.''

"You know, I'm starting to wonder if you aren't a dominatrix at heart after all.'' His smile was mocking.

"Stop it,'' she snapped. "I'd never done that before in my life.''

"Really? You did it very well, all things considered.'' An edge crept into his voice. "It took me half an hour to get those knots untied.''

"Are you going to cooperate on this or do I walk out and find a new job?''

"By all means, Mistress Ryan, tell me the rules."

Ryan glared at him. "Rule one, the Copley Plaza Hotel never happened."

"And the Beacon Hill Hotel," he cut in, a steely undertone in his voice.

"Fine. We met each other for the first time today." She stared at him as he leaned back lazily in his chair. "Rule two, no more innuendo, no more infantile games of one-upmanship. We work together like professionals and we focus on what's best for the project. Rule three, we deal with each other no more than necessary, over the phone whenever possible."

Cade rose to walk along the bookshelves that lined her wall, reading titles and picking up a framed photo of her with Becka. "When was this taken?"

"At my twenty-fifth birthday party. Stop changing the subject. Rule four—"

"Oh, there's a rule four, also?"

Impatience flared in her eyes. "Rule four. Hands off. Nothing physical. It's going to be hard enough to get things done without any hijinks going on."

Cade gave her a stare of amused disbelief. "Hijinks? Have you suddenly become a repressed schoolmarm overnight?"

She flushed. "Stop it."

"So let's see. Rule one, selective amnesia. Rule two, no talking. Rule three, stay away," he ticked them off on his fingers as he spoke, walking toward her desk. "And rule four, no, uh, what was it again?" He looked to her inquiringly.

"Hijinks," she muttered, her face flaming.

A corner of his mouth quirked. "Exactly." He stepped toward her chair and Ryan raised her chin to hold his gaze. "You know, anyone hearing this would think you didn't like me. But then, they wouldn't have been around at the

Copley, would they?'' She moved to rise but he dropped his hands swiftly onto the arm rests, pinning her neatly in place and leaning in close to her. ''Do you really think you can do that, put the genie back in the bottle? Do you really think it's as easy as that?'' His eyes mocked her. ''You can set up all the rules you want. I think you're going to be in for a surprise, Ms. Donnelly.''

She could smell the scent of his skin, feel the heat radiating from his body. He brought his mouth to within a hair's breadth of hers. The memory of his hands on her body was so vivid that she could feel them, could imagine him up against her naked, his weight atop her. Ryan licked her lips as her heart thudded. ''This…this is exactly the kind of thing I'm talking about,'' she managed.

''We might be working together, but you know what we're both going to be thinking about. Because however much I've ticked you off and you've ticked me off, we were good together. And it's going to take a whole lot more than a bunch of rules to make that go away.''

Her lips trembled, then parted until their breath mixed. Ridiculous to let a man make her feel like this.

Ridiculous to give up the chance of feeling it again.

Dark and turbulent, his eyes bored into hers. Then he abruptly released her, and turned to leave. ''That's the reality, so deal with it,'' he said, opening the door. ''I'll call you.''

And left her sitting in a silent office with a bloodstream full of adrenaline.

8

"OKAY, LET'S SPLIT UP IN pairs and try out the scripts for dealing with the twelve types of trouble employees." Ryan looked out across the rows of tables filling Meeting Room E in the suburban Boston Ramada Inn and forced enthusiasm into her voice. "One person plays the supervisor and one person plays the employee. We'll practice a bit, then break for lunch."

Ryan wondered what they'd say if she told them that each of the twelve types of problem employees was represented in this room to some degree. Then again, there were times that she felt like she embodied a few of the types herself—the clock-watcher, the dreamer, the early retiree. Not the prima donna, though. She was always the one to pitch in and get the job done. Sighing, she stacked up her morning notes and hoped devoutly that at that very second, her editor Elaine was reading the manuscript she'd sent to her. Until she got the phone call, though, she'd better pay attention to her job.

The first problem pair was easy to spot. "How's it going here?" Ryan drifted to a stop by a pale, rabbity-looking woman named Fran, catching the look of distress in her eyes.

Fran gulped, blinking rapidly. "Well, I'm trying to use your trouble talk script, but every time I start to talk she cuts me off."

The source of her distress was obvious—a formidable Type A brunette named Gloria. "I'm just trying to be the defensive employee," Gloria threw in—defensively. "It's what you told us to do."

"Okay, Fran, this is good practice for the real thing. Remember how we talked about comfort zones? This is where you move out of your comfort zone and try something different. Just trust the script. We've tested them in lots of situations."

"I just don't think I could say those things to my trouble employee. I'm not..." she leaned forward as though confiding a secret. "I'm not very assertive. It's hard for me to—" A boisterous whoop at the back of the room cut her off and had Ryan snapping her head around and frowning.

Every three or four months she ran across a student who was difficult to deal with. She focused on the back of the room where the pair she'd mentally cataloged as perennial frat boys scuffled with each other. Beefy and boisterous, they'd come in together, making it very clear that they had no use for the lessons she was trying to teach. God only knew why anyone thought they were management material. They couldn't even manage themselves.

Ryan checked her watch and raised her voice. "Okay everyone, looks like it's time for lunch. Let's meet back here at one-thirty." She stepped over to the pair as the other students began filing out. "You know, Brad," she said, reading the name off of the bright sticker on the ringleader's shirt front, "when I encouraged you guys to ad-lib on the scripts, I wasn't talking about channeling the Three Stooges."

Brad looked up from where he had his partner in a headlock. "I think I've got the coping strategies down, Teach." He gave a Neanderthal laugh as he released his friend.

"Impressive moves. I can see you've learned a lot from watching all those Friday night wrestling shows," she said dryly. "Now, I'd appreciate it and I'm sure the other students would appreciate it if you'd give it a rest. Not to mention Joe, here.''

Joe scowled and rubbed his neck. ''Hey, I'll see you at lunch, man,'' he said, walking out of the room.

Ryan waited until he hit the hallway and turned back to Brad. ''Cut the junior high stuff,'' she said flatly.

Brad stared down at her petulantly. He couldn't have been more than twenty-four or twenty-five. ''I don't see what good this class is going to do us. If someone reporting to me got out of line, I'd kick butt and take names, simple as that.''

''Which doesn't work in 80% of cases. Not a terribly effective strategy.'' She shook her head in disgust. ''Why are you in this class, Brad?''

''My boss told me to come.'' His gaze dropped to focus on her clavicles. Or points further south.

Ryan fought off an urge to cross her arms in front of her. ''Gee, did it ever occur to you that maybe your attitude toward reports is the reason your boss signed you up for this program?'' When he kept looking down, annoyance got the best of her. ''Hey Brad? I'm up here.''

At least he had the grace to look a little abashed. ''Ah, Dad's not even letting me manage anyone yet. He says I'm not ready.''

''Well, whether or not you're managing now, he's footing the bill for this course and I'm sure he'll expect you to come away with something.''

''I'd like to come away with something too, like maybe your phone number.'' Brad eyed her like she was a piece of meat. ''What do you say we go out for a drink after this is over? We can talk about prima donnas.''

Somehow he'd maneuvered her so she was between him and the display table of books and videos at the back of the room. How was it that creeps like him always knew the way to rattle her? She'd never dated enough to know how to deal with these kinds of unwanted passes—they just left her feeling vulnerable and powerless.

"So how about it, Teach?" Taking her silence for consent—or surrender—he reached up to toy with the silver pendant that hung at her neck. She flinched, heart hammering with a surge of adrenaline. Behind her, the table was a solid barrier. "How about we make a trade. I'll clean up my attitude and maybe you can show me a thing or two in private."

"How about you take your hand away before it gets taken off at the wrist," a voice behind her suggested evenly. Ryan whirled to see Cade Douglas staring at Brad with an icy, implacable gaze.

Ryan jumped. So did Brad. "Oh, uh, hey man, I was just fooling around." He put up both hands and backed away.

Relief warring with alarm, Ryan watched Cade's eyes. They didn't waver. Somehow the ice was more unsettling than anger would have been. Under the frost was a very real menace, especially since he topped Brad by about four inches.

"I think you need to apologize to Ms. Donnelly."

"Hey, I didn't mean anything by it," Brad's eyes skated away from hers. "I'm sorry. We'll, uh, keep it down this afternoon. I gotta go find Joe." He grabbed his cell phone and bolted out of the room.

Ryan turned to watch him go. Suppressing the surge of relief she felt, she swung back to Cade, who was impeccably dressed as usual in a blue-gray double-breasted suit. "I didn't know you specialized in intimidation. Did you moonlight as a bouncer when you were in college?"

Cade ignored the jab. "Are you okay? You look a little shaken."

"I'm fine," Ryan said, too quickly. In the aftermath of the adrenaline surge, the shakes were settling in. "I was handling it. It would have been nice if you'd left me to deal with things in my own way." Now that relief was ebbing, she was starting to feel annoyed at his high-handedness.

"That jackass was pawing you. And you didn't look like you were handling it at all." He didn't blame the idiot for trying. Dressed in a vivid violet suit with her glossy dark hair caught up in a clip to flow down her back, she was a shiny gem in the drab hotel meeting room.

"Touching my necklace is hardly pawing." All the same, her skin crawled a bit at the memory. "It's no big deal. He and his buddy were causing a problem and I was calling him on it. He was just trying to mess with me."

"It was out of line." She might insist she was fine, but she'd been obviously upset by the incident. And he was surprised at just how much that bothered him.

"It happens, Cade. I teach five or six thousand students a year. Sooner or later one of them pushes the limits of good behavior." She moved to step past him, away from the table. Somehow, being in open space made her feel less on edge. "It doesn't do Beckman Markham any good to have you intimidating students so they give negative feedback to their colleagues. We always have to think about referrals. Thanks to you, we've just lost one." It was easier, far easier, to be irritated than to admit that she still felt shaky, and that being protected by him had felt good.

"I can't imagine that one was going to bring you a lot of business."

Ryan shook her head as though she'd been doused with cold water. "What are you doing here? Why are we having this conversation? Did you come all the way over here to terrorize my students, or was this just passing coincidence?"

"I'd say Brad hasn't had enough terrorizing in his past or he wouldn't be such a pinhead."

"I come across his kind periodically. I can deal with them."

"That's fine," he said coolly. "I just don't like seeing my assets rattled."

"Your assets?" Her voice rose on the last word.

"Sure. We need you for this project. Like it or not, you're part of the deal."

"You want to know what you can do with your deal, Douglas?" she asked ominously.

"Careful, darlin'. Remember, Beckman Markham and eTrain have a contract." And the two of them had personal business to settle, as well. He wasn't about to forget about that.

Ryan forced herself to take a breath and calm down. "All right, fine. What do you want?"

He picked up one of the books for sale on the table and looked at the back cover. "I got sick of playing phone tag." He glanced up at her. "Mona sent me your schedule. I had a meeting out this way, so I figured I'd drop by."

"So great, you've found me. What do you want?"

"A couple of things. I want to talk about curriculum, but I figure it's also a good opportunity to see what works in the classroom."

"Not to mention terrorize my students."

"Terrorizing the jackass was a bonus."

She refused to be amused, Ryan thought stubbornly. She was practical enough to accept the inevitable, though. "I don't have much time, but if you want to talk over lunch, we can."

Cade nodded. "Good. Maybe I'll get a chance to give the eye of terror to young Brad." He spoke lightly, but he'd surprised himself. He didn't often get annoyed, certainly nothing like the blinding burst of anger he'd felt when he'd walked into the room and seen the young thug with his hand on her, seen her face pale and set. There was something hidden there. Not his problem, he told himself, even as his mind worried at it. Certainly Ryan wouldn't let him into her business. She'd be the first to tell him to take a hike. Perversely, something about that just gave him the urge to get in her way. Of course, there was also that elusive scent she wore, the one that whispered to him of black lace and sex in candlelit hotel rooms.

The hotel restaurant was doing a brisk business in sandwiches and burgers, harried waitresses trotting back and forth at a brisk clip. Ryan and Cade slid into a booth. "We haven't got a lot of time so we might as well get started," she said quickly, impersonally, pulling out her planner. "What do you need?"

The neckline of her cream blouse threw soft shadows on the fragile skin just above her breasts. He couldn't keep himself from watching her mouth and remembering the feel of her hands on his body. With a mental curse, he forced his mind back to the discussion at hand. He'd stopped letting his glands run his life years ago. "We want to set up a four-stage rollout. Stage one will be basic general courses, stage two will be basic technical courses, and stages three and four will be advanced versions of each category."

"I can break down our offerings according to those categories," Ryan said, making a note.

"What can I get you two?" A blowsy blonde stood at their table with a notepad. Ryan ordered, then checked her watch as the waitress hustled away.

"Problem?" Cade asked.

"I just need to keep an eye on the time. I like to be in the meeting room ten or fifteen minutes before we get started in case anyone has questions for me." She glanced at her notes, then looked up at him again. "Are you really planning to sit in on the afternoon session?"

His slow smile was a taunt. "Why, is it going to distract you?"

"Of course not. I just don't want your being there to disrupt the class."

"I don't know, it might actually help keep your friend in line," Cade said reflectively, glancing over toward Brad, who was eyeing him uneasily from across the room.

"Yes, well, I think you have him sufficiently in hand. Let's get back to business. What are you looking for from me? You could have handled this over the phone."

Cade shrugged. "Like I said, it was convenient, and we need to cover this ground. The online environment's very different from the classroom. We need to know the key elements of each class, what parts are self-explanatory and what parts you juice up in your presentation. We'll use that to power our online teaching assistant." He rubbed his chin. "We've got this little electronic blob that pops up with helpful hints during each lesson."

"Oh, ain't that sweet," Ryan gushed in honeyed tones.

His eyes narrowed. "Skip the sarcasm. The assistant is effective."

"And probably as annoying as Microsoft's obnoxious paperclip assistant. You know there are entire chat rooms devoted to people who loathe Clippy?" She reached out to take a sip of the iced tea the waitress set before her. "Cute is annoying. Unsolicited tips are annoying. Treat people like intelligent adults and put the information out where they can access it if they choose or ignore it. "

"Don't spare my feelings. Tell me what you really think, Ryan."

"Isn't that what you're paying for?" she shot back at him.

He couldn't help baiting her just a little. "I don't know," he said consideringly. "What else do you have to sell?"

She flushed. "Stop it. You agreed to be professional about this."

"But you're so entertaining when you're feisty," he said, his eyes unrepentant.

Now it was her turn to glare. "I don't know why you're

even bothering me," she said impatiently. "Most of what you want is on videotape. Barry's big plan last year was making a mint selling educational videos. We taped about four of the general skills classes before he decided it wouldn't fly. Mona can send you copies," she added.

Tapes or no tapes, he wanted to see her in the classroom, Cade thought as he watched her make notes to herself, clearly annoyed at being pushed into a corner. She brought animation and conviction to everything she said. Nothing by halves. When she was riled, you knew she was riled. When she was aroused, well, you knew that too. He glanced away just as the waitress appeared with their meals.

Ryan shook out her napkin and laid it on her lap. "So why online training? I'd have picked you for the high-powered financial shark type." She pulled her crock of soup in front of her.

Cade shot her a quick look as he picked up a French fry. "That sounds a lot like an insult."

"Just an observation."

"Well, I did my time in finance. I was head of mergers and acquisitions for Shearson Lehman a few years back."

"Didn't feed your soul, huh?" Her voice was dry.

His eyes narrowed. "Now you're definitely busting on me."

"Such a fragile flower." She took a sip of her iced tea. "Seriously, what made you switch?"

Cade gave her a skeptical glance. "I'm not sure I want to bare the tender little morsels of my soul to such a cynical audience."

"Really? You seem like the type who'd love to talk about himself." She ducked her head to take a quick spoonful of soup, trying not to enjoy his look of ruffled dignity.

"Now I'm definitely not going to tell you."

"Me? I'm harmless." She patted her lips with the napkin. "I swear. Come on, spill it."

He looked at her for a moment. "Well, I'd been doing the mergers and acquisitions job for about four years. In the beginning, it was fun. I liked the wheeling and dealing part of it, you know? Looking for the angle, swooping in for the kill."

"The swooping in for the kill part I can see. I bet you were good at it."

"Another insult, but I'll ignore it," he said mildly. "Actually, I was very good. I wound up as the youngest head of mergers and acquisitions they'd had in the history of the company."

Head of mergers and acquisitions? This was the job that his in-laws had disapproved of, Ryan remembered in surprise, studying the polished man across from her. Sitting on their family money, they'd had the nerve to look down on him when they should have been impressed by his accomplishments. It hadn't seemed to bother him when he'd told her, but suddenly, illogically, it bothered her. She took a swig of iced tea. "So what happened then?" she prompted, shying away from thinking about the sudden wave of protectiveness that had hit her.

Cade shrugged. "Somewhere along the line the fun went out of it. It all started seeming the same. I felt like I was just marking time." He shook his head at the memory. "I was making money, but wasn't involved anymore, you know? It was like I was detached from it all."

Ryan nodded. "That's when you know you need to leave a job, when you get to where you just go through the motions. So what happened after that?"

Cade dragged his eyes up from her mouth. "Patrick and I were buddies from college. We hooked up for dinner one night. He was working for a local Web page designer and wasn't any happier than I was." He pushed his hair back off his forehead absently. "We both needed a challenge

This was about the time that dot-coms were starting to be the hot thing.''

"So you decided to launch one of your own?" She propped her chin on her hand, her lunch forgotten. Somehow, she'd been drawn into his story, drawn into finding out just who he really was.

"I was having problems with a couple of my managers. They desperately needed training but we were having a hell of a time with the scheduling." And with her green eyes staring at him so intently, he was suddenly having a hell of a time keeping his mind off of getting her alone somewhere. "Anyway, Patrick and I started comparing notes at dinner that night. I don't know who came up with the idea first, but we decided to go for it."

"Are you glad you did?"

He nodded. "I can't imagine doing anything else. It's like one of those times when you don't know that you're missing something until you have it, and then you wonder how you ever did without it."

His eyes darkened, mesmerizing her, pulling her in against her will.

Someone cleared their throat. "Um, excuse me, Ryan?"

The sudden intrusion of the woman's voice made her jump. "What?" Ryan's head snapped around.

"Oh, I'm sorry, I didn't mean to interrupt. I'll just go..." Fran stood by the table, holding on to her notebook anxiously. She started to turn away.

"No, please, come back."

"I didn't want to bother..."

"It's no bother, really." Ryan gathered her wits. "What's up?"

"Well," Fran hesitated and Ryan gave her an encouraging nod. "I was just wondering if you had a few minutes to help me review some of the scripts before the afternoon session starts." She swallowed. "I want to try this out on my problem employee, but I want to practice."

Under normal circumstances Ryan would have felt triumph, but now, with her emotions in a blender, she could barely manage a smile. "Um, sure. Give me just a minute and I'll meet you in the classroom." She watched Fran walk away and turned back to Cade, eyes cool. "Well, thanks for making me look like a professional in front of my students," Ryan said brightly. "You bully one, you make me look like an idiot in front of another." She closed her planner and slid out to stand by the booth. "I hope you got your money's worth out of the meeting, Douglas. Next time, let's follow the rules and do our business over the phone."

Before she could turn away, his hand snaked out to grab her wrist. Heat licked up her arm.

"You know, when you get that tone to your voice, I get this urge to show you how quickly I could get you to forget all about those rules," he said. His voice was amused, but his eyes blazed at her.

Ryan's heart thudded in her chest. "Don't threaten me," she managed. "You know what I'm talking about makes sense."

"It's not a threat. Just reality." He held her wrist a moment longer. "You know, I can feel your pulse beating awfully fast. I wonder why that is?"

She was snared in the web of his gaze, tuning in to the staccato beat of her heart for long seconds before he released her. Without saying a word she walked away on legs that weren't quite steady, with a mouth suddenly gone dry with lust.

No, annoyance, she thought moments later in the classroom, not lust. And it was only the air conditioner that was trembling slightly when the afternoon session started just as Cade walked in and sat down in the back. It had nothing to do with nerves, certainly.

CADE SAT in the afternoon session and watched her move in front of the class. She was extraordinary, he thought. It was less teaching than performance, entertainment. She was a riveting flash of color caught up in connecting, and the students responded.

Oh yeah, she was good at connecting. It was just a matter of time, he thought. One of these days he was going to catch her when they were off the clock. And when he did, he was pretty sure that those rules of hers were going to go right out the window.

Finally, the afternoon wound to a close. Ryan stood at the front of the room, packing up books and notes, flipping through her evaluation forms. She gave him a wary glance as he approached. "What do you think? Did you find out what you needed?"

"I think you're very, very good at what you do. This puts a whole different spin on our strategy at eTrain."

Ryan shrugged, and he saw her unsuccessfully fight a smile. "It's just a class. We've got a dozen more just like it."

"No. Maybe you don't realize it, but it's the way you teach these classes that makes them memorable. I've got to talk with Patrick about a couple of options, and then I want to hook up with you again. What's your time like tomorrow?"

"Can't do it," she said in satisfaction. "I'm leaving for a conference in Manhattan. I'll be gone through Friday." She'd fought all afternoon not to let his presence affect her teaching, with little luck. No matter how hard she'd tried to throw herself into it, when she looked up his blue-black eyes were on her, reminding her of that moment at lunch when they'd clicked and she hadn't been aware of another person in the room. The thought that he could pull her in that much was somewhat frightening. She felt a little pulse of alarm— and adrenaline—at the thought of seeing him again.

"What's the conference?" Cade asked, his eyes on her.

She busied herself stacking her supplies into a box. "It's a meeting for training instructors."

"Training for the trainers?"

"Something like that. Building courses, organizing curriculum, classroom techniques and what have you."

Interested, he did a quick mental run through of his schedule. "It sounds like something I should be at. I need to do a quick study on this content stuff."

She slid her viewgraphs into a folder, checking to be sure they were in order. "Don't you have someone at the company who manages content?"

"We did, but he left two months ago and we haven't been able to replace him. I'm filling in until we can find the right person. Are you planning to fly or drive?"

Something skittered around in her stomach. "I'm driving down. It's a good excuse to get out of the city."

"Good," he said briskly. "We can go together. I can drive."

"No," she blurted, with a quick flicker of alarm. "I mean, I'm going to be leaving in the middle of the day. I'm sure you have meetings."

"Nothing I can't clear. If we go together, we'll save gas and money. It makes sense." His smile was mocking, his eyes challenged her. "Unless it makes you nervous to be alone in a car with me."

"Of course not," she said hotly, stung that he could tell what she was thinking.

"Great," Cade said in satisfaction. "I'll have my secretary take care of hotel arrangements. What time do you want to leave?"

She was trapped. "I was planning on about noon. It's the only way to beat traffic all the way down."

"Sounds good to me," he said, enjoying the frustrated look on her face. "Write down your address and phone and the name of the conference for me. I'll pick you up at your house.''

Ryan jerked her pen out of her planner. It was ridiculous to feel uneasy about the idea. There was the matter of his little challenge at lunch, but she'd put him in his place. They were professionals. They could be in each other's company without letting things get out of hand. And spending the next three days in his company wouldn't be a problem either. It was just business, that was all.

God help her.

''PATRICK, I'VE GOT IT.'' Cade breezed into the eTrain offices, completely unsurprised to see Patrick still at his desk at 8:00 p.m. ''I've got the perfect hook.''

''What hook?''

''Ryan Donnelly, the one who spoke at the meeting. She's hot in the classroom, absolutely hot. She has 'em eating out of her hand.''

Patrick stopped typing and turned to Cade. ''Is this the little dark-haired number in the purple suit?''

''Yeah. You should see her in the classroom.''

The puzzlement in Patrick's eyes bloomed into suspicion. ''When did you see her in the classroom? I thought you had a facilities meeting today.''

''I've been trying to hook up with her for a week and she was teaching right out by my morning meeting.''

Patrick gave him a level stare. ''So you just happened to drop in.''

''Yeah, I did. You got a problem with that?''

''Only the same one I had the other day.'' With a click of keys, Patrick saved the file he was working on. ''You're looking to me like you're mixing business with pleasure, buddy, and with seven million dollars on the line we can't afford to do that.''

''Patrick, this is work,'' Sure it is, said a mocking voice

in his head that he ignored. "Stop being paranoid and listen to me for a minute. I mean, her students get completely caught up. I've been to a couple of management seminars myself, but she's different. She makes it interesting and more to the point she makes it fun. She's the key to the whole thing."

"Well we can adapt some of her patter for the training assistant." Patrick hit a key and an animated blob bounced onto the screen. "Here's the newest incarnation."

Cade snorted. "You've got to be joking."

"Yeah, I didn't think it worked either."

"Too cutesy."

"Way too cutesy," Patrick agreed. "That's what we get for having Scoonie design it. You've got to wonder about a guy who honeymooned at Disney World."

"I thought it had a certain cartoon quality, now that you mention it," Cade said dryly, studying the blue blob. "At any rate, forget about the training assistant. You don't need that. What you need is her. Think about it. We could be the first online training site to offer streaming video." He remembered the sheen of her hair, the depths of her green eyes, the violet suit that was purple one minute, blue the next. Vivid, indeed. She made everything else look washed out by comparison.

"Streaming video," Patrick said thoughtfully. "It could work." His eyes began to light up the way they always did in the face of a technical challenge. They'd met when Cade was at Harvard and Patrick was a skinny MIT computer nerd who had infiltrated the university to play a prank. Coming home late one night Cade had seen the suspicious shadow slinking along the gaming field. Catching Patrick had been easy.

Ever the dealmaker, Cade offered the terrified freshman a choice—free calculus tutoring for the rest of the year or face the school authorities. The friendship that sprang up between the two had lasted long after the calculus final. Going to Patrick's home for the holidays had given Cade the first sense of family he'd ever had.

"So, can we do it?" Cade watched Patrick's face.

Patrick stared into space for a few minutes and then began nodding, a slow smile spreading over his face. "Oh yeah, baby, we can do it."

"Great. See you tomorrow." Cade turned to walk out of the room.

"Hey Cade?" Patrick called, turning once more to look at him. "I'm not trying to bust on you about Ryan. I know you're always looking out for what's best for the company. But there's something going on there with you and her, man, I know you too well."

"There's nothing going on I can't handle," Cade returned. "I know what the priorities are."

Patrick studied him for a moment. "I just don't want to see you do anything that either of us will regret, you follow me?"

Cade's eyes didn't waver. "Trust me, I won't." He stepped out into the hallway and headed for his office, stopping in the break room for a cup of coffee along the way. Unbidden, his mind filled with an image of Ryan. Maybe he knew what the priorities were, but his personal agenda had somehow undergone a shift. Two weeks before, he'd gleefully invented scenarios in which he'd had Ryan Donnelly squirming and at his mercy, seducing her in a public park, handcuffing her to a bench, touching her until she was begging him to take her over the edge, then leaving her to stew. Now, somehow, the urge to watch her squirm had been replaced by the drive to have her hot and eager against him.

Which Ms. Donnelly was likely to find as objectionable as any of his other scenarios, Cade thought, the corner of his mouth twitching up in a wry grin. Even if keeping hands off was the smart thing to do, it might be entertaining to crowd her a little, just to see what happened.

9

A FLOOD OF GOLDEN LIGHT flowed in through the bay windows of her bedroom as Ryan packed for the trip to Manhattan. Sheer curtains stirred in a soft, balmy breeze that blew through windows she'd opened for the first time all year. She felt a flush of spring fever, an antsy feeling that went all the way through to her bones. The earth was coming to life around her. Too bad she had to drive to Manhattan with Cade; she itched to be out running along the Charles River, feeling the sun on her shoulders and the breeze in her hair.

On the bed lay a cobalt blue suit, and atop it, the vivid magenta slash of a two-piece outfit that she'd bought on the way home the night before. Only because it was a good buy, she thought, smoothing her hand over the soft raw silk. The fact that it was sexy as all get out with its pencil skirt and snug bolero jacket was incidental. And if she grabbed her garter belt and stockings instead of practical panty hose, it was just her little indulgence. It certainly had nothing to do with Cade. She laid her clothes in the garment bag and zipped it closed with unnecessary force.

It was ridiculous to feel nervous about going down to Manhattan with him, she told herself, rummaging in the back of her closet for the shoulder strap to her garment bag. Being in the car with him didn't mean she was responsible for making conversation the entire time, and once they got to Manhattan, they could go their own ways. Work was work and she wasn't about to let an irritation like Cade Douglas get in the way of it.

Then the buzz of the front doorbell reverberated though her flat, sending her pulse galloping. She backed out of the closet, ran a hand through her disheveled hair, and hurried to the door.

One floor below, Cade stood on the doorstep of the blue and gray Victorian, staring up at the ornate gingerbread trim. He was a little surprised to discover how much he was looking forward to seeing Ryan. The idea of carpooling to Manhattan had been as much a way to bait her as anything else. Yes, he still wanted her, but as he'd assured Patrick, he wasn't about to let that get in the way of his common sense.

Flip-flops in her stomach were not the way to start out with the upper hand, Ryan thought as she looked at Cade. If only he'd been pallid and dough-faced instead of lean and purposeful, her life would have been a lot easier. A sheaf of black hair hung over his forehead, tossed there by the light breeze. The rolled up sleeves of his faded blue denim shirt showed tanned, sinewy forearms. His khakis looked like old friends. His eyes were vivid against his black eyelashes.

He gave her an amused look. "Are you going to invite me in or should I plan to just stand here until you're done?"

"Huh?" She'd been staring, she realized with a flush. "Oh, of course." She turned and led the way up the stairs to her flat.

There was an alarming sense of intimacy in having him in her space. He saw more than most people; in seeing where she lived, she had a feeling he'd learn more about her than she was ready for him to. She waved toward the couch. "Make yourself comfortable. I won't be a minute."

Ryan hurried to her bedroom and shut the door. She walked to the cheval glass in the corner, standing eye to eye with her reflection. If she was completely honest with herself, yes, she was attracted to him. She might find him infuriating, true, but something about him drew her. That much was chemistry. She could give into it, and him, or she could try to maintain some degree of control over the situation. Which was exactly what she intended to do.

Seconds later she stepped out into her living room to find Cade standing by her bookcase, flipping through the bound draft of the novel she'd just sent to Elaine. He looked up as she set down her garment bag.

"This you?" he asked, holding up the bound volume.

She crossed the room to him rapidly. "Time to go," she said curtly, reaching to pluck the book from his hands.

Cade lifted it out of her reach. "Some pretty sexy dialogue, here. He's got her stripped down to her Victoria's Secret lace and he's telling her he wants to kiss her on the—"

Face flaming, Ryan tried again for the draft and this time succeeded in snatching it from him. "I know where he wants to kiss her. I wrote the damned thing."

"Very hot stuff. Doesn't sound to me like you needed a gigolo for inspiration at all."

She shoved the draft to the back of the shelf with a thump. "Are you finished? Because it's getting late. I'd like to get started if you don't mind."

Cade gave her a speculative glance "They know about your sideline at Beckman Markham?"

"No." She looked at him belligerently as she grabbed her purse. "Why should they? There's no law against moonlighting."

She'd twisted her hair up and pulled on a boxy jacket the color of fuchsias, he noticed. The picture of the professional woman.

How was it that she still made him think of sex? He'd assured Patrick that he wasn't about to let desire get in the way of common sense, but somehow common sense was making less sense all the time.

"Well, I've got the directions, so we're set." He picked up her bag and turned toward the door. "After you."

The hell with women's liberation, Ryan thought as she stalked out the door of her flat and down the stairs ahead of him. The least he could do was carry her bag for her, especially when he irritated her as much as he did.

"My car's over here," he said as they started down the granite steps to the street. Sleek and black, a vintage Jaguar convertible sat by the curb.

"Well, I see you don't believe in denying yourself any of the finer things," Ryan said, brushing a hand over the graceful curving fender.

"I'm driving you to Manhattan and all you can do is insult me." Cade wedged her bag into the tiny trunk.

"I wasn't the one who had the bright idea of carpooling," she shot back at him as he opened the door so she could slip into the low slung car. The buttery smooth leather seat curved around her like a glove and she stretched her legs out with a little sigh. It was more like lying than sitting, she thought as she leaned her head back. Ahead of her, the long, black nose of the car swooped forward. Above her, tree branches arched overhead, covered with new green leaves. She stretched her arms over her head lazily.

Then Cade got in and the car suddenly became alarmingly small. Immediately, she tensed. The breath backed up in her lungs. She'd expected to spend the day sitting in a car with him. She hadn't expected to be nearly sitting in his lap.

He turned to her and they were practically lip to lip. "What's wrong?" he asked. "You look like a spooked bunny." She felt the throb of the engine as he started the car.

"I'm just thinking of all the stories I've heard about Jaguars breaking down," she lied. His hand brushed hers as he reached for the stick shift and she flinched at the flare of heat. The hairs prickled on the nape of her neck.

"You mean, does she go all the way for me?" His glance at her was sidelong.

"Cute." She narrowed her eyes at him. "All I'm asking is whether this thing will get us to Manhattan."

"Oh sure. She's a lady who's easy to deal with, unlike some I know. Relax, we'll get you there in a snap." He pulled the car out into the street.

She sniffed at him, then leaned her head back to look up into a sky so blue it hurt the eyes. Everywhere there was the sense of life bursting out, as though if you looked closely enough you could see things grow. "No one who doesn't live through northern winters can truly appreciate spring," Ryan said, forgetting that she'd vowed to herself not to speak to him the rest of the drive. "It's a perfect day for a convertible."

"I figure I ought to get to enjoy it for once instead of driving around freezing my tail off. New England is not a place for convertibles."

Ryan glanced at him curiously. "If that's the way you feel, why do you have one?"

He shrugged. "My grandfather left her to me when he passed away about six years back. She was his baby—he got her new in 1954." He turned onto Memorial Drive and headed toward the Pike. "I used to save her for sunny days until I sold my other car."

"Life in the fast lane gets expensive."

He shot her a hard look.

"Sorry," she muttered.

"We needed funding for eTrain, and it was too soon to go to the VCs. I probably should have sold her instead of the Beamer." He pulled to a stop at a light, and Ryan noticed the guy in the car next to them staring at the Jag with naked lust. "Collectors drool over her, but I just couldn't make myself do it."

"Memories?"

"My granddad used to take me riding sometimes. He'd sit me on his lap and let me steer." He gave her a sidelong glance. "Go ahead, tell me what a sap I am."

It hit her soft spot. "Not at all. Family's important. I can see why you'd hold on to it." She stroked the satiny smooth wood face of the leather-covered dashboard, a throwback to a more graceful time. "It's a gorgeous car," she said.

"She's a gorgeous car," Cade corrected. The light turned green and they rolled forward.

"Why is it that men always call cars and boats 'she'?"

"I don't know. I guess anything that demands so much of your time and care has to be female."

"If I didn't have to be in Manhattan tonight, I'd officially take exception to your sexist remark and storm out of the car," Ryan said lazily. "But then I'd miss cruising through the countryside with the top down and it's way too gorgeous of a day to pass on that."

"Well, then I guess it's lucky for you that I'm not going to give you a chance," Cade said, and accelerated onto the turnpike in a burst of speed that snapped her head back.

It was easy to get so caught up in city life that you forgot what it was like to get away from concrete and buildings, Ryan thought, watching the suburbs of Boston fall away behind them. The smooth stream of air flowed over the windshield and across her, teasing loose strands of hair.

A strain she wasn't aware of carrying ebbed away, and a softness whispered into her bones. For once, the tension between them seemed to be gone. Nothing that they said here could matter too much on such a glorious day.

"Are you from the country?" Cade asked. The wind eased high color into her cheeks. It suited her, he thought.

"No. I grew up in Newton, actually. My parents still live

there. I just know this road because we have relatives ou
in western Mass.''

''Whereabouts?''

''Stockbridge. Aunt Helen and Uncle Stanley. They have
twenty acres of sugar maples. Syrup is their business.''

''No kidding?''

''Nope, they have a sugarhouse and everything. A little
diner-style restaurant, too, but the big draw's the maple
sugar, especially in the fall.'' On the side of the road, for
sythia blazed gold against the new green leaves of the ma
ples. ''When I was a kid, it was my favorite thing to spend
a holiday weekend with them. The country out there is so
gorgeous. And at Christmas, they always had snow, whether
we'd gotten any back in Boston or not.''

He relaxed back into his seat, resting an arm on the door
''So you've always lived around here?''

''Except when I was in college.''

''Where'd you go?''

''Syracuse. Brown for my grad degree. In English,'' she
said in response to his questioning glance. ''I was going to
teach tomorrow's leaders at a prep school somewhere, bu
I found out the hard way that there are way more applicant
than openings.''

''Hence Beckman Markham?''

She shrugged. ''It's a living.''

''You would have been some teacher. I could see it yes
terday, watching you teach your class.''

She rolled her eyes but she couldn't block the little flush
of pleasure. ''What I was doing yesterday was hardly teach
ing.''

''No? Let me tell you something. You had everybody i
that room in the palm of your hand, even Mr. Personalit
and his buddy.'' He remembered her, a vivid presence, pac
ing back and forth, playing the room like an entertainer. ''I

night not be what you had planned to do, but you shine when you're up there.''

Ryan considered it. "I never thought about it before. I mostly do it because it's my job. I try to be good at it just because that's the way I am, but it's never felt like anything more than going through the motions.''

"You ought to give yourself more credit.'' He pulled the car into the left lane to zip around a truck. "So does that mean your heart lies with your writing?''

"Don't even start with me on that. We're actually having civil conversation. Be nice to keep it going.''

"No, seriously, you're a hell of a writer,'' he said. "I read a couple of pages of your manuscript while you were getting ready. It's good.''

"My dad keeps telling me I should write a cop thriller and make a million,'' she said dryly. "In my dreams I'd be writing full-time, but for now it's just a hobby.'' At least until she heard differently from Helene, she thought. Uncomfortably aware that the news she was quitting to write full-time would hardly be welcome, she cast about to change the subject. "So what about you, where are you from?''

He moved his shoulders. "I grew up in the Southwest.''

"New Mexico? Arizona?'' She thought of the bleached pastel hues of the desert.

"No. L.A., then Phoenix.''

"Is that where your granddad was from?''

"He was in Pasadena, just north of L.A.''

"The Rose Parade, right?''

He grinned. "You got it. A couple of times when I was little we spent New Year's Eve with Granddad and watched the parade the next day.'' At least he and his mother had. His father had usually cried off so he could be with one or another of his girlfriends.

"So is your family still there?'' she asked, turning to look at him.

"My father's in Malibu. My mother's in Arizona. The split up when I was a kid."

She thought of her parents, a comfortable unit so soli that she couldn't for a moment imagine them any way bu together. What would it have been like to grow up withou that certainty, without that utterly solid underpinning to he life? Cold, she thought. And lonely. "I'm sorry. That mus have been tough."

The compassion in her voice arrowed into him. Cade ad justed his sunglasses restlessly. "It was a long time ago."

"Don't you miss being out where you can see them eas ily?"

He couldn't quite suppress a snort. "We stay in touch a much as we need. I mean, how often do you see your fam ily?"

"Me?" She thought for a minute. "I talk with my parent every couple of weeks. I mean, it's not like I'm tied to thei apron strings or anything. I just like them." Thinking of he mother and father, she smiled. "It's fun to pop by for dinne or just to say hello." Her voice trailed off self-consciously "It probably sounds silly to you."

He shook his head. "No, it sounds good." It sounde like family, Cade thought, like a real family. He felt th whisper of longing that hit him sometimes around Patrick' people. A wistful wish to belong.

When he'd first met Alyssa, he'd mistaken her pride i her patrician roots for love of family. Then he got to kno her and realized that it was just a sense of misplaced su periority. He'd only discovered his mistake when it was to late, then berated himself for thinking that he could get tha family feeling off the shelf like a can of soup. Either yo were born to it or not. He'd grown up with dysfunctiona parents who taught him everything he knew of family; h couldn't just toss that aside and suddenly develop skills he' ever had. He cut off that line of thought and turned back to the conversation. "So, is it just you and your parents?"

Ryan heard the wistful note and wondered. "Irish Catholics? Hardly. My sister Colleen runs a bed-and-breakfast in Maine with her husband. We don't see her much except during holidays. My little sister's in San Diego, at the Scripps Research Institute. I've also got twin brothers—Brendan is finishing his residency at Mass Eye and Ear and Matt is an engineer in Texas." The thought of her siblings made her smile. They may have squabbled growing up, but each of them was an important part of her life. "Do you have any brothers or sisters? Did your parents remarry?"

How did he answer a question like that? How could he explain his father's five marriages without sounding a California cliché? And the icy wasteland his mother had made from her life? He was like the poster child for the dysfunctional family.

The silence stretched out a beat too long.

"You don't have to answer that," Ryan said apologetically. "I'm sorry. Sometimes I ask too many questions. I don't mean to pry." She looked out of the car, watching the greening trees rush by.

Cade searched for words. "It's not prying. My family's just hard to explain. And no, there's nobody else but me." He'd wondered sometimes if it might have felt different growing up if he'd had a brother or sister near when his parents were screaming at each other and throwing things, or when he and his mother had moved to Phoenix, a place wholly alien with no one he knew, leaving his grandfather far behind in Pasadena.

"So, I guess it must have been quite a change to move out here from California," Ryan said brightly. She'd said something wrong when they were talking about families, but he couldn't figure out what. He'd gone so far away he was in a different time zone. She should have been happy to have silence, but she wanted the easy flow they'd had earlier. "What brought you all the way out here?"

"I came out to go to school."

"That's a long way to go at eighteen." She thought of herself as adventurous, but she couldn't quite imagine leaving everyone and everything familiar on the other side of the continent.

"Actually, I came out for prep school when I was fourteen."

"You moved away from your parents at fourteen? How could they let you do that?" She blurted it out before she could stop herself. It shocked her, she couldn't help it. What kind of parents would let their fourteen-year-old boy go three thousand miles away? There had to have been a good school closer to home.

Cade smiled humorlessly. "Are you kidding? They couldn't get rid of me fast enough." He wanted to take the words back as soon as they were out. They held too much of the truth. He shrugged and tried to soften it. "They had their own lives, and I just wanted to get out." He glanced over his shoulder and flipped on his blinker to pass another truck.

Her heart broke a little for that young boy, lost and alone, knowing no one cared enough to keep him close.

"Prep school was fine," he continued, shifting back over into the travel lane. He shrugged. "It helped me get into Harvard, and then I met Patrick and here we are today." He reached over and turned up the volume on the stereo.

Something was still missing for him. She'd heard it in his voice. He'd shut down, though, as clearly as though he'd put up the Closed sign in a shop window. The topic was not open for discussion.

All she could do was look out the window and let the miles go by.

MANHATTAN WAS ITS USUAL crowded, cluttered, exciting self. Ryan stepped out of the car in front of the Essex Midtown, stretching her stiff muscles and watching the bellhops scramble to take their luggage. Amazing the treatment money brought, Ryan thought, as Cade handed his keys to the valets.

He caught her staring. "What?" he asked as they walked through the front doors and toward the registration desk.

She shook her head. "Nothing. I'm just thinking about how they would have acted if I'd driven up in my Toyota."

"Jealousy is so unbecoming. Look at it this way. I'm just trying to make sure that you're treated properly while you're on the eTrain account. It's my job to keep you happy." They stopped in the registration line and he eyed her up and down. "Interesting that we continually seem to meet up in hotels, don't you think?"

Ryan threw him a sharp look. "Don't start with me, or you'll undo all the good collegial feelings I built up for you during the drive."

"Okay," Cade said, "next topic. What's on the docket for this little shindig?"

"There's a mixer at six-thirty. Tomorrow, I think sessions start at eight and run through six."

"Okay." A redheaded desk clerk beckoned to him. He started to walk over then abruptly stopped and turned. "Want to have dinner?"

Caught by surprise, she only blinked. "Dinner?"

"You know, when you sit down at a table and eat?"

"Miss?" A different clerk waved to Ryan. Cade held up a hand to the redhead and glanced back at her. The people in line behind her shifted restlessly.

Ryan gave up. "Um sure, I guess."

He flashed a grin. "Good. We can catch up with each other at the mixer and go from there."

Trying not to think about the little bolt of excitement that his grin had sent through her, Ryan walked up to the desk clerk. Just then, the previous guest returned to contest the room rate. So it was that she was back in line when Cade walked by with his room folio.

"What happened?"

Ryan pointed to the guest, who was now arguing fervently with the clerk.

"Oh." Cade paused to watch for a moment. "Do you want me to stay?"

"No, go on up. We can meet at the mixer, like you said."

"Sounds good." He gave a wave to flag down the bellhop and glanced back at her. "See you later."

Ryan couldn't help watching him walk away. The man had himself a fine rear view. She jumped when the person behind her gave her a nudge to make her notice the desk clerk calling her. She walked up to the counter and set her purse down. "Checking in, name of Ryan Donnelly."

"Sorry for the delay, ma'am. Let's just bring up your name," said the clerk, a young man with a brilliant smile whose name badge said he hailed from Auckland, New Zealand. "Donnelly, Donnelly, Donnelly...hmm." He clicked keys rapidly, then frowned and typed some more.

She felt a flutter of disquiet and dug through her briefcase for the folder that held her confirmation. "Is there something wrong with the reservation? I checked it yesterday."

"Well, it appears to have been changed since then. Looks like you've been upgraded to concierge level, in room...oh, that's it." He looked at her and smiled. "You don't need to check in. Apparently you're already registered in the suite of one of our guests."

"That's wrong," she said positively. "You must have mixed me up with another guest. Check again, please."

"I already have, ma'am. We have you listed in the suite of a Cade Douglas."

For a beat, everything seemed to stop, then the blood

rushed to her cheeks. "I didn't authorize a change to my room." Her voice was quiet but anger slammed through her.

"I see that here. Mr. Douglas is an Essex Rewards member. It appears that one of our reservations operators made the change as a courtesy." He clicked the keys some more. "Normally, we could put you back in a single room, but unfortunately, we're fully booked because of the conference. We'll be happy to get you a reservation at another hotel in Manhattan." He stopped a moment and frowned. "Only thing is, I happen to know there aren't any openings close by. It's just a bad week. We can look, but it will be a few minutes. Do you want me to do that?"

Ryan forced her jaw to move. "Not just yet. What is the number of the suite I'm supposed to be in?"

"May I see your identification, ma'am?"

Ryan struggled to hold on to her temper as she pulled out her driver's license and slapped it down on the counter.

"Thank you. You're in room 4042. I can't give you a key, though," he said apologetically. "You'll have to get it from Mr. Douglas."

She really was reaching the end of her rope. "Do I need a passkey to get up to concierge level?" she asked carefully. After all, it wasn't the clerk's fault. Oh no, she knew exactly whose fault it was.

"Normally you use your room key, but we have passkeys for visitors." He handed her the plastic card. "The elevators are just ahead to your left. If you change your mind about wanting to switch to another hotel, ma'am, just give us a call or come back down and we'll take care of it. I'd suggest you do it quickly, though. There's a big electronics conference in town at the Javits Center and rooms are almost nonexistent at the better hotels."

Ryan thanked him and left. It felt good to burn a little energy walking across the enormous lobby to the elevators. It helped her hold back from breaking something or screaming. The nerve of the man, she fumed. If he thought she was going to sleep with him just because they were in a hotel together, he was very much mistaken. She slid her passkey into the slot on the elevator control panel and punched the button for the fortieth floor. The car zoomed upward and Ryan stared at her furious face, reflected in the gold-toned mirrors that covered the elevator doors.

Then the car stopped at the concierge level and she walked out onto the plush floor. The concierge sitting behind the desk looked at her inquiringly. "May I help you, ma'am?"

"I'm looking for room 4042."

"And the name of the guest, ma'am?"

Ryan wanted badly to hiss. Instead, she maintained her calm. "Cade Douglas."

"Ah. Down the hall and to the right."

Ryan headed swiftly down the hall to 4042 and knocked on the door so hard her knuckles hurt.

Cade opened it a moment later, as she was nursing her bruised knuckles. "Hi. I wondered if you—"

Ryan pushed past him into the room without waiting for an invitation. "Where in the hell do you get off screwing up my reservation and—" she broke off. It was a palace built into a glassed-in corner of the hotel. Windows faced two walls of the living room, offering a stunning view of midtown Manhattan and the East River. Conversational groupings of soft gray sofas and black chairs sat on an art deco patterned rug over deep burgundy carpet. Mottled silk wallpaper gleamed richly. Ahead, sliding doors opened onto a balcony surrounded by waist-high planters spilling over with vivid geraniums and lush ivy. To one side, an open door led into what she assumed was Cade's room.

And her garment bag sat just inside the door.

Her fury reignited. "You are out of your mind if you think I'm going to sleep with you just because you got cute and put us into the same room. Did you really think I'm so stupid that I'd just roll over for you? Was that the whole reason you decided to come along on this trip? A trip that I had set up well in advance without you, thanks very much.'' She paced as she talked, flattening a little path in the plush rug. ''I can't believe you. Thanks to you my reservation is gone and they can't find another anywhere around here because of some big show in town. And I was stupid enough to actually like you for an hour or so this afternoon.'' Her voice rose.

''Are you finished?'' Cade's voice was deceptively calm, but his eyes sparked with temper.

Ryan opened her mouth and shut it. ''Please, by all means, talk. I'm dying to hear this one.''

He smiled thinly. ''Good. First of all, I asked my secretary to have them move you to concierge level as a courtesy gesture. I do a lot of traveling, so I get certain perks. I didn't expect anything then and I still don't.'' Her skeptical sniff only tested his control further. ''I got a suite for myself because I have some meetings with our venture cap people tomorrow and I needed a professional space. I never intended them to move you into my suite.''

''Oh, sure.'' Sarcasm dripped from her words.

''It was an accident.''

''An accident?'' She stalked into his bedroom where her garment bag sat. ''Oh, like it's an accident that that's sitting here?''

Irritation flashed into his eyes. The fact that he couldn't help just for an instant imagining her lying naked on his bed did nothing to improve his mood. ''Do you think for one minute I'd believe that I could seduce you with an absurd story like this? Give me some credit.'' He stalked toward her. Step by step she retreated until her back was against a connecting door. He gave a feral smile, leaning his forearms against the door on either side of her head.

"When and if I decide to try to seduce you, trust me, I'll be much more direct than that."

Her heart thumped so loud she could hear it pounding. Her breath jerked unsteadily. "Don't try to intimidate me."

"Don't insult me." God, he wanted to lean in and feel her body against him. He wanted to feel her moving under him, hear her cry out when she came like she had the last time they were together. He spun around and grabbed her garment bag and walked her into her room. "There. I'm sure you can unpack yourself. Here's your passkey for the room." He slapped the cards down on the dresser. "And in case you're worried about your virtue, which I assure you, is perfectly safe, you'll notice you have locks on both of your doors."

"Fine," she snapped, and slammed the connecting door on her side. It was infantile, but satisfying. When the companion door on Cade's side thudded into the latch, she jumped. Shortly after, she heard the front door shut, but she refused to examine why she felt bereft.

It was only when she was at a conference that she remembered how relentlessly boring they were, Ryan reflected, and how much she disliked what she did. It didn't help that she spent the morning watching for Cade. He was either a very late sleeper or an early riser, because she hadn't seen or heard a trace of him that morning. Now, she didn't see him anywhere.

The problem was, she was beginning to feel more and more foolish and unreasonable for blowing up at him. The hotel had made a mistake. The more she thought about it, the more probable it seemed. He was right, she thought with a little shiver of arousal. If he wanted to seduce her, it certainly wouldn't be with the hotel equivalent of running out of gas on a lonely road. She had a growing suspicion that she'd made a perfect fool out of herself.

Finally, at the afternoon coffee break she saw him. Approaching him took work, but she'd always believed that unpleasant things were best done quickly. Eating humble pie definitely fell into the category of unpleasant, she reflected as she crossed over to where he stood near the wall. His eyes flicked up as she approached, though his expression was noncommittal.

"I was beginning to wonder if I was going to see you around here today," she said brightly, feeling miserably uncomfortable. "How did your meetings go?"

"Fine," he said briefly, wondering what she'd cooked up now. Mouseketeer bright was not a normal part of Ryan's repertoire, that much he knew about her. It put him on his guard. He'd spent the night tossing and turning, knowing she was near, unable to stop thinking about the first time he'd been in a hotel with her. "Enjoying yourself?"

She moved her shoulders restlessly. "Not really. Some useful sessions, I guess. Nothing that's blown my skirt up."

He flicked a glance at the skirt in question. She wore a vivid magenta suit today, the snug pencil skirt flowing up into the tight bolero jacket. It would take a lot of doing to blow that skirt up, he thought, but didn't say it. The first few times he'd seen her, she'd been wearing suits in which the color shouted sex but the cut said don't see me. Now both cut and color were sending the same message, one it would take a better man than him to ignore.

Especially when she was sleeping a dozen feet from him.

Just get it over with, Ryan, she told herself. Maybe if she said it quickly it wouldn't be so bad. "Well, the real reason I came over here was that I owe you an apology."

"Come again?"

She looked at him blankly.

"I didn't understand a word you said. Could you repeat it?"

She gave him a narrow-eyed stare. "I wanted to apologize."

"Really?" He looked at her a moment, then put his coffee cup on a nearby table. He leaned against the wall, crossing his arms and shifting a few times to get into a comfortable position. "Go ahead."

"You're not making this very easy."

"I'm not? Sorry. It's just such a novel experience I wanted to savor it."

"Look, do you want to hear this apology or not?" she snapped.

Cade grinned at the bright flare of temper in her eyes. "Now that's a face I recognize. The Mouseketeer stuff was scaring me."

"It might surprise you to know that I rarely lose my temper with anyone," she said icily.

"I feel special, thanks. But really, don't let me distract you," he said encouragingly. "Please, continue."

Ryan drew a breath. This was excruciating. "I was out of line yesterday. I jumped to conclusions and I'm sorry. I should have gotten the facts first." There. It was out. She was relieved to have it over with. "I'm, um, also sorry for implying that you were…that you might have been trying to…"

"Get you between the sheets?" he offered helpfully. "Take you for a tumble? Boff your brains out?"

Ryan scowled at him. "Look, if you're just going to—"

"Faking you out with a hotel room story is not my style," Cade cut her off. "Believe me, when I go to seduce you, you won't have any doubt."

How did he do that, she wondered. Without ever moving, he suddenly seemed much, much closer, close enough to start that slow buzz of arousal deep inside her.

Cade's gaze ran lazily down her body. "Of course, a person could start to think that the reason you're bringing this all up is because you're really hoping that I'll do just that.''

"You can get lost," Ryan snapped.

"I'd rather get lost with you. It seems to me that I still owe you dinner. How about tonight?"

"Sorry, I have a date tonight," she said with satisfaction. With Helene, but he didn't need to know that.

Cade raised his eyebrows. "Really?" The sting of jealousy took him by surprise.

Something in his tone raised her hackles. "I'm sure it won't put a crimp in your social life. You can always go out with Melissa." As soon as she'd said it she could cheerfully have cut her tongue out.

Cade gave her a blank look, then quickly glanced to where the cool blond conference organizer stood across the room. "Melissa? How did she come into the conversation?"

"Well I thought…I just…" Ryan floundered. "I saw you two at the mixer last night. I just figured you went to dinner after."

The smile of pure enjoyment that spread over his face had her grinding her teeth. "I had no idea you were watching that closely. I was just asking Melissa about content resources. I suppose I could find out if she's free for dinner tonight, though, now that you mention it," he added thoughtfully.

"That's a little more information than I needed to know," Ryan muttered.

"Well, since it's obviously been troubling you, you should know that I went out on my own last night," he said, enjoying her discomfiture.

It shouldn't have made her feel better.

It did.

People began drifting out of the hall, back toward the meeting rooms. "Well, it looks like the sessions are starting again, so I guess I'll see you later,'' Cade said, brushing his thumb across her lips. ''Don't do anything I wouldn't do.''

Ryan slanted him a cutting look as he walked away. ''Don't worry, Dad, I'll be home before curfew.''

10

RYAN SMOOTHED DOWN HER swingy miniskirt as she walked through the hotel lobby, her hair a loose tumble of sable. The warm weather was like an aphrodisiac, making her blood run faster and her muscles loose. A bellhop turned to watch her as she walked past, though she suspected it had more to do with her low-cut summer sweater than anything else.

The bar was mobbed with conventioneers, but it didn't take her long to spot Helene; she was the chain-smoker sitting near the bar with a waiter dancing in close attendance. Helene grinned as Ryan shouldered her way through the crowd. "Hey kid, I was just about to give up on you," she rasped and pulled Ryan in for a quick, hard hug.

How ever much she might occasionally be pressured by her, Ryan thanked her lucky stars for Helene. The woman had believed in her when she was starting out, and had encouraged—and occasionally bullied—her through the early days. It wasn't an act. It was real, she honestly did care.

"It's so good to see you." Ryan squeezed Helene's hands and dropped into a chair. "I'm sorry I'm late. The sessions ran over."

"I tried to call you but they said you weren't staying here. If I'd known you were in another hotel we could have met there."

"No, I'm staying here. Figures he wouldn't put my name on the room," she muttered under her breath. She saw Helene's eyebrows go up and she cursed herself. "It's not what it sounds like. There was a mix-up with the reservations. I'm staying in a suite with a colleague."

"Oh really?" Helene drew out the words with relish.

The waiter standing by the table cleared his throat. "What can I get you ladies?" he asked, setting down a bowl of pretzels and a couple of napkins.

Helene leaned over to be heard over the hubbub. "I'll have another glass of the chardonnay and my friend will have..." she looked at Ryan in question.

Ryan thought, then gave a slow smile. "A martini. I'll have a dry martini with two olives."

"I'll have that for you in a jiffy," he said and disappeared.

Helene settled back in her chair and crossed her legs. "So, a suite at the Essex Midtown? That must be some colleague. Anyone I know?"

"It's not like that, Helene. He's a pain and it's just business.

Helene smiled. "Ah, so it is a he. Come on kid, don't hold out on me."

Ryan hesitated, eyeing her.

"Come on, Ryan, spill it. I know all your other deep, dark secrets. Why stop just when it's getting good?"

"Oh, all right. But I'm telling you, you're not going to believe this one." Sighing, she started with the meeting at Beckman Markham, watching Helene's eyebrows go higher and higher with each twist. "So then it turned out that the hotel had screwed up the reservations and I had the choice of his suite or a room across town."

"And you believed that?"

"The hotel verified it this afternoon," Ryan said defensively, looking around for the waiter. Where was her drink? "In the grand scheme of things it's not nearly as ridiculous as some of the other things that have happened recently. I should face it, my life has turned into a seriocomedy.''

''Or a romantic comedy.''

''Give me a break, Helene.'' She raked her hair back with impatient fingers. ''He drives me crazy, and anyway, I've got to work with the guy. I'd be out of my mind to sleep with him again now, even assuming I wanted to.''

''Which you do.''

''Okay, maybe I've thought about it,'' she acknowledged. ''But nothing's going to happen.''

Helene shook her head. ''I wouldn't be so sure.''

''I would.'' But Ryan's mind vaulted down forbidden pathways, imagining moonlight streaming through the windows as she opened the connecting door to Cade's room. And ran smack into his door. Okay, so it was her fantasy. Little details like architecture were negotiable. In her fantasy there was only one door, and she was dressed in a transparent scrap of negligee that ended at midthigh, standing in the moonlight and reaching out to turn the handle—''

''Earth to Ryan.'' Helene waved her hand in front of Ryan's eyes.

''Sorry, I got distracted.'' Ryan shook her head, then smiled at Helene. ''It's good to see you. I was beginning to think that you had just become a voice on the phone.''

''Not me, I'm one hundred percent here in the flesh.'' Helene turned to look for the waiter, then turned back to her. ''You're looking great, kid. What are you, taking special vitamins?''

''Nope. Just fresh air and clean living.'' Ryan took a closer look at Helene. ''You know, you look pretty good yourself.'' Despite the garish red hair and the lines carved in her face by smoking, Helene had a buoyancy to her that had been missing the last time they'd been together. ''What's your secret?''

''Oh, polluted air and clean living,'' Helene said airily.

"With some honest to goodness canoodling thrown in." She gave a bawdy wink.

Ryan's jaw dropped. "Helene. Tell me you didn't go to the gig—"

"Escort," Helene cut in, unoffended. "No, I've actually got a volunteer, believe it or not. He owns the company that installed my hot tub. You know, something kept telling me I needed to get that tub." She gave a deep laugh.

"Oh my god, Helene, you've got a boyfriend!" For the five years Ryan had known her, Helene had been single and steadfastly devoted to the memory of her late husband. She'd always dodged any questions about dating, maintaining that she'd had her run and that was that. Apparently her opinion had changed.

"I figured I'd been a widow long enough," she confirmed. "I'm sure that H.L., God rest his soul, approves."

"What's his name?"

"Leo. Leo Morelli."

The waiter appeared with their drinks. "Sorry for the delay, ladies. It's a madhouse in here tonight. Let's see, we had a chardonnay?" He handed the wine to Helene. "And a martini, dry, two olives." He settled the bill rapidly and whisked off into the crowd.

Ryan leaned closer to be heard over the hubbub and raised her glass. "Well, here's to hot tubs."

Helene winked. "And everything that comes with them."

They clinked glasses, and Ryan settled back in her chair and crossed her legs. "So, tell me about Leo."

Helene's eyes softened and for a moment she looked almost girlish. "He's as good as they come. He's a little rough but he's kind. He makes me laugh." She took a sip of her wine. "He...surprises me," she said slowly. "That's the biggest drawback about being alone, you know. You can't surprise yourself. Everything becomes too predictable." She smiled at some private memory.

"He sounds great," Ryan said enviously. "Does he have a brother?"

Helene snorted. "One to a customer, kid. You've already got a fellow."

"Cade Douglas is not my fellow," she said emphatically.

"For not being your fellow, he spends an awful lot of time with you." Helene studied her judiciously. "He's on your mind."

"So's a headache." Ryan waved her hand, dismissing the topic, and picked up her martini again. "Let's have a better toast. To Leo Morelli, long may he wave." She clinked glasses with Helene and raised her drink to her lips.

"Martinis can be dangerous, you know," Cade's voice came from behind her just as she swallowed. Surprise had her choking on the liquid.

"Didn't your mother ever tell you not to surprise people?" she asked between coughs, then coughed some more when she caught Helene's wink.

"No, mine was bigger on teaching me to use the right forks at dinner. Why don't you introduce me to your friend?" Cade asked, nodding at Helene, who was watching avidly.

Ryan cleared her throat and took a cautious sip of her drink. "Um, Cade, this is Helene Frost. Helene, this is Cade Douglas. A colleague."

"The one with the suite?" Helene's eyes were bright with speculation.

"That would be me. And you're the dinner date?"

"You got it."

They sized each other up and grinned entirely too companionably for Ryan's taste. "Well, so much for introductions," she said briskly. "Don't let us keep you, Cade. I'm sure you've got plans."

He shrugged, studying the display of scotches over the bar. "Not really. I'm sort of at loose ends for tonight. I figured I'd stop in here and scare up a drink before I go find dinner.''

"Oh, gee, that's too bad. Well, see you tomo—''

"Why don't you eat with us?" Helene asked genially, ignoring Ryan's laser glare. "You've got time for a drink before we go, if you grab yourself a seat.''

"Well…" He hesitated, then deviltry crept into his eyes. "All right, don't mind if I do," he said, ferreting out an empty chair in the crowded room and bringing it over.

"I'm going to the ladies' room," Ryan muttered in disgust. Let them get bored with each other. After his behavior that afternoon, the last thing she wanted to do was spend any more time with him.

Cade stopped in the middle of ordering a drink to watch her go. She definitely had legs worth watching, he thought, blessing the inventor of the miniskirt.

"So what do you do when you're not impersonating a gigolo?" Helene spoke without preamble.

Cade winced. "I see our storyteller has been practicing her craft.''

"I'm her agent. I was the one who had the service ripping me a new one because Ryan had stood up their best boy.''

"Ah. That would make you the one who arranged for the meeting in the first place," he said, eyeing her steadily.

"It seemed like a good idea at the time," Helene said mildly. "Ryan's an adult. It was her decision to do it.''

And do it she did, Cade thought to himself, flashing briefly on the feel of Ryan's naked body against him.

"So yes, I had the agency rep screaming at me about her not showing up just before I had Ryan on the phone all giddy telling me how wonderful the fellow they'd sent was.''

Guilt pricked at him. He hadn't intended to, but he'd hurt her, and that was difficult to live with. "And your point?''

Helene's gaze chilled to ice. "Ryan's one of my nearest

and dearest. You mess with my people, you mess with me.''
She took a strong draw on her cigarette and blew smoke to
the ceiling. ''And despite my soft, girlish exterior, believe
me, buddy boy, you don't want to mess with me.''

Cade eyed her a moment. ''Now Helene, why would a
stand-up guy like me want to mess with your people?''

Helene stared at him for a moment, then humor crept back
into her eyes. ''Good. Then we'll get along.'' She took a
sip of her wine. ''So what do you have planned for our
girl?''

Cade blinked. ''Is this like the part where the father with
the shotgun asks my intentions?''

''Possibly, though Ryan has a daddy of her own who's
probably quite capable of taking after you with a shotgun
if you've got it coming to you.'' Helene blew a few smoke
rings to amuse herself. ''I'm just asking because I'm her
friend and I'd like to see her happy and not jerked around.
So what do you have planned for her?''

Cade frowned. ''We're working together. Right now, I'd
say I don't have much of anything planned for her.''

''That's what she says, too.''

''I guess you have your answer, then.''

''You're going to let a skinny little thing like her do all
the deciding for you? I'd say an enterprising young fellow
like yourself could turn her ideas around if he was of a mind
to.''

It was a good thing his drink had appeared. He took a
good, solid swig, letting the bourbon slide down his throat.
''I have yet to figure out whether I'm of a mind to. Is that
what you're suggesting?''

''I'm suggesting that you'd better act fast if you're going
to act at all. Ryan's one in a million, but she's been living
in the background until now. Being with you was good for
her—it woke her up. And people are noticing.'' She turned
to watch as Ryan walked back into the bar, past a table of

men whose heads swung in unison to watch her. "She's not hiding her looks anymore. If I were you, I'd figure out whether I wanted to go after her before the decision got taken out of my hands."

Cade gave Helene an opaque look. "Look, I know your intentions are good, but—"

"Hey," she raised her hands in front of her. "Just some advice from an old broad. It's worth exactly what you paid for it." She tapped her cigarette against the ashtray and gave a wary glance toward Ryan, who was now a few feet away. "So, this your first time to Manhattan?" she asked in a voice that was artificial and carrying.

They looked thick as thieves, Ryan thought as she walked up, and the guilty grins on their faces suggested they'd been talking about something besides sightseeing. "So have you finished dissecting me? Is it safe to come back?"

"Don't be like that, kid," Helene flapped a hand at her. "You know how it is when you just meet someone. You look for the things you've got in common. In this case, we started off with you, and now we're on to New York."

"Glad the topic's changed," Ryan muttered. She wished, how she wished that she could get out of this. The two sides of her life were colliding, and the result could be disaster. And anyway, she wasn't at all happy that they seemed to be getting on like old friends, trading notes on favorite hangouts. Just her luck that he had gone to Columbia for his MBA, Ryan thought sourly. The tiny hope she'd held out that he'd get bored and cry off dinner seemed to be shrinking by the second. In which case, she thought resignedly, they might as well move things along and get it over with. The sooner they got done eating, the sooner she could get back to her room. And lie awake, to think about Cade next door. "So, when's dinner?"

Helene glanced at her watch. "Our reservation's in about twenty-five minutes. That do you, Mr. D?"

"Sure," he said easily.

"Good. Then we should roll." She got up to leave and gasped in surprise. "Leo!"

Ryan blinked as a graying man with a lived-in face wrapped his arms around Helene. He gave her a soft kiss and brushed a stray strand of hair out of her face before turning toward Ryan and Cade.

Helene's cheeks quickly tinted pink and clashed with her hair. "Ryan, Cade, I'd like you to meet Leo Morelli. Leo, this is Ryan, the one I've told you so much about, and her friend Cade."

"Pleasure to meet you." Leo nodded at Ryan and shook hands with Cade.

Ryan scanned his face, liking what she saw. He had a weathered look, a bit like a nightclub bouncer, but the wrinkles on his face were from laughing, not from frowning. His eyes were clear and steady, and softened when he looked at Helene.

Helene laughed delightedly. "I thought you were playing poker tonight."

"Oh, you know…" Leo shrugged. "I cancelled. I can see those guys anytime. I wanted to meet your friend, and I wanted to see you." He gave Helene a squeeze and looked around for a chair. In the crowded bar, there wasn't another one to be had. He turned back with a roguish grin, then sat in her empty chair and pulled her giggling onto his lap.

Ryan choked on the last of her martini.

"Are you okay?" Leo asked, his arms around a beaming Helene.

Cade thumped Ryan's back. "She has this problem with martinis."

"It's a sad thing to see a drinking problem in such a young thing." Leo shook his head in high good humor. He glanced around the crowded bar. "So how's your convention going? These folks look like a barrel of laughs."

"I think I saw someone snickering over by the bar when I first came in," Cade returned, deadpan, "but I think they threw him out."

Leo grinned. "This your first time in the Big Apple?"

"Cade here is practically a local," Helene answered for him. "He's lived here before."

"Welcome back. Where do you live now?"

"Boston."

Leo's eyes narrowed. "Sox fan?"

Cade nodded. "To the death. Yankee fan?"

"Since I was born."

There was a short silence while the two gave each other flinty stares from opposite sides of the oldest rivalry in baseball. Leo broke first, with a contagious laugh that had Cade joining in.

"Okay, so baseball's off-limits," Cade said.

"Good idea," Leo agreed. "So where are we going for dinner?"

"Little Kashmir," Helene said, checking her watch again. "And we have to go if we're going to make our reservations."

"Little Kashmir?" Leo asked with a grin for Helene. "Did you warn them what they're in for?"

"Hottest curries I've ever had in my life. That all right with you, kid?"

Ryan nodded slowly. She was all for Indian food, she just wasn't so hot on this sudden buddy-buddy thing they all had going.

Helene got up off of Leo's lap. "Come on, then, drink up and let's go."

Outside the hotel, a breeze caught at Ryan's skirt as she stepped into the cab, flashing a glimpse of black lace to anyone on the block, she thought in mortification as she slapped the fabric down and scooted onto the seat.

Cade slid in next to her. "Nice gams, Donnelly," he murmured into her ear, settling his arm around her shoulders.

Face flaming, Ryan smoothed her skirt down as Leo gave directions to the cab driver.

"So you're Ryan's agent?" Cade asked Helene.

"You betcha. And I'm here to tell you, this kid's got the goods."

"I know. I read part of her last manuscript. She spins a pretty sexy yarn."

Helene's eyebrows rose. "Really? Ryan didn't tell me she'd shown it to anyone."

"You can stop talking about me as if I weren't here," Ryan put in.

"I picked it up when she wasn't looking," Cade continued, ignoring Ryan's words.

"Do tell," Helene said, her eyes flicking to her client. "And here I thought you two just worked together."

"Close collaboration always improves team performance," Cade said blandly.

"I can imagine. Well, you'd better collaborate with her while you can, because she's getting serious about her writing."

"Really." Cade gave Ryan a long, speculative glance. "That's interesting. She didn't mention that."

"Cade doesn't need to hear all about my writing hobby, Helene," Ryan put in, trying to subtly head off a potentially disastrous disclosure.

"Hobby, hell. You know yourself that when that multibook deal comes through you're going to say goodbye to teaching Quark for dummies. I say more power to you."

Ryan's mouth dropped open, but there was nothing she could think of to say. Helene had already said it all.

"So you're going to be quitting any day, huh?" Cade looked at her consideringly. "Nice of you to let us know."

"Helene's exaggerating," Ryan said uncomfortably, just as the cab pulled to a stop.

They got out at a storefront restaurant where ropes of jingling brass charms screened the door. Passing through the portal was like walking into another land where sitar music played quietly in the background, exotic spices perfumed the air, and rich tapestries adorned the walls. A dark-eyed, lovely woman clad in a paprika-colored sari led them to a table.

Ryan cleared her throat. "Cade, could you step into the bar for a moment? We need to talk."

He eyed her steadily. "I think that's a good idea."

They walked under a stone arch into a cavelike room. Cade slid onto a stool and nodded to the bartender. "Sam Adams, please." He glanced inquiringly at Ryan, who nodded. "Make that two."

Ryan looked at Cade uneasily. She moistened her lips. "I know what you must be thinking, but it's not the way it sounds."

"Just exactly how is it?"

Honesty or diplomacy? That was the question. "Helene's a little confused," Ryan began. "I'm not going to…" Her voice trailed off. Somehow the false assurances wouldn't come out. The two of them had connected the day before. She owed him more than false platitudes.

She took a deep breath and began again. "Okay, the truth is that I've always wanted to write, ever since I was little. I've been working toward doing it for a living for the last four years, so I'd be lying if I told you I didn't plan to quit if the contract comes through. Or when."

"When?"

She gave him a mischievous smile. "When. You were very effective at providing inspiration."

"I'm happy I could be of service," he said dryly. The

barkeep set their beers in front of them. "Does Barry know you might quit?" Cade asked, tossing down a bill.

Ryan shook her head. "No one at Beckman Markham knows. The last thing I wanted to do was take a chance on losing one job before I was sure of the other. Until we…spent time together, I wasn't sure I was going to be able to finish the first book in the series, and the rest of the contract hinges on whether the editor likes it." She lifted her beer and took a long drink, trying to ignore a quick spurt of uneasiness. Cade's expression remained calm, though, giving her the courage to continue. "The thing is, all this came about before I got involved in the eTrain project. I know you and Patrick signed a contract based on a package deal, and I don't want to compromise that."

Cade shrugged and took a drink of his beer. "Beckman Markham is the one on the contract, not you. You're under no legal obligation."

She raised her chin. "I make good on my commitments."

He studied her for a long moment. "I meant what I said earlier. You're a good writer. If it's what you love and you have a chance to do it full-time, you'd be a fool to let the chance go by. Go for it. We'll work it out some way."

Whatever reaction she'd expected from him, it hadn't been that. Fairness, maybe. Not support. Ryan swallowed. "Why are you being so nice about this?"

He centered his glass on the beer mat then looked at her soberly. "Don't forget, I know what it's like to work at a job that feels wrong. It eats away at you, you know that. Your heart's in your writing." He traced a finger down her cheek. "That's what you should be doing."

His voice was husky and compelling, drawing her in. "I'll consult or do whatever needs doing to build the eTrain product, you have my word."

"We'll be fine, especially if you agree to make sure we have the notes and material we need to work off of. In the meantime, you have my word that I won't say anything about it. Is it a deal?''

Ryan stared at him in surprise and gratitude. ''Absolutely.'' She put out her hand to shake, but he raised it to brush his lips over her knuckles. A little shudder of heat raced up her arm.

''Why did you do that?''

He shrugged. ''I don't know, it seemed appropriate. Why, would you rather I kissed you somewhere else?''

She had a flash of herself standing at the window of the Copley Hotel, Cade on his knees in front of her. ''Well, I—''

''Hey, are you guys going to get out here, or should we order dinner on our own?'' Leo asked from the bar's archway.

''We're all set,'' Cade said, taking her hand to walk her in to dinner.

Helene leaned toward her as soon as she sat down. ''Did I screw up in the cab?'' she asked in an anxious undertone. ''I wasn't even thinking that it could be a problem for you, Ryan. I'm so sorry.''

''It's okay, Helene, we talked about it.'' She looked over at Cade and smiled. ''Everything's just fine.''

THE REMAINS OF DINNER LAY scattered around them, and Ryan wasn't sure her tongue would ever be the same. Fiery hot was a pallid descriptor for the blazing concoctions that had come out of the kitchen. And the company—the company had been warm and steady. Sitting around the table with Helene and Leo felt immensely cozy and natural. It wasn't a date, Ryan reminded herself, but when Cade sent her a smoky glance, she felt the flutter in her stomach just the same.

''Well, I'm going to step outside for a quick cigarette while we're waiting to clear the tab,'' Helene said, rising as the waiter carried off her credit card and a quietly efficient busboy began clearing their table.

"You know those things are no good for you, doll," Leo said. "How 'bout if I come outside and try to be a good influence." He glanced at Cade and Ryan and winked. "You guys can keep yourselves entertained for a little while, can't you?"

Ryan turned to watch them go with a little sigh. "It's like they've been together all their lives. Or in a previous life, if you're into that sort of thing."

She rolled her eyes then and flashed that quick, addictive smile that always got to him. The dim lighting of the restaurant added mystery to her eyes and shadows beneath her cheekbones. "They seem to suit each other," Cade agreed. The way he was beginning to think she suited him, he thought.

For the short term, anyway.

"They do work, don't they? I'm so happy for her. She's been alone ever since I've known her." She smiled again. "It's so good to see her with someone. I hope it lasts for the long haul."

Cade finished the last of his water, then moved the glass around restlessly, watching the way the shadows fell on the soft curve of her neck. He knew how silky smooth the skin was there. "I don't know. I'm not sure there is such a thing as the long haul."

Ryan propped her chin on her hand, studying him. "Why not? When a relationship is right, it lasts."

"Theoretically. But it seems like all I ever hear about are divorces. I've got one friend who's happily married, but a whole string that are divorced. I bet it's the same for you. Tell me one you know of that really works."

"My parents," she said without missing a beat. "They're like something out of a fairy tale. They fell in love at first sight, married after two weeks, and after thirty-six years they *still* take walks holding hands.''

''So why aren't you hooked up if it's such a hot ticket?'' His head tilted speculatively.

Ryan flushed. ''I could ask you the same question. Anyway, I'm a bad example. I told you before, guys don't notice me.''

''I don't buy that one for a minute. I think if you wanted to be involved with someone, you'd be involved.'' He picked up her hand and began rubbing his thumb idly over her fingertips.

All the thoughts in her head scattered like a flock of startled birds. ''What...do you mean? I'm open to being involved,'' she managed.

''Oh yeah?'' He leaned forward. Too close, Ryan thought hazily. He was too close for her to think straight. ''Then why is it that you spend all your time telling me hands off?'' He kissed her fingertips and her body went liquid. ''The only time you've let me touch you was at the beginning, when it was safe and controlled. When nothing could really happen.'' His mouth brushed over her knuckles, his eyes riveted on hers. ''I think a guy would have to be out of his mind not to want you. I don't see all that many crazy guys walking around Boston. So I figure it must be your choice.'' He drew closer to her, closer to her trembling lips. ''So I have to ask myself, what does it take to get you to let go and just say yes. What does it take, Ryan,'' he whispered hypnotically, leaning in to take her mouth.

The chimes at the front door jingled as Helene and Leo came back in, laughing boisterously. ''Hey you two,'' Helene called, ''We—oops. Looks like we came back in too soon, Leo.''

Ryan jumped. ''Oh, hi,'' she said foolishly, her brain still mired in the heat from Cade's mouth.

''Well, it's looking to me like you two could use some

time alone," Helene said, noticing Ryan's flaming cheeks. She grabbed her credit card and signed the charge slip with a flourish. "It's Cinderella time for all of us. Everybody out to the curb."

Helene hurried them out of the restaurant and before Ryan knew it, she and Cade were in a cab and waving goodbye. Cade leaned back against the seat and turned to watch Ryan. "Hyatt Midtown," he said to the driver, without glancing away. His gaze on her was molten.

Ryan watched Central Park flow past her windows, only as an excuse to look away from him. It was too much, too much to feel. Then she felt his fingertips slide lightly along her jaw to the point of her chin, turning her to face him. His eyes were dark pools in the dim, shifting light of the cab. Streetlights strobed over his face, the contrast weirdly magnetic. She found herself leaning toward him without volition.

"Why did you do that?" she asked.

"I like to look at you," he replied. *And I want to taste you* he thought.

They reached the hotel sooner than she'd expected. Ryan stepped out almost as soon as the vehicle stopped, breathing in the night air to clear her mind while Cade paid the driver.

Then Cade walked up behind her and took her arm to walk her into the hotel. She couldn't stop the little shiver that ran through her. "All set," he said. "Do you want to stop for a drink or go on up?" His question was weirdly intimate. Going upstairs to the rooms they shared, just as in another hotel at another time they had gone upstairs to make love.

The suite suddenly seemed perilous, and yet she was weary of restaurants and bars. Besides, there was always her room. She could just say good-night, shut the door, and go to sleep. *Liar,* a voice in her head taunted her. *If you go up there you know you're going to do more than sleep.*

"Let's go on up. We can have a drink there." She walked to the elevators slightly ahead of him, utterly conscious of every motion of her body, of the swish of the miniskirt against her legs, and of Cade walking next to her.

In the elevator, he slid his passkey into the slot, pushing the button for the concierge level. A slow, hot pulse of arousal ran through him. He wanted his hands in her hair, he wanted to feel her yielding body against him. The elevator carried them smoothly, silently upward to the top floor. When the doors opened, Cade gestured to Ryan to go first, resting his hand on the small of her back as she stepped through the door. They passed the empty concierge desk, the carpet muffling their steps as they headed down the hall.

Cade opened the door into the dark living room of the suite. Beyond the floor-to-ceiling windows, Manhattan spread out in a jeweled panorama of light. Ryan caught her breath. "Oh, don't turn the lights on, please. This is wonderful."

She crossed to the sliding glass doors and stepped out on the balcony, into the soft, balmy night air. The barest touch of a breeze brushed softly against her cheeks. And against her arms she felt the cool leaves from the planters, as she leaned on the railing and watched the slow-moving barges on the river. Then she heard Cade step behind her.

He watched her for a moment, the moonlight glimmering on her hair. Then he moved just close enough to catch a hint of her scent. "Looks almost peaceful from up here, doesn't it?"

"It's exquisite." She turned to find his mouth disquietingly close. They had only to move a fraction to be touching. Ryan froze as the long beat of seconds passed.

"The moonlight turns everything into magic." Cade stepped over to gaze out across the city, then turned around to stare at her. She looked like a moon goddess, he thought, with her raven hair and pale skin. Her breasts rose and fell with her breath. He couldn't help himself, he reached for her. "Do you know how much I've wanted to have my hands on you?" he asked softly. "I look at you and all I can think about is the Copley Hotel. I can't get it out of my head, any of it. I remember exactly how it felt every time we touched."

His eyes were dark, his voice intense and compelling. Desire pulled at her, drawing her toward him until her palms were against his chest. For an instant, she held back, pushing herself away. Then she surrendered and slipped her arms around his neck. Her eyes closed and she fell into the kiss.

His mouth was feverish and demanding, whirling her around though her back was pressed to the railing. Why had she been fighting this when it was everything she craved? One of his hands slid around to cup the nape of her neck, the other ran down the length of her back, molding her to him, and she plunged into all the sensations she'd tried so hard not to want. She moaned to feel the heat and the hardness of his body against her, to feel his arms pulling her tight, so tight. She felt like the desert after a rainstorm, all the desiccated parts of her pulsing with life and flowering at once. The slight coolness of the night breeze whisked around under her skirt. Then his hand was under the fabric, stroking the bare skin of her thighs, sliding over her lacy bikini bottoms.

Desire throbbed through him as he felt her soft skin and the silky smoothness of the satin and lace. It wasn't enough, he thought, driven to plunder. Her head fell back, her lips parted and he tasted her tempting, secret flavors. So sweet, so warm. Her mouth was alive under his, teasing a thousand nerve endings with the promise of more. It did nothing to sate him; the hunger only grew. Then he brushed his mouth across her cheek and down her neck, feasting on the delicate skin, inhaling her scent until it made him dizzy. It was amazing to feel her close again after waiting to touch her for so long. He could feel her fingers running through his hair, clutching his shoulders as his mouth moved lower, to the soft swell of her breasts.

Ryan reeled, lost in the overpowering sensation. He opened the top of her sweater, then unsnapped the front of her bra to let her breasts tumble free. She gasped at the heat of his mouth on her, moaned as his tongue swirled and teased her, starting that slow, inexorable tightening in her belly. Dwelling on first one peak, then the other, he drove her higher and higher. His hands stroked the tender flesh, the roughness of his five o'clock shadow scraped against her. The contrast between the beard stubble and his mouth made her moan.

She wanted to feel him against her, craved it, Ryan thought feverishly as she unbuttoned his shirt with shaking fingers. She pulled it apart and ran her palms up his smooth, hard chest. Then she sank against him, her breasts crushed into the heat of his skin.

Cade groaned and fisted his hand in her hair, fastening his mouth on hers. He wanted her, *he wanted her* there and then. He needed to be a part of her, to bury himself deep inside of her until neither of them knew where one body started and the other left off. He sank down to the floor of the balcony, pulling her with him, and slid his hand under the edge of her lacy briefs to find her wet and ready. It brought him to the edge of control. Thinking only of tasting her, he reached over to pull them off.

And suddenly light spilled onto one side of the balcony. They both jumped as a burst of music and voices floated across from the suite next door. "Wow, great place to have people over for drinks," a woman's nasally voice said. "It's really romantic up here."

Or it was before you came along, Cade thought with a groan, rolling onto his back.

Ryan sat up hastily, fastening her bra and sweater before

he could reach her. She shook her head like she'd been doused with water. "I must be out of my mind," she muttered, getting to her feet and heading toward the sliding glass doors.

"They couldn't see us." Cade said mildly, following her inside.

"What, are you kidding?" she asked, turning on a lamp. "Who cares about those people next door? This is New York. With my luck, someone was out there with a telephoto lens taking shots for the Internet that my mother will find by accident when she's surfing the Web."

Before she knew what he was doing, Cade pulled her close for a quick kiss. "You're cute when you're provincial," he whispered, releasing her before she could scratch, like a bad-tempered cat.

She glowered at him. "Don't even start with me."

"Hey, you're the one who said leave the lights off." He stepped toward her.

Ryan backed up until she'd put the couch between them. "Oh no, you, keep your distance." The man was lethal within a five-foot range. She was better off staying across the room from him. Hell, who was she trying to kid. Across the room wasn't enough. Out of the building wouldn't be enough.

"Don't start with that." He shook his head. "You were into it as much as I was and you still are. Don't even try to stand there and tell me you haven't been thinking about this ever since we saw each other again." He started toward her, but she stepped nimbly to the other side of an end table.

"Of course I've been thinking about it, and I've been trying to ignore it, which, I might add, you've been making as difficult as possible." She gave a huff of frustration at his unrepentant look. "All I'm trying to do is get some work done and not spend every moment thinking about sex." That would have been a lot easier, of course, if he'd buttoned up his shirt, she thought, dragging her eyes up from the smooth, hard planes of his belly.

"We're already spending every moment thinking about sex," he threw back at her. "I say the only thing that makes sense is to take our clothes off and make love with each other until we completely get it out of our systems." He stepped toward her. "Want me to demonstrate?"

She backed up a pace. "I don't want to sleep with you just to scratch an itch," she said hotly.

"Honey, scratching an itch is how we got into this whole thing in the first place."

"That's exactly my point," she snapped. "Now if you'll excuse me, I'm going to bed before we do anything stupid."

"And you know you'll be thinking about it all night," he shot back at her, heading for the minibar and a brandy that might help him sleep.

"In your dreams, Douglas."

"No." His smile fed the slow flame she couldn't extinguish. "In yours."

IT DIDN'T HELP HER disposition the next morning that the man was right. She felt virtuous for having stuck to her principles, but she'd have felt better if she'd gotten some sleep. Convincing herself that playtime was over hadn't been the same thing as convincing her body. The only small bit of satisfaction she gained was from hearing Cade's bed creak as he tossed and turned also.

She wasn't about to tempt fate—or herself—by spending another night in the suite, Ryan thought, considering ways and means of getting home. Cade was up; she'd heard him moving about while she was showering and getting dressed. Now she took a deep breath and walked into the living room where the aroma of coffee beckoned to her.

"Good morning," he said, leaning against the kitchenette counter with mug in hand. "Sleep well?"

"Like a baby," she muttered. "You?"

"Never better," he lied.

She stepped into the kitchenette, doing her best to keep her distance. "Is there any more coffee?" Caffeine was critical. After that, she could begin thinking about getting home.

"Help yourself." He gestured to the pot but stayed in her way, grinning when her elbow brushed him and she jerked. "Hey, how would you feel about leaving as soon as the conference is done today? Something's come up. I need to be in Boston first thing tomorrow morning." He took a drink from his mug. "The conference gets done at six-thirty. We could be home by ten."

"Actually, I was thinking about taking a shuttle home tonight from LaGuardia."

"Skipping out?" His smile was mocking. "Coward."

"It has nothing to do with you," she answered too quickly. The hell it didn't, she thought, and he raised one eyebrow as though she'd spoken aloud. "It just seemed efficient. There's nothing on the schedule tomorrow that I need to see." And there was no way she was going to stay another night here with Cade. There was only so much a person could take, and she didn't trust herself.

"Well that settles it, then. We can check our bags and meet in the lobby at seven. That way we'll only hit the end of heavy traffic." He took in her skeptical expression. "Oh come on. It's three hours. You'll waste at least that taking the shuttle, assuming you can even find a ticket at the last minute. If you discipline yourself, I'm sure you can get through the drive home without jumping me."

She couldn't quite suppress a smile. "I think I can hold myself back."

"Make sure you do. I don't want people thinking that I'm easy, you know." He pressed a light kiss to her lips before she could react, then sauntered off into his bedroom to pack.

11

SHE PROBABLY SHOULD HAVE felt reassured that she could be gone for three days and come back to find that nothing had changed, Ryan thought as she walked into the Beckman Markham offices. Instead, she felt suffocated. If she'd been a different kind of person, she would have just played hooky, since she wasn't due back in the office until Monday. No one would have been the wiser, and she'd have had a day to get Cade Douglas out of her system.

Unfortunately, she'd been raised with a conscience, which was why she found herself walking in bright and early on Friday morning. Her faint hopes of sneaking into her office unnoticed were dashed when she saw Barry standing at Mona's desk, files clutched in his stubby fingers.

"Ryan, what are you doing here?" Mona asked, with as much relief at the interruption as enthusiasm, Ryan noted. "I thought you weren't back until Monday."

"Yeah." Barry glanced up from his files. "Whadja do, skip out early?"

"Today's sessions were mostly about real estate certifications, so I figured it made more sense to come on back. It'll give me some time to work on that new course I've been building." She picked her mail up off the counter and started to head toward her office.

"Hey, speaking of classes, Douglas called this morning," Barry called.

Ryan turned around and frowned. "What did he want?"

"Wants to tape your courses. He was saying something about putting video up on the Web site."

"He wants to tape me?" Ryan asked blankly. "Why?"

"He seems to think you're a hot ticket in the classroom, I don't know," Barry shrugged. "All I know is whatever he wants, we give him. Speaking of which, are you guys forming a team for that corporate charity shindig this year?"

Ryan sighed. "If you mean the Boston Corporate Games, Barry, they're next weekend. Adam sent you the team list a month ago, when you turned down our request for the sponsorship. Why, did you change your mind?" She couldn't suppress a quick flick of hope. "I've got all the lists in case you want to match us." The annual charity games funded a variety of worthy causes by getting local businesses to sponsor teams to compete in various athletic events. In the case of the Beckman Markham team, the money always came from friends and family—Barry had a selective deafness that he put into practice when his employees came looking for donations.

He flapped a hand through the air. "Naw, I just wanted to make sure we were going to have people there." He smoothed the sparse strands of his comb-over. "Douglas and his company are sponsoring part of the games. It'd look good for us to have a presence."

Ryan almost groaned aloud. She was cursed, basically. She should just resign herself that every place she went, Cade would be there. And temptation would follow. "Well, three of us are doing the 5K, and a friend of mine has volunteered to be the fourth. Without sponsorship, we couldn't drum up enough interest for a softball team, so all we're doing is the run."

"I want you to be sure to stop by and check in with him," Barry said, ignoring her comment. "Let him know that we've got people there. He sounds like one of those guys who's big on that kind of thing."

Barry, of course, wasn't, which didn't stop him from trying to cash in on the fact that his employees were. Ryan resisted the urge to grind her teeth. "I'm not leading the team this year, Barry. Adam is."

"I don't care," he said obstinately. "Douglas doesn't know Adam from...uh, Adam. You he knows."

Including in the biblical sense, Ryan thought, which was where all the problems started.

"You know, Barry, if you really want to look good you could have Beckman Markham sponsor the team or match the money we've raised," she said lightly.

"Nah, I think it's enough that he knows we're there," he said over his shoulder as he walked away toward his office. "You make sure you stop by and talk with him, all right?"

She sighed. When it came to Barry, subtlety was lost. Cocking her head, she caught a burble of noise from her office. "Whoops, that's my phone," she said hastily, giving Mona a quick wave.

Hustling into her office, she glanced at the caller I.D. to see Cade's name. She grimaced as she snatched up the receiver.

"Videotapes?" she asked without greeting. "You want to make videotapes?"

He didn't miss a beat. "Sure, if that's what turns you on. I'm thinking we rent a hotel room, get a good videographer and we can sell 'em on the Intern..."

"Very funny," Ryan said sarcastically.

"Hey, you brought it up." He smiled into the air, looking out the windows of his office to the daffodils nodding in the flowerbeds lining the front walk.

"Why videotapes?" Ryan's voice squawked out of the receiver. "I don't even like talking into the camcorder at weddings, for heaven's sake."

"You were the one who gave me the idea." He leaned

back in his chair and turned it sideways so he could prop one leg on the other knee.

"I meant to help you with the online content," she said aggrievedly. "Besides, the tapes I was talking about were already made, with a different instructor."

"I don't want another instructor. I want you." Didn't he just, thought Cade. She may have spent the previous night in her house a dozen miles away from him, but he hadn't slept any better than he had when they'd been in Manhattan, despite the fact that he'd worked until 2 a.m. on materials for his emergency facilities meeting that morning.

"I don't want someone out there taping me."

"Why not? You're amazing in the classroom. You have them eating out of your hand." Idly, he traced patterns on the polished top of his desk, feeling the smooth wood against his fingertips.

"How am I supposed to be able to think with a camera staring at me?"

"No whining," he said mildly.

"I'm not whining. That was a legitimate question. It was specifically not a whine." Cade grinned at her affronted tone. "I'm going to look like a goob."

"Trust me, you won't look like a goob," He reassured her in amusement. "After a few minutes in front of the camera, you'll relax and everything will be fine."

"It'll distract my students."

"Then we'll tape without them," Cade returned easily. He could field her objections all day until she ran down. He had no intention of letting her off the hook. "We need this as a resource for the future in case we lose you, remember? We'll use the Beckman Markham classroom. Mona says next Monday's good for you, so I've lined up a video team."

"I'll look like a goob," she muttered again.

"No you won't. I'll make sure of it."

There was a short silence. "Tell me you're not planning on coming to any of these tapings."

"Wouldn't miss 'em for the world."

"We don't need you there," she said darkly.

"You say that now, but you never know when you're going to want help. I wouldn't dream of leaving you guys to go it alone this early in the process." He grinned, imagining the expression on her face. "I'll finalize things with Mona. See you Wednesday, cupcake."

"That's Ms. Cupcake, to you," she retorted.

RYAN SAT IN FRONT OF HER home computer in T-shirt and jeans, working on the beginning of her latest novel. She was dying to know how her manuscript was faring with Elaine. It wouldn't help anybody, though, if she just sat around twiddling her thumbs until she got the call before she started writing again. She needed to get cracking now. Already, her characters had come to life in her head. They'd struck sparks off each other and come back for more. Now they were having their first kiss.

Unfortunately, all writing the scene did was make her want Cade.

On the stereo, the sounds of Dwayne Allmann and Eric Clapton blasted forth in bluesy guitar riffs that were the aural equivalent of hot and nasty sex. Which she'd almost had the other night. She wasn't sure if the fact that she hadn't was reason for congratulations or regret. Her opinion changed from minute to minute.

She'd dreaded the ride home from Manhattan, expecting three hours of tension and sparring. Interestingly, it hadn't been even remotely awkward. The Red Sox were playing the Yankees at Fenway Park, so they'd listened to the game all the way home, first from the Yankee broadcasters, then from the Red Sox network. The distraction hadn't stopped her from thinking about sex periodically—she'd have to be comatose before being near Cade didn't make her think about that—but it was at a manageable level. He'd focused on driving, not staring at her with those unsettling eyes. It was almost relaxing.

Until he pulled up in front of her house and walked up the front steps with her suitcase...

The doorbell rang, startling her out of her reverie. Ryan looked at the clock and smiled, then hustled out of her flat and down to the main door, opening it a crack. "What's the magic password?" she asked.

"Sam Adams?" Becka answered, holding up a six-pack of beer.

"That will certainly do for a start," Ryan grinned, stepping back to swing the door wide. "Come on in. I picked up a copy of *Pearl Harbor* at the video store on my way home. All we need is a pizza and we're ready to go."

"I thought infatuation killed your appetite," Becka said once they were up the stairs and inside Ryan's flat, setting the beer on the kitchen counter and tossing down her purse.

"I'm not infatuated," Ryan said, too quickly.

"Yeah, right." Becka pulled off her jacket and walked out into the living room to hang it up, then stopped. "Ryan," she called in an aggrieved voice, "what are you doing with the computer on? I can't believe you're working on a Friday night. Don't you get enough of it during the week?" She came back into the kitchen.

"That's not work, it's my latest book."

Becka plucked a pair of bottles of beer out of the six-pack and put the rest in the refrigerator. "What's the word on the contract?"

"Any day, or so Helene says. The delay's driving me nuts." A fleeting frown of impatience flitted over Ryan's face as she dug in a drawer for a bottle opener. "Anyway, I wanted to get a jump on things. Figured it would keep my mind off waiting for the call."

Becka leaned a hip against the counter. "What's this one about?"

"Head of a charity organization meets a dot-com entrepreneur."

"Dot-com entrepreneur?" Becka's eyebrows rose in exaggerated surprise. "You don't say. Gee, were you inspired by anyone I know of, Miss I'm Not Infatuated?"

Ryan flushed. "I told you, I'm not hung up on him." She slapped the bottle opener in Becka's hand.

"So says the woman who called and told me come to dinner, you've got to hear the latest," Becka said, rolling her eyes.

"I'm simply looking for your insight on a work situation," Ryan said with dignity. "And now, if you're finished, I'm going to order dinner." She picked up the telephone receiver and punched in a number she knew by heart. "Hi, I'd like a large pepperoni—"

"Veggie," Becka called over her shoulder as she opened bottles of beer.

Ryan sighed. "Sorry, make that a large veggie pizza." She reeled off the address and hung up the phone. "Honestly, Becka, any normal person breaks down and eats junk food once in a while."

"I eat junk food sometimes," Becka said defensively. "I got a turkey sandwich at the deli last week."

"Some people consider a turkey sandwich to be a healthy meal," Ryan muttered.

"That's why Americans are in such pathetic shape. Only maybe ten percent of the people in this country eat properly," she returned.

"We can't all live on lentils and wheat grass juice like you do." Ryan poured them both glasses of water. "You're a sick woman, Becka Landon."

"Oh, shut up and drink," Becka ordered, handing her a beer. "We've got a pizza coming, what more do you want?

Now let's kick back on the couch and you can tell me what happened with loverboy this week.''

"He's not my loverboy. Anyway, first you have to fill me in on the new job." Ryan stuck a package of popcorn into the microwave and punched the start button.

Becka beamed. "It's great. The team isn't exactly clobbering the competition, but they're all really young. It's like watching puppies playing ball. They're about that cute." She took a swig of her beer. "A bonus I didn't know about is that if any of the trainers for the Sox get sick, they call us up to the main club."

Ryan shook her head in amazement. "I can't believe you get paid for this."

"And paid well." Becka laughed. "I keep waiting for someone to pinch me so I wake up. I can't believe I've been so lucky."

"It wasn't luck. You earned it, and you should enjoy every minute," Ryan said. Behind her, in the microwave, the first kernels of popcorn began to pop. "At the risk of shooting a hole in your bliss, what's going on with Scott?"

"Speaking of waking up," Becka said with a grimace. "I've decided to break things off with him. I'm telling him Monday night after he gets back from his muscle show."

"Really?" Ryan stopped to stare at her. "What happened?"

Becka shrugged. "Nothing, really. Just cumulative frustration. The only person in Scott's life is Scott. Everyone else, including me, is support crew." She gave an impatient sigh. "Don't get me started. It's the same stuff I talk about every time. I've just gotten smart finally and realized that I deserve better," she said decisively, pushing her red hair out of her eyes. "So tell me about Cade, it's got to be more interesting."

"Yeah, there's an old Chinese curse that says 'May you live in interesting times.'" Ryan pulled the popcorn from the microwave and dumped it into a bowl. "Let's go si down," she said, grabbing the beers and heading toward th living room.

By the time the pizza arrived, they were sprawled com fortably on the couch and Ryan had reached the point in he tale at which she and Cade had arrived back home.

"So we get to the house and I don't know what to expect I figure I'll get this big, heavy seduction routine again, an he just carries in my suitcase, gives me a peck, and wishe me sweet dreams." She carried the pizza box into th kitchen and set it on the counter.

Becka slanted her a look as she pulled plates from th cupboard. "You know, to a person who didn't know yo well, it would almost sound like you didn't want the big heavy seduction routine. Come on, this is me you're talkin to." She set the plates down. "I don't believe for a minut that you weren't turned on by what happened in that hote. Can you honestly tell me that if those people hadn't com out onto the balcony that you wouldn't have had sex wit him? Can you?"

Ryan looked down at the linoleum.

"I didn't think so. So my question is, if he wants to slee with you and you want to sleep with him, then why aren' you? I mean, this is exciting, romantic, all the stuff you'v always talked about wanting. So why are you pushing hir away?"

"I don't know," Ryan said helplessly. "I don't know i he really wants to be involved or if he just does it to ba me. I mean, this is my job we're talking about, Becka. don't want to screw it up. And I really don't want to mak a fool of myself with someone I've got to work with." Sh put a couple of pieces of pizza on each plate and carrie them out into the living room.

"So what do you think happened?" Becka grabbed a cou ple more beers and followed.

Ryan blew a strand of hair out of her eyes. "I don't know. He said he had an early meeting. Maybe he meant really early, you got me. It figures, you know? The one time I want him to make a pass at me, he doesn't." Sighing, she settled on the couch. "I suppose it was for the best, but jeez, you know, what's really wrong with sleeping with him? It's not like he's my boss, at least not technically." She stopped for a beat and threw up her hands. "What am I, nuts? I work with the guy. I'm crazy to be thinking about sleeping with him. But god, I just can't get my mind off of it."

Becka lifted a slice of pizza to her mouth. "I don't know, babycakes, it sounds to me like you're passing on something good." She took a bite of pizza and made a little purring noise of pleasure.

"Yeah, but then I think about how one minute he looks at me like he wants to have me on toast, the next he turns around and tells me he doesn't believe that love can last."

"Maybe he's confusing love with lust."

"Maybe I am." Ryan bit into her pizza.

Becka looked at her sharply. "You're not saying you're falling for him, are you?"

"Not even," Ryan said hastily. She wasn't, was she? "I do think about him more than I should. But that's probably natural, don't you think? I mean, he's the first guy I've had anything going with in years. Part of me—okay a lot of me—wants to sleep with him again," she confessed, and grinned. "I've been having some really randy dreams."

"You go, girl," Becka said, clinking her beer bottle against Ryan's.

"It's just that, I don't know…" she sighed. "Sleeping with someone for the sake of sex sounds all well and good, but at the end of the day I want more than that."

"I told you the first time we talked about him, you're a

romantic. You're always going to look for love, whether it's this guy or someone else.''

"Believe me, it's not this guy." Of course it wasn't. Chemistry, yes, and maybe a bit of liking, but not love. They turned on the movie and Ryan sighed and bit into her pizza. Life had been so much easier when her sex life consisted of feature films.

12

RYAN STOOD AT THE FRONT of the classroom at Beckman Markham, watching the video crew set up the microphones and minicam. She studied the black electrician's tape that they'd put down on the carpet to indicate where she should stand, her stomach roiling with nerves. Just knowing that Cade was going to walk into the room at any moment had tension thrumming through her. The unblinking eye of the camera was nothing compared with the emotional chaos he made her feel.

"Just relax and pretend we're not here," said the cameraman, a youngish bearded guy named Pete, as he focused the lens. What would be better, she thought, would be to relax and pretend that *she* wasn't there, to take herself far, far away. Willing the nerves to subside, she looked at the chairs in the first row and tried to organize her thoughts.

"Take it easy," Pete said. "Don't worry if you mess up. We can always edit it or start again." He checked the lens one last time. "You all set?" he asked. At her nod, he switched on the camera.

Ryan never used a script when she taught, only an outline of the major points. The rest, the important parts, she ad-libbed as she went along. For her, teaching was about connecting with the people in her class, about communicating. Now, with the gleaming eye of the camera on her and no students in sight, she had no connection to play to. Words deserted her. She knew she was supposed to look into the lens, but the gleaming purplish black circle only made her freeze up. She groped for the easy tone of her usual introduction.

Then Cade walked into the room and every thought flew out of her head.

"Cut," the cameraman called.

Cade flashed her a smile. As usual, he wore an exquisitely cut suit, this time camel-colored. An earth-toned tie in an architectural motif, the sleek gold sweep of a tie chain, the gold cufflinks winking at his wrists, all of it built up the picture of the perfect gentleman. Then his blue-black eyes met hers and she had a sudden, vivid memory of how he'd looked with his shirt unbuttoned and hanging off his shoulders as he stood in the darkened suite in Manhattan. Hastily, she glanced down at her note cards, hoping her face didn't betray her thoughts.

"Sorry I'm late, my meeting ran over," Cade said, unbuttoning his jacket. "What's the status?"

"We're just getting started," answered Pete, helping his partner reposition the microphone.

"Just give me a minute," Cade said over his shoulder, and walked up to Ryan, making her pulse accelerate with every step he took. "How are you doing?"

"Great. Fine. Couldn't be better," she said quickly, suppressing the urge to step back to where she could think for a minute. The slight whiff of his scent, something clean and spicy and male, sent the butterflies in her stomach fluttering. A sheaf of dark hair fell over his forehead. Her fingers itched to run through it and push it back into place. Instead, she willed herself to focus on the job at hand.

She looked jittery, he thought. It wouldn't do to think of all the ways he'd like to relax her, touching her until she was hot and damp and mindless.

"You're going to do great," he said reassuringly. "Don't think about the camera. Just pretend you're talking to a room full of students." Pretend you don't want that lush, clever mouth under yours, he thought to himself. Pretend you're not imagining the feel of her breasts in your hands. "It'll be a piece of cake, you'll see."

"Easy for you to say. There's no one here for me to talk to."

"There's me." His eyes darkened. "Just think of me as your student. I'm sure there's a thing or two you could teach me." He stared at her just a beat too long then walked back toward the rows of desks, pulling his coat off and tossing it over a chair. Ryan caught the flash of silk suspenders, the kind that hooked to his trousers with leather loops. The kind she'd always thought were unbearably sexy. Underneath, his body was lean and powerful.

Cade hooked a finger in his tie to loosen it. "I always thought if I ran the company I'd wear suits less, not more," he muttered ruefully, dropping into a chair in the front row of tables and rolling up his sleeves. "Okay, chief, let 'er rip."

Ryan stared at him sitting there, one arm hooked over the chair back, looking like an advertisement for *GQ,* and felt like laughing at the sheer impossibility of running through a class when she had a distraction like him in the room. It was nerves, she told herself with a flare of impatience. Nerves had her off balance, thinking of Cade when she should be focused on work. Clearing her throat and trying to ignore the steadily tightening thread of desire that ran through her, Ryan began.

He gave her what would have been an encouraging smile if it hadn't been as wolfishly sexy as a come-on. All her words dried up in a heartbeat, leaving her stuttering and mentally cursing herself. "Look at the camera," Pete had said, but she couldn't keep her eyes off Cade.

Finally she stopped. "I'm sorry, can we start over, please?"

"Okay, once more from the top," called Pete. He rewound the tape and she began again. Then her eyes met Cade's, just for an instant, and everything else receded. She felt his gaze like a physical touch. For just a moment, it felt like they were the only ones in the room. Everything else became completely irrelevant.

"Cut," Pete said again and sighed. "Look, why don't we take five, let you get your thoughts together, then come back to it?"

Ryan stood absolutely still at the front of the classroom. She'd never been so embarrassed in her entire career. She was blowing it, big time. She, who prided herself on her competency, her ability, her professionalism. It was part of who she was. Or had been, before she met Cade.

He was watching her with those blue-black eyes, reminding her of all the things she didn't want to feel, just when she could least afford to feel them. Before he could rise, Ryan made a beeline for the sanctuary of her office, breathing a sigh of relief as she dropped into her chair. Nervous tension had her rising to stalk to the windows, staring out at the street below, fighting to get past the frustration that had enveloped her. Up to now, she'd never run across something that she couldn't do. Up until now. Calm, she thought. She had to calm down or she'd never be able to think.

"What's the big rush?" Cade stood in the doorway. He stepped into her office, swinging the door shut behind him.

She didn't jerk in surprise at his voice. She'd known he would follow her. Turning to look at him, she found it impossible not to think of the last time she'd been this close to him. What they'd done. What she wanted to do again.

He crossed the room to her with easy assurance.

Ryan reached out to touch the window frame for support, feeling the cool of the metal against her palm. "This isn't working. I can't do it." It took work to keep the unsteadiness out of her voice.

"Sure you can."

His voice was low and smooth. She remembered the way his throat had vibrated under her mouth when she was kissing him and he groaned. Unconsciously, she ran the tip of her tongue over her lips. "I just can't get into the flow. I don't know what's wrong." It was a lie, she thought. She knew exactly what was wrong. It was her own mind betraying her. He'd wound into her thoughts, laid claim to her body. At a time when she should have been concentrating on work, she was helpless to stop thinking about him.

"You just aren't used to the cameras. You'll do better after the break."

Frustration flooded through her. "No, I won't," she said positively. "The setup's all wrong." Unable to stay still, she paced restlessly across the office.

"What do you mean?" He turned to watch her walk.

Ryan spun to face him. "I can't teach in a vacuum." She spread her hands out. "I need students, I need to be interacting with people."

His eyes glinted devilishly. "You can interact with me."

Images of being naked and wrapped around him billowed up in her mind. Color stained her cheeks. "That's hardly what I'm talking about, and the last thing I need is more distractions, thank you very much."

"What's distracting you? There's hardly anyone in the room. Just Pete, the sound guy, and me. Are they bugging you?" he asked softly, and stepped closer to her. "Or is it me?" Hunger for her twisted in his gut. He could feel her skin against his palms, the memory was so clear.

Ryan edged backward until she felt the bookshelves at her back. Her heart pounded, in alarm or excitement, she couldn't tell. "We're in my office, Cade. This kind of thing is hardly appropriate."

"I'm just asking a simple question."

It wasn't fleeing, just a strategic retreat, she told herself as she slid past him to go to her desk. Her hand brushed his in passing, and she caught her breath and flinched as she felt the sizzle. She dropped into her chair and shook her head. "This isn't going to work. If you want to tape me, come to one of my classes and set up in the back of the room. I'm teaching next week out in Worcester. We can do it then."

Cade pondered the notion for a moment. He rubbed his jaw thoughtfully and walked over to her desk. "Okay, assuming Pete and his buddy are available."

"Okay. But you tell them to just turn on the cameras and let it roll," she warned. "No interrupting or calling 'cut.' Your cameraman will just be a fly on the wall."

"We'll be so discreet you won't even notice us."

The day she didn't notice him would be the day she was stone cold in her grave, Ryan thought. Looking at his mouth made her think of the Copley Hotel. Looking at his hands made her think of the balcony in Manhattan. All at a time when she should have been getting her act together so she could perform the way she was paid to do.

A sudden fury swept over her. She'd tried to set down rules at the beginning and he'd just laughed at her. Now she, who'd always prided herself on doing her job well, was suddenly screwing it up big time. Ryan set her jaw. He was not going to wreak havoc with her life and her career. She was going to ignore him and get her act in gear, that was all there was to it.

"What have you got here?" he was looking at the notes on her desk, outlines for a new course she was preparing.

"None of your business," she said sharply, flipping the folder closed.

He dropped into the chair across from her desk and studied her. "You mind telling me what's wrong?"

"What's always wrong?" she snapped.

"Ah." He eyed her steadily. "We're playing by your rules. What's the problem?"

It was too late for the rules to help, she thought. That was the problem. It had been hard enough when she was merely attracted to him. After the drive to Manhattan and the time they'd spent there, she was in way deeper than she could handle. Distance was what she needed, but it was the last thing she could get.

And if she was honest with herself, she knew even distance wouldn't help.

"Talk to me," Cade said quietly.

Ryan blew out a breath. "I'm sorry, I'm just frustrated with myself." She made a sudden, vain wish that he didn't look so good and stood up. "Come on, let's go back and try one more time."

THE SOUND OF VACUUM cleaners from the custodial staff echoed through the empty halls of Beckman Markham. Ryan looked up from her computer and rubbed her eyes. She'd stayed at her desk well after the rest of her colleagues left for the day, trying to make up for the time she'd lost. The aborted taping had consumed the better part of the afternoon, but she doubted that much of it would be usable. No matter how she'd tried to focus, she'd only wound up getting distracted by his face, his hands, by wondering what he was thinking about.

By wanting him.

Her frustration level rose with every mistake. Every time Pete called "cut" her patience grew thinner. They finally gave up, making plans to meet in Worcester the following week. When she got back to her desk, her nerves were completely ragged. Trying to concentrate on the course was a labor and her progress was almost nonexistent.

It was beginning to be impossible to work.

She focused again on the computer screen where she was

putting together a list of bullet points for the new class. "Managing a project from start to finish," she muttered to herself. Rule number one, don't sleep with your team members before the project starts. Rule number two, communicate with your team members as little as possible when they only make you think of climbing all over them. Rule number three, don't think about how it felt when you were both naked and he was sliding your legs apart, putting his mouth against you, sliding the tip of his tongue against your...

Ryan slapped her hands on her desk top in frustration. It had to stop, that was all there was to it. The question was how? The rules didn't help at all. Trying not to think about making love with Cade worked about as well as the childhood game of not thinking of elephants. She'd tried to keep him at a distance, but he wouldn't listen. Now because of him, her work was suffering. Her sanity was suffering.

What she was doing didn't seem to be working.

Maybe it was time to go bag herself an elephant.

RYAN JERKED HER CAR TO A stop in front of condos that sat on the Cambridge side of the Charles River, like a jumble of glass and stone building blocks tossed down by a child. The sun was a fading glow on the western horizon, the air still unseasonably warm. Apple trees nodded with blossoms but she had no time to admire them. She stomped into the lobby and checked for Cade's name. His condo was on the top floor. Naturally.

She'd see him and they'd hash this out, she thought, riding up in the elevator. And if that meant sex, so be it. She strode out onto his floor, stopping when she found his door. She rang the buzzer and waited, then, impatient, rang it again. Finally, she heard the sound of feet approaching.

The door swung open to reveal Cade. He wore an old cotton shirt that might once have been navy, hanging down over faded jeans. Behind him, slow blues played. Pale gold wine filled the glass in his hand. His feet were bare.

"Ryan." For a moment he stood and simply looked. She wore the skirt from the ripe red suit she'd had on earlier that day, but somewhere along the line she'd stripped off the jacket. Her silk blouse looked soft and smooth as cream, almost as smooth as the skin he knew lay beneath it. His eye followed the long line of her throat down into the now-unbuttoned neckline to where the soft swell of her breasts started. Her hair, once pinned up neatly, tumbled loose and wild over her shoulders as though she'd raked her hands through it. Her eyes blazed with a wildness all their own.

Desire flooded over him.

"Can I come in?" she asked, her heart thudding in her chest.

"Sure." He moved back and pulled the door open for her. "Something wrong?"

She stepped in the hall. "We need to talk."

Tension vibrated through her, humming in her voice and putting him on alert. He took his time shutting the door and throwing the deadbolt, then turned to her. "First things first, you look like you could use a drink."

She followed him down the hall. A flight of stairs rose to her right, a golden oak baluster gleaming faintly. The stairs that led to his bedroom, she thought with a little thrill of heat. A deep blue hall runner muffled the click of her heels. To her left, an arch led to a spacious, airy living room that looked out on the river. A glass sculpture, a flowing ribbon of translucent scarlet, sat on a pedestal near the window, the last beams of sunlight turning it to flame.

Cade turned into a cleanly efficient kitchen in tones of pale gray and burgundy, setting his glass down on the counter. He took a moment to put the wariness aside and enjoy the look of her in his house. "I've got a pinot grigio cold, or I can open a red."

"No, white is fine." A glass of cold, clear wine to cool her mind and let her think. Except that she didn't want to be cooled down. She wanted to be hot. She wanted Cade.

He set a tall, slender wineglass on the granite counter, filling the glass with pale gold liquid and handing it to her. Picking up his own wine, he leaned against the counter. "To clean living," he said, and clinked his glass against hers, the crystal ringing.

Ryan took a reckless gulp, then looked at him. "I think we should sleep together."

He didn't react for a moment, and she rushed on. "Look, we've spent days dancing around it and it's making me crazy. I couldn't get anything done today and neither could you." She knew she was talking too fast but the words wouldn't stop spilling out. "I thought it over and you were right in Manhattan. We should just do it and get it out of our systems."

Cade just leaned against the counter and watched her quietly.

"I mean, it's just sex," she said, reasoning aloud. "It shouldn't rule our lives. We had a good time with each other before and lived to tell the tale." Unable to stand still, she began to pace, her heels ringing on the marble floor. "Lots of people just have casual sex. Why shouldn't we? We go to bed, we have a good time, and we burn it out."

She stopped to take a gulp of wine, then she couldn't stand his silence any more. "What do you think?"

For a moment, he simply looked at her. Then he pushed away from the counter. "I think we should go sit down." Ryan followed him, as he walked down the hall. She drifted toward the living room arch, expecting him to turn in. Instead, he turned left to mount the stairs. Adrenaline pumped through her. She'd thought she meant what she'd said, but she hadn't expected him to take her at her word, no further conversation. It was too fast, she thought wildly.

Upstairs, he turned down a short hall and into the master bedroom.

"Wait," she blurted, trailing him into the room.

Cade stopped and looked at her inquiringly, his hand on the latch to a sliding glass door. Beyond it, a wooden deck overlooked the river.

"Oh." Ryan breathed a faint sigh of relief.

"What?"

"Nothing. I just thought…"

A corner of his mouth curved up. "Worried that I wasn't wasting any time?"

"Something like that."

He stepped up to her, so close she could hear the soft sound of his breath over the pounding of her heart. So close she could feel his heat. "Well, I suppose we could get right to it if you really want to, but I think we'd be better off talking about it first." He moved back to slide open the door and walk out onto the wooden deck. Ryan followed him.

Citronella candles perfumed the air. The blues music she'd heard downstairs played quietly from wall-mounted speakers. Robert Parker's latest lay face down between a pair of forest-green Adirondack chairs. The river glimmered beyond.

The wineglass felt cool against her fingers. Though the day was just a glow on the horizon, the night air remained warm. She stared across to the lights of Boston. "This is wonderful."

"It sold me on the place." Cade closed the slider and crossed to where Ryan stood. He leaned against the rail. "So talk to me."

"What about?"

He tilted his head and looked at her. "When I'm in negotiations with someone and they make a one-hundred-and-eighty degree turn for no apparent reason, I usually get suspicious."

Ryan's eyes narrowed. "We're not in negotiations."

"Oh no?"

Leaning against the waist high barrier in the fading dusk, Ryan stared out into the evening. Instead of the lights of Manhattan, she saw the lights along the Charles River. This time there was no moonlight, but the city lights set up a glow about them. She took a sip of her wine and relaxed fractionally.

Cade watched an evening jogger run down the trail by the river, safety beacon bobbing up and down in the dusk. "Wasn't it just last week we were on a balcony standing just about like this?" He took a drink and set his glass on the broad wooden railing. "I seem to recall someone telling me she didn't want to sleep with me just to scratch an itch."

Ryan raised her chin. "Maybe I changed my mind. If we just set some rules up front—"

"Ah, rules again."

Her eyes flashed. "You have a problem with that?"

"They didn't help last time." He reached over to toy with her hair.

"Maybe if you'd followed them they would have. Maybe then we wouldn't be standing here having this conversation." She thumped the wineglass down on the railing.

Before she could react he'd pulled her close, his smile quick and dangerous. "Sooner or later we would have had this conversation no matter what."

"Let me go," Ryan hissed.

He ignored her. "I thought you came here to have sex," he said, tracing his fingertips down her throat and into the V of her collar. "Seems to me like holding you ought to be part of the proceedings. Personally, I kind of like holding you." His hands slid down her back, molding her to him. "It's something I've been thinking about a lot lately. That's the point of all this, isn't it? Burn it out, you said." He nibbled a line of kisses over her jaw. ''That's going to take some doing.''

Ryan felt every inch of his body against hers, felt his arousal growing. The barrier around the balcony was a solid wall behind her. His hands were warmer than the night air, heating her skin through the thin cloth of her blouse. Under his touch, her frustration melted away. It felt so right to be here with him, no matter what happened after. Ryan caught herself. What was she, nuts? Cade ran a hand back up to tangle in her hair, pulling her head back to plunder her mouth. ''Wait,'' she managed. ''We need to make sure we both agree on what's going on here.''

He stopped for a moment. ''Back to the rules, hmm?'' She felt his lips rub lightly, teasingly against hers, then nibble across her cheek. ''Okay. Rule number one, we get to be naked together as often as we both want. And I can tell you right now, I'm going to want it a lot,'' he whispered, then his lips took possession of hers and pulled her away on a whirling journey of passion. Hot and demanding, his mouth plundered hers ruthlessly until arousal pulsed through every cell of her body. The rough scrape of his beard against her chin inflamed her. His hands were in her hair. He tempted her to give, then to take until she was dizzy with pleasure.

There had been a point when she'd thought she could turn away from this whirlwind of sensation, the night she'd walked away at the Beacon Hill Hotel. Now she knew she'd been fooling herself to think she could do without this feeling. To think that she could do without him. It was impossible to consider walking away now. She'd been running to this point since she'd seen him in the conference room at Beckman Markham. However much she tried to convince herself otherwise, he'd written himself indelibly into her mind and onto her body. With his mouth on hers, she met him with a moan.

"Rule number two," Cade murmured as he broke the kiss to nibble her earlobe, "we get to have each other any way we want to." His hands stroked down over her breasts, hot and demanding, sliding over to free the top buttons on her blouse one by one. The fabric parted and his fingers were on the warm curves of lace-covered flesh, making her catch her breath. She pressed herself against him with abandon, feeling the warmth of his hands contrast with the tepid evening air. Then he slid his hand up slightly, and she could feel her heart pounding against his palm.

Passion dragged him beyond gentleness and she followed willingly. This was the product of days of longing and nights of pent-up desire, this maelstrom of passion that had overtaken them both. Caught in the whirling frenzy, she could only cling to him, closing her mouth over his as though they could breathe through each other. His touch was rough and she gloried in it. She felt his hands sliding her skirt up around her hips, heard his murmur of approval as his finger slipped over the tops of her stockings to run up the garters she wore. The stroke of his fingertips over the soft flesh made her shiver. The thought drifted through her head that she should tell him to stop, but the words turned into a moan and she ran her hands up his back to rake them through his hair.

"Rule number three, no backing out tomorrow." God, how had he managed to keep his hands off of her when she felt so gloriously, wonderfully right, Cade wondered as Ryan ran feverish kisses down his neck. After weeks of watching her and wondering, the answer was that the reality made his memories pale in comparison. She unbuttoned his shirt, sliding her smooth hands against his chest and he groaned at the brush of her skin over his nipples. She tempted him to push farther, to take them both to the edge and beyond.

Ryan gasped as his clever fingers slipped under the edge

of her lacy bikini underwear to find her slick and hot. He stroked her there and she writhed against him. "Oh," she gasped and parted her legs to give him better access. Then his fingers were pulling the scrap of lace between them aside, driving her up toward the point of absolute pleasure. Dimly, she heard the sound of his zipper, and he pulled her up until her legs were wrapped around his waist, her back braced against the barrier.

"Rule number four," Cade said in her ear, his voice strained, his breath ragged. "I get to have you. Now."

13

HIS MOUTH WAS on hers, taking, devouring. Then he raised his head. ''Let's get inside,'' he said. ''Hold on tight.'' With her still wrapped around him, he turned and walked across the balcony to the slider, then stepped inside. A swath of moonlight from the skylight shone across the bed and up one wall. He crossed the room and tumbled Ryan back onto the smooth cotton coverlet.

She'd barely registered the feeling of the bed beneath her before he was on her. His hands were relentless, touching her, sliding against her until she moved her hips without volition, crying out, caught up in sensation. He was hot and hard against her, his mouth bruising hers. Gone was any pretense at gentleness. Now it was only naked desire and insatiable hunger that drove them both, as he pushed her up, up and over the edge in a burst of exquisite pleasure that only left her wanting more.

Even as the aftershocks coursed through her, she felt Cade lean away from her and heard the sound of a drawer opening. Then he was back against her, pushing up her skirt, stripping off her lacy briefs. She gloried in his urgency, as she tore open the buttons of his jeans, reaching in to feel the hardness and pulsing heat in her hand, unbearably aroused by knowing that he wanted her so much. She heard the crackle of plastic and then he moved her hand away to sheath his shuddering erection.

And sank himself into her in a slick rush that tore the breath from her lungs.

Nothing that had come before had prepared her for this. The climax from moments ago had been just a teaser for the sensation that overwhelmed her now. The pressure of his body, the exquisite friction of him sliding in and out of her combined in a glorious molten flow of pleasure. His face was pure and tight with desire. The tightening began again in her body, intensifying with every stroke until she was clinging to him mindlessly, legs wrapped around his waist, fingers clutching the sweat-slick muscles of his back as they bunched and flowed. She gasped as she felt him thicken, heard him groan, and then he was surging against her, impaling her on the mattress even as she shuddered with her own ecstasy.

CADE ROLLED OFF onto his side, sliding out of her in a slick rush that only made him hard again.

"Where—"

"Shh." He leaned over her and kissed her long and lingeringly. "God, you're amazing. All I want to do is make love with you again." He backed away to strip his shirt and jeans off, then came back to her. "But first, we've got to get you out of all these clothes." He traced his tongue down her neck, unfastening the remaining buttons on her blouse. Stripping it off, he tossed it to the floor. The low-cut lace bra she wore beneath was anything but demure. Ryan reached down and unsnapped the front clasp and Cade peeled the cups back to uncover the smooth, soft skin of her breasts.

The silky soft feel of his tongue in contrast with the rough scrape of his beard did delicious things to her. Ryan ran her hands down his arms, glorying in the feel of the smooth, hard muscle, then gasped as his tongue teased first one then the other nipple to a tight, hard point. She raised her hips to help him strip off her skirt and the scrap of lace she wore beneath, leaving her clad only in stockings and garter belt.

He lay on the bed next to her, amazed at the luxury of

her smooth warmth pressed against him. This was what he hadn't been able to get out of his mind, the heat and intimacy of being close to her. He ran his hand lightly down her body, his fingers rising and falling over her breast, fanning out over the slight curve of hip. One at a time, he unsnapped her garters and pushed the stockings off.

"Right now, I just want to feel you," he whispered. He leaned in to kiss her, and the feel of her warm, mobile mouth under his excited him again.

The hard length of him nudged her thigh. Ryan reached down and wrapped her fingers around him until he shuddered, amazed at the fact that she could arouse him so.

Ryan stared up at his shadowed face as he moved to lie between her legs.

He'd imagined this moment so many times. None of it even came close to the pure glory he felt as he looked into her eyes and drove himself into her, sliding in so slick and fast it took his breath away. For an instant, he stayed absolutely still, lost in the pleasure and heat, lost in being a part of her. Then slowly, slowly he began to move.

The sensation threatened to overwhelm him, but he'd sworn that he would savor the experience, he would give them both a chance to absorb what they were feeling before it was over. He felt Ryan tightening around him, moaning, her fingers clinging to his shoulders. Higher and higher they rode the motion until he pushed both of them over the peak to plummet in a spinning spiral of pleasure, crying out with release.

The warm weight of his body was an intimacy beyond description, Ryan thought drowsily as she floated into sleep feeling him still a part of her. Cade pressed a kiss to her temple and followed her down.

THE BRIGHT LIGHT OF morning flooded into the room, pulling Ryan into wakefulness. She became vividly aware of the warmth of Cade's body behind her as she lay spooned against him. Every nerve ending registering the texture of his skin, memories of the night just past crowding in on each other.

She may have been celibate for eight years, but in the previous hours they'd made up for lost time. The night had been a pattern of making love, then dozing long enough to make love again. Each time they had dropped off, one of them awoke enough to brush a caress over skin sensitized to the touch, starting the cycle all over again. Desire gave way to laughter, which dissolved back into blazing passion in the blink of an eye.

It was amazing, and she wanted more.

It was terrifying, and she had no idea what came next. How would it be when he awoke? They hadn't come close to hashing things out the night before and she had no idea what to expect from him. Going to bed and getting it over with had sounded like a good idea when she started out for his condo, but now here she was in bed with him, and her desire for him was far, far from burned out. All she was certain of was that she wanted more.

Cade muttered in his sleep and pulled her closer, wrapping his arms around her.

She'd never woken with a lover before, never been in a man's bed with the coming of dawn. Her feeble college experience, utterly meaningless in retrospect, had begun and ended one night after a party. She had no experience greeting the morning with another. After a lifetime of waking alone, the reality of waking in the arms of her lover was utterly extraordinary.

Nerves gradually began to erode the golden glow, though. How Cade felt, where things stood now, she had no clue. She'd come to his house intending to talk first and act later. Instead, they'd fallen into bed without sorting anything out, with no more understanding of where things stood than the first time they'd been together. Who knew what he was expecting? She'd said burn out the chemistry. Maybe it was done for him, in which case waking up in his bed was too embarrassing to contemplate. Ryan craned her neck to look for the clock and saw it blink to 6:10 a.m. She had a nine o'clock class to teach and she was halfway across town from her apartment and a change of clothes. What had she been thinking of?

Anxiety dug its fingers into her as she tried to ease out of the bed without waking him. He only pressed his lips against her in sleepy reflex and tightened his arms in response. She pulled against him again, scooting toward the edge of the bed. Finally, she managed to slip loose. He turned over, and sank back into sleep.

Ryan padded quietly across the bedroom floor, fishing for garments she recognized from the tangle of cloth strewn on the floor. Slipping into the bathroom, she closed the door with a quiet click and snapped on the light. She had the bare minimum of clothes to make her decent, though her garter belt had somehow gone missing, not to mention her underwear. Hastily, she washed in the sink then slipped into her clothes, smoothing her skirt down over her hips, her hands echoing the feel of his touch. She glanced at herself in the mirror and a goofy smile spread across her face. No matter what came next, it had been a glorious night.

Quietly, she turned off the light and opened the door to see Cade still sleeping. She walked quietly across the room, bending to retrieve her shoes. Spying one of her stockings tossed in a corner, she scooped it up and looked around for its companion. Then she spied the end of the garter belt. Of her underwear, there was no sign, but it was little enough to sacrifice.

She stopped and stared a moment at Cade's sleeping profile. Leaning down, she brushed the barest of kisses over his temple, then turned to go.

And an arm swept around her waist from behind.

"Running out on me?"

Surprise sent adrenaline rocketing through her system even as she registered his voice, rough with sleep. Before she could react, he pulled her back onto the bed for a long, lingering kiss.

The kiss reignited all the need she'd felt the night before. Far from being burned out, the wanting was sharper, more vivid for knowing just what she was missing in all its particulars.

Cade broke the kiss off and looked at her. "The rules said no backing out in the morning."

"I have to get to work." Ryan pulled away to stand up.

Cade followed her, pulling her close to him again. "Saying goodbye doesn't take long."

"I wasn't sure we'd have much to say this morning. We said we'd burn it out. I thought maybe last night was enough."

"To burn this out? I don't think so." He began unbuttoning the front of her blouse. "I don't know about you, darlin', but I'm very far from burned out on this. In fact, I think we're going to have to try a whole lot harder to get through this because right now I've got a regular bonfire going."

She glanced down, following his eyes, and saw the evidence for herself. "Wait," she said desperately as he tossed her blouse on the floor and unfastened her bra. "We rushed into things last night without figuring out what's going on. Let's not do it all over again." Then she caught her breath at the feel of his hands on her breasts.

"I think I know what's going on. It's very easy," he said, nibbling down her throat. "I want you, pure and simple. You want more rules?" He unzipped the back of her skirt.

"I'll take you to dinner tonight and we can hash out the rules to your heart's content."

"Dinner?"

"You know, where you sit down at a table and eat? Seems to me like I still owe you one." He slid her skirt down over her hips to find nothing but bare flesh beneath. "Mmm. I see you didn't find all of your clothes this morning."

At the touch of his hands, Ryan gave up her efforts to leave. "I was pressed for time," she breathed, sliding her hands down his back.

"Well then we need to get you showered and on your way," he said, tugging her toward the bathroom. "Come with me. I'll help you figure out how the bar of soap works."

THE HOURS HAD GONE BY so quickly since then, Ryan thought, as she dug in her desk for her purse at the end of the day. She'd never realized the entertainment possibilities of soap and water, she thought, her lips curving in memory. By the time they'd finished, only rushing flat out had gotten her to work in time to prepare for her class. And now, as she locked her office, she was heading out to meet her lover, to reap her reward for getting through another dutiful day of work.

And what a reward it was, she thought twenty minutes later as she came up out of the underground parking and saw him waiting for her in front of the restaurant. It was hard to force herself to walk when she wanted to fly into his arms.

Then she was there, wrapped around him, her mouth fused to his.

Cade kissed her long and thoroughly, wiping away the memory of the daytime hours that had dragged by while he had been distracted by thoughts of the night just past. At some point he really needed to think about the rush of pleasure that the sight of her brought to him. For now, it was enough just to feel her against him, to smell her hair as he kissed it, to take her hand to walk her into the restaurant.

"Who was it that had the bright idea of meeting here for dinner instead of at one of our houses where I could have torn your clothes off and had my way with you?" he asked as he held the door for her.

Ryan slanted him an amused look. "That would be you."

Cade nodded. "I thought as much. Just for the record, even *I* am sometimes wrong."

The restaurant was elegant and expensive, a mix of soaring white walls, blond wood, and brushed aluminum. An enormous bronze urn held a huge palm, its fronds arching over the reception area. The maitre d' led them to a table next to a wall of windows overlooking the avenue, where the golden light of late afternoon flowed in.

Cade seated her, then kissed her lightly on the lips before taking his chair. Without consciously thinking about it, Ryan reached her hand across the table to link her fingers with his.

She looked around her and sighed in pleasure. "When I was a kid I always dreamed of going to a restaurant like this."

"Well I'm glad that I'm able to make one of your dreams reality."

He'd done that many times over, she thought, locking eyes with him. Passion of the type she'd only dreamed about when she'd written her novels had come to life for her the previous night. Now, finally, she knew what it was like to make love all night, to have the desire be inexhaustible. Long seconds slid by as they swam deep into each other's gaze, stopping only long enough for Cade to deal with the wine list.

Cade looked at her as the sommelier walked away. "You know, you're the most vivid person I've ever known."

"What do you mean?"

He nodded toward the other diners in the restaurant. "Look at all of them. They're all in the Boston uniform of black and khaki. Monochrome, or darned close. Then there's you, dressed like a peacock. You light up every room you walk into."

Self-conscious, Ryan looked down at her sleeveless fuchsia shift. During the day, she had subdued it with a cream jacket, but she'd taken it off when she'd left to meet him. "Everyone's got their weakness. Bright colors have always been mine. I must have been a parrot in a previous life."

He considered the idea then rejected it. "No. Parrots are too raucous. I see you more as a tropical fish, the sleek kind that swirls around coral reefs and flirts with divers." He ran his fingers over the palm of her hand, teasing the sensitive skin there.

"And what kind of an animal were you in a previous life?"

"I don't know. I've never thought about it. Maybe an eagle or something. Some kind of a loner."

"No, you'd be something more feral. A panther, maybe. One that sits on a branch all sleek and coiled, waiting to spring."

The measured stroking was pulling her down into a sensual haze and she began to tremble. Just then, the sommelier approached with their wine. The next few minutes were occupied with the ceremony of label, cork, and tasting, affording her a chance to get her heart rate down where it belonged. Then they were left with their wine and a basket of breads.

Cade raised his glass to her. "To tropical fish."

"And panthers." They clinked glasses and she savored the cool, crisp taste of the wine on her tongue.

Cade grinned. "Seems like we've been going at this backward."

"How so?"

"Well, usually a dinner date is the first thing on the agenda in an affair, not the last." He took a drink of wine.

"And are we having an affair?" she asked, with a quick flip of nerves.

"After last night you ask that?"

"There are such things as one-night stands. We said we'd burn it out." Her face flamed, but she forced herself to continue. "I thought that might have been enough."

"Enough?" He considered. "Nope, not by half." He raised her fingers to lips and lingered over them, his eyes on hers. "I want you. And I'm pretty sure I'm going to keep wanting you for a while."

Butterflies whirled and danced in her stomach. "Same goes for me."

"Good. That saves me the time of convincing you." He wanted his hands on her, he wanted her against him.

"You had me convinced last night." The words came out in a husky whisper.

The waiter cleared his throat. "Hi, I'm Troy, I'll be your server tonight." He flashed brilliant white teeth and rattled off a list of specials so quickly Ryan could barely keep up.

She opened her menu. "I haven't even had a chance to look at this thing yet. Could we have a little more time?"

"Sure thing. Take as long as you like." He nodded and left.

Cade glanced down at his menu and made a selection. Then he closed it and set it aside. He had much better things to look at than a menu. "So what are you doing over the weekend? I'm trying to figure out exactly how much of it we can while away in bed."

"That's three days from now."

His teeth were very white as he smiled. "I've already got plans for you each of those nights."

"You're nothing if not efficient."

He drew her hand to his mouth and sucked on her fingertips. "Efficiency is the least of my talents."

A warm tide of arousal washed over her at his words.

"So you didn't answer my question," he said in amusement.

"What?" she asked blankly. "Oh, um, this weekend. Well, Saturday I'm going to the Boston Corporate Games for Charity. We've got a team in the run."

"We're going to be there too. You should bring the team to have lunch with us. We're a sponsor." He brushed a kiss over her fingers.

"I know. Barry specifically asked me to look you up and bond with you." She rolled her eyes. "He seems to think it will impress you."

"Anything you do impresses me, darlin', but I'm glad to hear that Barry's turned matchmaker."

"A matchmaker who will remain blissfully ignorant of what's between you and me, thank you very much," she said primly.

"Of course." He gave a short laugh and shook his head. "Patrick, now, Patrick's going to have a field day with this one."

"Why does he need to know?" Anxiety tightened her voice. "I think we should keep this off the work radar. You own your company. I don't. It could be a problem for me."

"I wouldn't do anything to compromise your work situation. Patrick will keep quiet. He may take some of my hide off, but he'll keep quiet." Cade broke off a piece of bread from the loaf in the basket and buttered it. "He's my partner and we go too far back for me to lie to him if he asks."

"Why would he ask?"

"He's been telling me to stay away from you for the past two weeks."

"From me?" she asked blankly. "Why?"

"He could tell that you were on my mind. Sometimes Patrick knows me a little too well." He raised his glass again to drink. "He's just concerned that something might happen between us to impact the project. Is it going to be a problem for you, working together?"

A smile tugged at her lips. "It's a little late to ask that now, isn't it?"

"Oh, I don't know. I figured you'd want to set some rules."

"We keep the two separate. It's as simple as that. Otherwise, I kind of liked your rules from last night. Especially the part about getting to be naked together whenever we want."

"I liked that one, too."

She looked at him consideringly. "Do you suppose it would be really bad form to take the bottle of wine to go?"

"It might be a first for them, but I've always been one for blazing trails." His eyes gleamed as he rose and held out his hand for her. "Your place or mine?"

14

RYAN SHIVERED AS SHE stood with Becka near the starting line of the Boston Corporate Games' 5K. The day had dawned sunny and clear, but the morning air still held a chill as they waited amid a crowd of runners. The nasal honk of the air horn shattered the quiet and the pack broke away.

As with most 5Ks, it took a minute or two for the foot traffic to disperse enough for them to move beyond a slow jog. The delay didn't make Ryan as impatient as it usually did—her mind was on waking earlier that morning with Cade.

"You've got that I've-got-a-man-on-my-mind kind of look, girlfriend," Becka said. "Come back to Earth and tell me what's going on. Did you have a talk with our boy?"

Ryan gave her a sidelong glance. "Nah, I figured I'd just jump him, instead." At Becka's astounded look, Ryan broke into a delighted laugh.

"I can't keep up with you." Becka shook her head in amazement. "One minute you're doing the solo chick thing, the next you're tying the guy up, and now you're taking him to bed." Becka gave her an admiring look. "I've got to hand it to you, Donnelly, when you decide to break out of a rut, you do it right."

Ryan nodded, waiting for the pack around them to thin out until there was some privacy. "It's wonderful. He's wonderful. I haven't a clue why I waited so long."

"Now do you understand why I've been hounding you

to have an affair all these years?'' Becka bounded along in high good humor. "So when do I get to meet him?"

"Today, if you want to." Ryan glanced over her shoulder before moving to pass a runner ahead of her. "He's invited our team to have lunch at the eTrain tables."

"Oh this is excellent. I can't wait. Ryan's got herself a man and I want to meet him."

"It's only temporary," Ryan cautioned. "We just agreed to try it out for a while. It could be over tomorrow for all I know."

"That's true of any relationship," Becka reasoned. "Don't borrow trouble—enjoy it while it lasts."

"Speaking of borrowing trouble, how did the breakup with Scott go?"

"Ugly in a very Scott-like way." All the exuberance drained from Becka's face, leaving her uncharacteristically subdued. "It was all how could I leave him, how could I abandon him just when the muscle show season is getting going, didn't I care about his career at all." Becka's jaw set as she upped her speed a notch.

Ryan looked at her sympathetically. "No 'I want you,' 'I love you,' 'I need you'?"

"Nope. I don't think considerations like that enter into his head." She shook her head as though warding off disappointment. "I still can't believe I stuck with him for so long. It was just empty. I feel really good that I'm out of it, though. I just want to be on my own for a while, not make another mistake by rushing into something."

"I know everybody says the same thing, but the right guy is out there for you, Becka. Now that you've broken up with Scott, you're free to find him."

"And have you found the right guy, hmm, Ms. Romantic?" Becka asked teasingly.

Ryan flushed. "It's too soon to even begin thinking that way. I feel good when I'm with him. I'll take that as enough for now.'' But part of her wondered if it already felt too good to be with Cade. In just a few short days, he'd become a fixture in her life. When he was around, she felt light enough to walk on air, free enough to be herself, and amazingly, that was what he wanted.

She thought of it again after the run, as she sat watching the softball tournament with the rest of the team, nibbling on a banana and bobbing her head to the reggae music playing over the loudspeakers. Only a few hours had passed since she'd left Cade, yet she was already wondering how soon she could discreetly go find him.

Next to her, Becka stirred. ''So what time is lunch? I volunteered to help out at the rubdown table, so I should get over there.''

''I'll go with you,'' Ryan said, hopping to her feet with alacrity. She glanced at her colleagues. ''I'll see you guys in a little while. Barry wanted me to check in with the new clients, so I have to go and make nice.''

''That was slick,'' Becka said admiringly as they walked toward the massage area, passing the rows of booths from corporate sponsors. ''I take it you and Cade are in stealth mode?''

Ryan nodded. ''What they don't know won't hurt them. I've got to find his booth. Come with me?''

Becka grinned. ''How old did you say you were again?''

''Two months older than you, Landon,'' she retorted, ''and still big enough to make you cry uncle.''

''In your dreams,'' Becka scoffed.

''Probably so, the way you work out.'' Ryan seized Becka's wrist abruptly. ''Oh, there's their booth, over there.'' It took her a conscious effort to amble up casually, taking her time. It was a letdown to realize that only Patrick was there.

''That's him?'' Becka whispered in a disappointed tone.

"Shh. No, that's his partner." Ryan gave Patrick a little wave as they walked up to the table.

"Ryan Donnelly, right?" Patrick asked before she could speak. "I didn't know anyone from Beckman Markham was here."

"Wouldn't miss it for the world," she said easily, and introduced Becka. "Becka was part of our team in the 5K. How are you guys doing?"

"We had some people in the run. Our softball team got eliminated last weekend, but that wasn't much of a surprise. We kind of sucked. It was still fun, though," he said, without visible regret. "And hey, our volleyball team is kicking butt. Cade seems to think we might make it into the semi-finals."

Ryan picked up an eTrain leaflet and flipped through it idly. "Oh yeah? Is he around?" she asked in an offhand tone.

Patrick's gaze sharpened. "Cade, you mean?" He gave her a penetrating look. "He's on the team. Check over at the volleyball courts if you want him."

If she wanted him? She was beginning to do nothing but. With Becka in tow, Ryan walked over to where string and nets marked the four volleyball courts.

"What does he look like?" Becka asked. "You've never told me."

"Oh, you know, tall, dark, good looking…" Ryan's voice drifted off as she scanned the teams playing, trying to find the group from eTrain. Then she saw Cade and the breath left her lungs.

Even though she knew what he looked like naked, somehow it was even more provocative seeing his rangy body half clothed. He wore beat up khaki shorts that just accentuated his muscled legs. His dark blue T-shirt draped over a torso that tapered from muscled shoulders to lean hips.

Sweat darkened the cloth in an oval circle on his back. Sunglasses hid his eyes.

As they watched, the eTrain team got the ball and Cade moved into serving position. His forearm muscles flexed as he tossed the ball up in front of him, then brought his other arm around in an arc, open hand smashing the ball into the opposite court. Players on the opposing team made stabs for the white sphere as it flew past, but it thumped into the grass before they could react. Cade's teeth flashed white as he grinned.

"Which one is he?" Becka asked.

Ryan merely pointed. It was too hard to talk with her tongue hanging out.

"Good god, that's the man you were telling to take a hike?" Becka watched Cade ace another serve. "What were you thinking of?"

"Shh. Try to be a little more discreet, will you?" Ryan asked without turning her head. "I work with him, remember?"

The referee called game point, and Cade served again. A furious volley ensued, punctuated by grunts and thuds, both teams grimly intent on victory. The ball nearly hit the ground on the eTrain side of the net but Cade dove for it, pounding it back up into the air so that the front line could drop it neatly over the net for the final point.

There was a chorus of triumphant cheers from the eTrain team. Cade stood up grinning, brushing grass off the front of his shirt. Slapping high fives, they all walked off the court.

Ryan felt the giddy rush of pleasure as he broke off from the group to grab a bottle of water from a barrel of ice near the court. She watched his tanned throat move as he swallowed the spring water, and remembered how tight and smooth his skin felt there, how thick his hair was as it curled through her fingers when they were in bed. He finished drinking and wiped his mouth, then he glanced up and their eyes locked. It threw her back like a physical contact. He picked a towel off the grass and walked over.

"Hi," he said, wiping his forehead and pleasing himself by letting his eyes roam over her.

Ryan tried unsuccessfully to wipe the smile off her face. It was absurd how good it felt to see him. "Congratulations."

He grinned. "Thanks. We're on a roll today."

"I can see that."

"It's good to see you."

Dark stubble shadowed his jaw, making him look rough and just a bit dangerous. The desire to kiss him was nearly overwhelming. Belatedly, she remembered her manners. "This is Becka Landon, a very dear friend of mine who volunteered to round out our 5K team. Becka, Cade Douglas."

"Nice to meet you." Becka eyed him speculatively. "Where'd you get that serve?"

"I played in college." He took another swig of water. "I'm hoping to get the rust off in time for the quarterfinals in about half an hour."

"You guys keep playing like that I'd say you've got it sewn up."

"Thanks." Cade looked back at Ryan. He'd awakened with her wrapped around him just that morning but it felt like weeks had gone by. Having her near now felt right. "So how'd you folks do?"

"Faster than I expected," Ryan said. "We might actually place."

He glanced at the sleek lines of her legs, remembering when she stood in front of the window in the Copley Hotel, wearing only gossamer hose and a garter belt. "With legs like that, I'm not surprised."

She blushed. Becka looked at her and grinned, then

glanced at her sports watch. "Cade, it was nice to meet you. I'm sorry, but I've got to dash. I'm supposed to be working the rubdown table. Ryan, where do you want to meet for lunch?"

Ryan looked at Cade in question. "Where do you want us?"

Anywhere I can get you. The thought was immediate. For now, though, he'd have to damp his urges until he could have her to himself. "Our tables are over near the booth. Just bring the whole team." The rest of the team didn't matter. She did.

"It's really nice of you to invite us."

"No trouble, really. You're our partners." His gaze went through her skin and into her bones.

"I'll see you guys later," Becka said, but they barely heard her, intent on each other.

He stepped just a bit closer. She couldn't help but imagine him closer still. "You left too early this morning," he said softly.

"I had to get here to meet the team."

"You should have stopped by when you got here. We had bagels and muffins." And he would have seen her that much sooner, he thought, taking another drink from his water bottle, eyes on hers.

"Are you sure you're going to have room for us at lunch?"

"Not a problem." The rest of the eTrain team was filing back, preparing for the quarterfinal. Someone called Cade's name.

"I should let you go." She wanted him with an intensity that stunned her. "Good luck with your game. I'll bring the rest of the team over later."

"Good idea. You know where to find us."

They stood staring at each other, unwilling to part without touching, unable to do anything but. It was ridiculous to feel bereft when she knew she'd be with him that night, Ryan thought, but that didn't change the way she felt. She gave a little wave, then forced herself to go.

Cade watched her walk away. Stupendous legs, just stupendous. And as for the rest of the package, well, that was as fine as it came too, he thought, as the team began bumping balls around to warm up. When he'd turned around and seen her he'd felt like he'd conjured her up by thinking about her. She'd been on his mind nearly nonstop since he'd seen her off that morning. The burst of pure, uncomplicated pleasure that had hit him then gave him pause for thought, though. Desire was only part of the feeling; most of it was knowing that he was going to be in her company again. When had that happened, he wondered.

She stayed on his mind even through the quarterfinal, which didn't keep him from leading the team to a win. She'd become such a part of him in such a short time, he thought, walking back to the eTrain booth with the rest of the team. They were together nearly every minute they weren't at work. He kept waiting for burnout to set in, but it hadn't happened yet. Still, given his family history and track record, it was just a matter of time. And that, he thought, would be a very great shame.

"Congratulations," Patrick called when Cade reached the booth. "I hear you guys made the semifinals."

"With this kind of talent, did you ever doubt it?" They went through the high-five ritual, slapping palms and bumping fists.

Patrick rolled his eyes. "Sorry, guess I forgot about your twenty Olympic gold medals and lifetime career achievement award."

"I don't hold it against you," Cade said genially, taking a swig from the bottle of Gatorade he held. "I figured I had to spread a little magic for the company."

Patrick's smile faded. "Speaking of the company, Ryan

Donnelly from Beckman Markham stopped by. Did she find you?'' He reached under the table to pull out some more brochures.

The attempt at casualness was completely unconvincing, Cade thought. ''Yep. I invited her to bring the rest of the Beckman Markham team over to our area for lunch.''

Patrick slapped the brochures on the table. ''Is that really a good idea?''

''Patrick, we're working a deal with them. Why wouldn't we want to hook up with them if they're here?''

Patrick shrugged. ''No reason, I guess.''

''Good.'' Cade took a deep breath. ''The other part that you should know about is that we've gotten involved.''

Patrick spun around to face him, genuine anger on his face. ''Goddammit, Cade, you said…''

''I said it would be okay, and it is.'' His voice held an emphatic edge. He looked steadily at Patrick until the irritation in his friend's eyes began to ease. ''Look, this isn't a one-night stand, okay? I like this woman, a lot. The job's getting done. What we do on our own time is our own business.''

''Not when it impacts the company you're running.'' Patrick folded his arms in front of him like a high school teacher reasoning with a difficult student.

''It's not impacting the company. The work is going fine.''

''That's great for now, but what about—''

''Patrick, I like being with her.'' Cade's voice was shaded with intensity. ''You know how long it's been for me since I've wanted to be around anyone? Cut me some slack here.'' He paused. ''I need to do this.''

Patrick stared at him a moment, then nodded reluctantly. ''Okay. Just be careful. I don't want the business screwed up and I don't want you to get messed around over this. I don't want to hear that—''

"Uncle Cade!" A pair of dark-haired moppets hit Cade simultaneously from opposite sides. Patrick sighed as his kids hugged Cade. "Uncle Cade, take us for a rocket ride," piped the older one, a boy perhaps of four or five years.

"Wottet wide," echoed the toddler with him, pushing her face into Cade's leg.

"Let's go away from the table, Cameron." Grinning, Cade gave Patrick a helpless shrug and obediently picked up the boy, carrying him safely away from the table before whirling him up into the air.

"More," cried the boy, screaming with laughter. "More."

"Me," the little girl cried, holding her arms up. Patrick picked up his young daughter and hoisted her onto his shoulders. "There you go, Sydney, you can watch Cameron and Uncle Cade from the penthouse suite."

"Wottet wide!" she cried, clapping her hands together. And watching his best friend with his child, Patrick couldn't help smiling, despite his doubts.

RYAN BROUGHT THE OTHERS to the eTrain tables, introducing them to the handful of people she knew from meetings. Trying to ignore the flutters in her stomach, she walked toward the booth, looking for Cade. Then she saw him, whirling a squealing little girl around with abandon. Her jaw dropped at the scene. Cade swung the tiny girl again then set her down. A dark-haired little boy dancing at his side tugged on his T-shirt for a turn. Somehow, she'd never thought of Cade as the family sort, but he looked carefree and delighted. His face was absent its usual intensity, relaxed in a way she'd never seen before. She found herself charmed, utterly and completely. "What cute kids," she murmured.

"Thanks. We like them." Ryan jerked around to find Patrick giving her an assessing look. He looked beyond her to where his children were swinging on Cade's arms, using him as a human jungle gym. "They're mine. They've known him all their lives, so they pretty much act like they own him."

Cade glanced up and saw Ryan and Patrick standing together. Letting Cameron down, he straightened up and walked over to them. The children danced along beside him, swinging on his hands. He locked eyes with Ryan. "Hi."

"Hello." A moment slid by while they simply looked at each other and grinned. Patrick watched them, and his mouth softened into a reluctant smile.

Cade snapped out of it first. "Did you bring the others?"

Ryan nodded. "They're over at the tables. How did the quarterfinals go?"

"We won. Onto the se—wait," he stopped, looking at her intently. "Hold still a minute. You've got a bug in your hair."

"What kind?" Ryan's voice rose in alarm as she cringed. She'd always had a horror of wasps and hornets.

Cade spoke soothingly, catching her shoulder. "Nothing that stings. Just hold still." He reached over to untangle an early Japanese beetle from her hair and held it out. "Just a beetle, see?"

"Oh." Ryan flushed. "Sorry. I have a thing about bites and stings."

"Let me see," Cameron cried.

Cade knelt down and held his palm out so that Cameron and Sydney could crowd around. They stared at the beetle in fascination. As the insect crawled over his hand, Cade tipped it so that they could continue to watch. "Put your finger out, Cam," he said.

"It tickles," Cameron squealed when the scratchy legs touched him, and dropped the beetle back in Cade's open hand.

Staring at the scene, Ryan felt something constrict in her

chest, like there wasn't enough room for her heart. She glanced away to see Patrick looking at her as though she were a science experiment he was studying.

"Patrick?" a redhaired woman called as she walked across the grass toward them. "Time to get the kids over to lunch, hon." She came up and gave Patrick a quick kiss, then knelt down to stare at Cade's hand with the children. "Whatcha looking at?"

"It's a beetle," Cameron answered importantly. "Isn't he cool? He's all shiny and coloredy."

"Neat stuff," she agreed. As though tired of being the center of attention, the beetle raised its wings and took off into the air. There was a chorus of protests from the children.

"It's okay," Cade said. "He was late for lunch."

"Like us," said the woman, straightening up and pushing a strand of hair out of her eyes. "You going to introduce me to your girl, Cade?"

Patrick stiffened and Cade shifted.

She looked from one to the other. "What, did I say something wrong?"

"I'm just a colleague," Ryan said quickly. "Ryan Donnelly." She extended her hand.

The woman blushed. "I'm so sorry. When I looked over and saw you two together I thought...oh, I jump to conclusions sometimes. I'm Amy Wallace, mother of those two crazy kids there."

Patrick stepped up behind her to put his arms around her neck. "You forgot the most important part," he said, dropping a kiss on her hair. "She's also my adoring wife."

Amy turned to look at him, eyes sparkling. "You bet I am, buster," she said and kissed him. "You just bet I am. Now let's get this crew to lunch."

"Cade, can you do something about the leaflets so they don't blow away?" Patrick asked as he walked away.

"Sure."

The foursome headed off across the grass, the children skipping ahead.

"They seem really nice," Ryan said. She turned to Cade, and saw him watching Patrick and his family with a kind of wistful longing in his eyes.

"Huh?" He responded a beat too late. "Oh, yeah. The kids are fun. Patrick and Amy have it golden." He glanced at them one more time, then turned to her and smiled, his eyes clear again. "Come on, let's go find your friends and eat."

She didn't see the look return at lunch, when they laughed and joked through the meal, or in the afternoon, when he led the eTrain team to victory. And as she lay in bed next to him that night, she wondered if it had all been in her imagination, but she knew it hadn't. Somewhere deep inside him was a longing for what he thought he couldn't have. Somewhere inside him was a longing for family.

15

"SO WHY DO WE CARE ABOUT determining your employees' personality types?" Ryan was up in front of the class, loose and enjoying herself. It was a particularly good group, one that she'd connected with right off the bat. Or perhaps she'd just connected with Cade, who watched her avidly from the last row. Every time she glanced his way, she felt bathed in a special glow. The lens of the camera that winked at her from the back of the room didn't bother her. She hardly noticed it.

"The answer is that the more you understand them, the more effectively you can work with them. It's all about give and take." She glanced at the faces in the class, and once again found herself unable to keep from looking at Cade. The smile on his face made her mouth curve in return. "In case you haven't figured it out, as a manager you have a relationship with your reports, just as you do with someone you're involved with. And like any relationship, the key issues are communication, understanding and willingness to be flexible. As boss, you may be calling the shots, but if you want to get the most out of the relationship, you'll find a way to accomplish your goals by helping the employees under your supervision accomplish their goals.

"You have to define the relationship." Like she and Cade had defined their relationship. Only now, she found herself wanting more. The feeling wasn't burning out. It was only getting deeper and stronger. "There's got to be trust. They have to know they can depend on you to be honest with them, to be fair, to look out for their interests."

Cade rubbed his jaw and she felt a quick surge of butterflies in her stomach. Suddenly all she could think was how much she wanted him, just a few moments alone with him. "All right, everybody, it's ten-thirty. Let's take a break. I'll see you back here in fifteen minutes." Ryan watched the students file out of the hotel meeting room and breathed a sigh of relief.

Pete turned off the camera and flashed her a smile. "You're doing great. It's like night and day compared to last week. This is going to be amazing when I get it edited."

"You were right," Cade said, "the audience makes all the difference."

She flushed with pleasure. "I'm lucky. This is a particularly good bunch."

Pete yawned. "Hit traffic and got here too late to have coffee. I'm gonna go grab some before I fall asleep." He wandered out the door followed by the sound man, leaving the room empty but for Cade and Ryan.

Cade approached her as she walked toward him and pulled her back into a niche hidden from the doorway. "Why is it I feel like it's been weeks since I saw you rather than just a couple of hours?" he whispered, fastening his mouth over hers.

It continued to amaze her, the heat his kisses stirred up. One minute she was in front of the room, calm and collected, aware of him at a level of quiet happiness. The next, she was thrumming with desire. Emotion burst through her with an intensity she'd never expected. She'd never realized that a love affair could satisfy on so many levels.

Love affair? Love? Ryan stiffened. They had agreed on a purely physical affair. Love didn't enter into it. It couldn't.

She was very afraid it already had.

"What's wrong?" Cade murmured, his lips against her neck.

"Nothing," she said unsteadily, trying to pull away. "I just remembered...I need..."

"What's going on?" He started to protest, but just then his cell phone jangled for attention and they broke apart. "Douglas," he answered in clipped tones, brushing his hand over his mouth absentmindedly to wipe away Ryan's lipstick.

If she could just get her bearings, she'd be okay, Ryan thought, grabbing her purse and fleeing to the ladies room. How had it crept up on her? The physical attraction she was comfortable with. It was the way she'd felt watching Cade with Patrick's kids at the Corporate Games that had ambushed her. It was the quiet pleasures and the passions of the week gone by that had caught her unawares. Now, there was nothing to do but keep the sudden surge of feeling to herself and let it fade away. Hand shaking, she repaired her lipstick as best she could.

CADE WALKED AWAY from the classroom, searching for better reception. "Okay, that's better, you're not breaking up so much. Calm down, Patrick, and tell me what happened."

Patrick's words came out in a rush, his voice strained. "It was the VCs. They called up for a progress report and I talked to them since you weren't in. They wanted to know what was new. I told them about the streaming video."

Cade closed his eyes. "Tell me you didn't try to do a demo with them, Patrick. That feature's not ready to show, you told me that yourself."

"I told them it was a new feature, just in test mode."

Cade took a breath and searched for patience. "Patrick, we talked about this. These guys are flinchy. The last thing we want to do is spook them by showing them something that doesn't work. Call them back and tell them you can't do it."

There was a short silence. "It's too late," Patrick said finally.

"Shit."

"I'd just been through it three times earlier this morning and it worked fine," Patrick burst out defensively. "I didn't have anything else to tell them about and they seemed to be expecting something." He hesitated a moment as if searching for words. "I gave them the URL and started to walk them through a tour."

Cade stared at the ceiling and searched for patience. "And it blew up."

"Worse. The server crashed. We're dead in the water. Ravi and the guys are working on it. The problem is that it went down when I was demoing it to the VCs."

"Who were not impressed."

"Well." Tension vibrated in Patrick's voice. "They actually got pretty agitated. I mean, our original schedule for the live rollout of phase one is in two weeks. They're freaked out that we might not be able to meet schedule. Frank Briamante, especially, was acting really pissed. They want to talk with you, pronto."

"We're doing a taping here."

"They said now, Cade. I don't know if they can pull funding at this point, but I don't want to give them a chance."

"All right," he said wearily. "I'll call them."

Five minutes later he was on the phone to New York, soothing Briamante, the head of the venture cap group. "What you saw today was an anomaly, Frank. The rollout isn't for two weeks. We'll be fine."

"That's not good enough." There was an edge to Briamante's words. "We've put seven million dollars into you guys, in the expectation of getting it back in the IPO. I need more than just your assurances."

"The content is solid, and that's what's going to sell this whole thing."

"Prove it to me." Briamante was brusque. "I'm taking the shuttle up tonight. I want to meet with your content people and I want to see a demo tomorrow that works. In this market, a dot-com IPO isn't a guaranteed success. I need to know this is going to fly.''

Cade sighed. There went his hopes for a quiet evening with Ryan. ''No problem. When you get your flight set up, let my secretary know. I'll pick you up at the airport and we can go to dinner.''

Cade ended the call and stood a minute. Then he stepped out into the deserted courtyard and released a quiet and heartfelt string of profanity as he dialed Patrick back up on the cell phone.

CADE STOOD IN THE classroom doorway watching Ryan flip through viewgraphs, her mouth firm in concentration. As much as she turned him on when she was naked and avid against him, there was something he downright adored about her precise, serious business persona. Maybe because he knew how just a touch from him could affect her. Maybe because, much to his surprise, she was becoming something of a fixture in his life. The lovemaking was incredible, the intensity never seemed to dim. But he'd never really known the quiet pleasure of sharing the events of his day with a lover, and in turn sharing her triumphs and challenges. Ryan had brought that to him. She had brought his days to life.

She sensed him before he was even through the doorway. When she looked up to find his eyes on her, the truth of her newfound self-knowledge pulsed through her. Love. Whether or not it was right, it simply was. Her heart hammered. ''Exciting phone call?''

''You don't know the half of it. What's your schedule look like tomorrow? Do you have time for a meeting?''

''I've got the second half of this class all day.'' Just as well. She needed time away from him to recover her equilibrium.

''That's right. I forgot.'' He paused a moment. ''Got plans for dinner tonight?''

Her decision to duck out was born of self-preservation. "Um, sort of, why?"

"Some eTrain investors are coming up from New York. They want to have a meeting with our content providers. I called Barry, but he's booked. Which isn't necessarily a bad thing. I don't think Barry can do what I need done in this meeting." His eyes were on hers, sharp and direct. "I need you to represent Beckman Markham. Will you do it?"

Ryan blinked and instantly changed her mind. "Sure, I'll do anything you need, you know that. But what could they possibly want from me?"

"Mostly reassurance. We tried to demo the streaming video for them today and it crashed and burned pretty spectacularly." He paced restlessly. "We're scheduled to go live in two weeks. All the marketing is built around that launch date. Now they're feeling nervous about their investment."

"How much of an investment?"

"Seven million."

Ryan gave a low whistle. "I'd be a little nervous too."

"They'll get it back during the IPO next year," Cade said dismissively. "They've got nothing to worry about. We do, though, if they pull out and leave us without funding." He hesitated. "I need your help. I need to send these guys away confident and happy. Between the two of us, we should be able to do it. We probably won't even get much into the business aspect of things. They'll just want to see that you've got a strong content list and a clear idea of where you're going with it."

"Do I need to do a presentation?"

He shook his head. "Like I said, it'll just be dinner. Can you change your plans?"

"Of course," she said, without hesitation. "What time?"

"I'm not sure. I'll leave a message on your voicemail." He brushed a quick kiss over her lips. "I have to get back to the eTrain offices and do some damage control, then get them at the airport. You're in good hands with Pete, though. Meet us at Radius?''

"I'll be there."

RYAN SAT AT THE TABLE IN the quietly elegant restaurant at the heart of the financial district, toying with an earring and watching her dinner companions. Graying and powerfully built, Frank Briamante was the picture of the successful financier. Energy buzzed around him; he seemed a man ill at ease with inaction.

Royce Littleton, his lawyer, was younger, with a sharp-toothed smile that reminded her of a snapping dog. Where Briamante sat with an easy authority, Littleton bridled at his side with nervous energy, like a schnauzer on a leash.

Briamante looked at Ryan. "So you're head of the content side?''

She nodded. "I'm the content manager for Beckman Markham. We're contracted to provide a two-level curriculum for eTrain.''

"You seem awfully young to have held that position for long,'' Littleton said patronizingly. "Have you had any experience building these courses or are you just parroting what's there?''

Ryan gave him a look of faint surprise mingled with distaste. "Age doesn't define capabilities, as I'm sure you're aware. In answer to your question, over the last five years I've developed course concepts and materials for nine of eTrain's courses.''

"What's your background?'' Briamante asked.

"A master's from Brown in English, psychology minor. Teaching certificate. I had plans to teach at a prep school.''

"Just exactly how does an English degree qualify you for—'' Littleton began.

"Put a lid on it, Royce,'' Briamante said easily and smiled at Ryan in genuine pleasure. "So you went to

Brown, hmm? That's my alma mater. There used to be a little greasy spoon right off campus…''

"Lila's Diner?''

His eyes lit up. "Yeah. Is it still there?''

Ryan grinned and nodded. "I think there would be a riot if they tried to close Lila's down.''

"Best greasy breakfasts in town,'' Briamante said nostalgically, and took a pull on his drink. "So why Beckman Markham instead of a straight teaching job?''

She shrugged. "The right opportunity at the right time.''

He seemed to accept this. "Are you sorry you didn't go into the prep school track?''

"No. I think dealing with adults is more challenging,'' she answered, realizing as she said it that it was true. "I like reaching people, and knowing the courses I'm building can change their professional lives.''

"Once you build a course, your role is done, though.'' He stated it as though it were a fact.

"Oh no, I'm in the classroom regularly. It's the only way to see what works and what doesn't. The dynamic is different every time. The students drive the personality of a class.''

"Looks to me like it's driven by your personality,'' he said with a smile.

Cade watched her parry Briamante while charming him, and felt an upwelling of pride, salted by the frustration of having to share her. At being unable to touch her. She excited him in a way that no other woman ever had, not just his body but his mind.

"So you're providing summaries of courses for the eTrain site?'' Briamante asked.

Cade cleared his throat. "Actually, Ryan is the one we're taping for the streaming video applications. She's dynamic in the classroom. You'll get to see some of it in the demo tomorrow.'' Which he devoutly hoped would work.

The waitress approached to take their order, cutting off

the conversation until they'd each selected their dinners. After she left, Briamante turned back to Ryan.

"I had some great times at Brown," Briamante said reminiscently. "Used to play on the soccer team. After the games sometimes, we'd go down and have a clambake on the beach." He gave a surprised chuckle. "You know, I haven't thought about that in years. Come to think of it, I've got a reunion coming up. I think I lost the announcement, though," he muttered.

"Try looking on the Brown Web site," Ryan put in. "I checked it out a couple months back to track down an old classmate." Her eyes brightened. "You know they're giving thought to putting some courses online."

"No kidding."

"Yup." She racked her brains for a moment. "I remember reading a study that said that in five years, more than fifteen percent of all education was going to be delivered through the Internet."

Cade stirred. "Twenty percent."

"Really." She looked at him in surprise and tried to ignore the now-familiar rush of emotion as their eyes locked. "You guys were so smart to get in on the ground floor." Unconsciously, she'd became more animated, talking with her hands and eyes. "I wish we'd thought of it at Beckman Markham, but then we don't have the software infrastructure to carry it off. I get calls all the time from people who want to take our courses but just can't find a day or location that works, or they can't sacrifice a whole day, even though they need the training."

Cade watched her across the table, her green eyes snapping with excitement. He felt a surge of amazement that she was here for him, that she'd be there for him after the meeting was over.

Briamante countered, "There's still no substitute for a classroom."

"From an experiential point of view, no," she conceded.

"But when you're a professional with a job to get done and deadlines to meet, you have to take your educational opportunities where and when you can. I mean, don't get me wrong. Every so often I try to get back to Brown just to soak up the atmosphere, walk around the campus."

"I loved those ivy-covered walls," Briamante said fondly, taking a sip of wine. "Something about going to a school like that makes you take it all more seriously, I think. Royce here went to UCLA. A little too new for my tastes."

Ryan jumped in before the slight could sink home. "UCLA is a good school. One of my brothers went there."

Littleton stirred. "For law?"

"No, medicine. He just finished his residency at Mass Eye and Ear and is going to start a position at Cedars-Sinai in a couple of weeks."

"Can't stay away from L.A., huh?" Littleton asked.

"I think he got a little too wimpy for New England winters when he was out there," she said with a private, fond grin. "He told me he even learned how to surf."

Watching the affection on her face, Cade felt a sudden wash of emotion. He shook his head, forcing his mind back onto business. This was no place for personal feelings, and he sure as hell couldn't risk screwing things up because he hadn't paid attention. Ryan had them eating out of her hand. She'd dealt with the Internet discussion subtly and deftly, lingering over it just long enough to make them relax. With luck, the demonstration the next day would go as flawlessly as it had today, and he could send them on their way reassured.

As for Ryan, he'd deal with his feelings for her later.

RYAN STOOD IN HER candlelit bathroom, tipping bath oil into the water that steamed in the claw-footed tub. She loved this bathroom, with its marble-topped counter and delicate Victorian sconces on walls covered to the picture rail with wainscoting. She set down the glass of wine she'd poured and slid off her silk robe to step into the tub. She knew she'd had too much to drink already that night, but the cappuccino she'd had with dessert had her wired. The fluid heat of the steaming water rose nearly to her shoulders as she sank down to lean against the slanted porcelain and sip her wine in a sybaritic paradise.

The evening had gone well, she thought, though it was hard to say for sure since she didn't know the investors. But she knew people. When they'd arrived, they'd been tense and brusque. By the end of the evening, they'd been relaxed and expansive. Much to her surprise, she'd enjoyed Briamante's company, though Littleton was pompous and self-absorbed to the end. Still, she could make nice with the best of them.

It had been the oddest feeling, though. She and Cade had been working on the same project from the time they'd reconnected at Beckman Markham, but this night, for the first time, they'd seemed like a team. Somehow, she'd felt closer to him than before, perhaps because he'd brought her into a different part of his life, perhaps because he'd admitted he'd needed her help.

Perhaps because she knew that she was in love with him.

And yet, she had no idea what he was thinking. She'd hoped he would come by but hadn't wanted to expect anything, hadn't wanted to ask in case she seemed like she was pressuring him. How could she feel what she felt for him when she didn't know whether their affair would even last another week?

Over the past ten days they'd spent nearly every waking minute together, trading off nights at her home, then at his. She was shocked at how quickly the habit had formed, and how empty her apartment had suddenly seemed when she'd returned after the business dinner. Maybe it didn't feel like a habit to Cade, though. Maybe it felt like being confined. The thought was unbearable, but how did she know she wasn't right? An evening to herself would give her perspective, she thought, feeling the warm water loosen her tense muscles.

She was still soaking an hour later when the doorbell sounded, making her jump. Hastily, she stepped out of the tub and wiped off most of the water before slipping into her robe and trotting down stairs. She couldn't help the surge of excitement she felt at seeing Cade on the front stoop.

Pressing her mouth to his, she breathed in his scent. "I didn't think you were coming tonight. I figured you'd just drop off the VCs and head home."

He'd thought so also, but somehow when he wasn't paying attention he'd made the turn to her house. He stepped inside and pulled her to him for a hard, quick kiss. "Mmm. This is nice," he murmured, running his fingers over the soft skin exposed by the red silk, then raised an eyebrow. "You're wet."

"I was in the bath."

He ran his lips over her jaw. "No wonder you took so long to come to the door. Is there room for two?"

It felt so good, so right to have him there. "Why don't you come up and we'll find out."

On the table in her entryway, a bowl of tulips that he'd sent earlier in the week blazed scarlet. She stopped to admire them, then turned to wrap her arms around his neck. "Thank you again for sending the flowers. They're lovely."

"Don't be so surprised. It's little enough, especially now, considering the stellar job you did charming the VCs."

She blushed and turned the pot to show off the flowers to their best advantage. "I just didn't expect this kind of thing from…our kind of arrangement. It's the first time I've ever gotten flowers from a man."

"You're kidding."

Embarrassment flooded over her. "I told you, I haven't dated much."

"The men you've been around have been idiots," he muttered, then swept her up in his arms.

"What are you doing?" she squeaked.

"Just getting you to the bathroom the best way I know how," he answered, heading down the hall.

In the bathroom, he set her down and hastily stripped off his clothes. Then he kissed his way along her throat and down her quivering stomach, ending on his knees in front of her. For a moment, he clasped her to him, resting his face against her. A wave of tenderness came over him. She'd known so little affection from men, then they'd started this blatantly physical affair. He hadn't shown her romance and sweetness, just sex and fire. Yet she'd been there for him unhesitatingly that evening, pitching in to help him succeed. She deserved more than he had been giving her, and tonight he'd see that she got it.

He kissed her lightly, softly, stepping into the tub and drawing her in after him.

The silky, smooth water enveloped both of their bodies. Ryan leaned back against his chest and sighed with pleasure at the slippery stroke of his hands. She could feel the emotion swirling inside her, the words bubbling on her lips. Because she knew it was the wrong time to say what she felt, she tried to change the conversation. "So are you happy with the way the evening went?"

He kissed her hair. "Shh. Let's talk about it later. For now, let's just be with each other." Slowly, gently, his hands moved over her body, teasing the nerve endings awake in the warm oil-infused water with a soft caress. "When I walked into that restaurant tonight and saw you, I couldn't believe how beautiful you were. I couldn't believe you were waiting there for me." His lips were warm on her shoulder. "I didn't want to share you."

In a giddy rush of pleasure, Ryan turned her head so that she could kiss him, and tried to turn her body.

"Uh-uh," he said softly, kissing her on the eyelids. "We're always in a hurry, going rough and tumble. This time we take our time." Slowly, hypnotically, his hands stroked her body. "Relax and let me take you," he whispered, sliding his fingers down her flat belly, across the tender insides of her thighs.

Whether it was the wine she'd had or his touch, the urgency melted away in a haze of sensation. His hands rose up over the rounded fullness of her breasts, his lips were warm on her cheek, her neck, her shoulders. Instead of the usual rocket of sensation, though, it was like being carried on a warm, swelling tide of feeling.

Ryan gasped when his slick fingers moved through the folds between her legs. Instead of stroking her to madness in the way she'd come to know, his fingers slipped inside her warmth. Mouth fused to hers, he stroked her smooth inner center, finding an exquisitely sensitive hidden place that she'd never known existed. An immense heat grew within her, as much a part of the feeling of his arms around her as of his fingers within her, like emotion made physical. There was no him, no her, just a golden cloud of feeling made up of the two of them.

"Cade," she whispered, startled.

"I know, sweetheart," he said with a soft groan, "oh, I know."

Later, on her bed, instead of making love to her, he began to massage her body, lingering over each limb, each muscle, his hands kneading her into mindless pleasure. His touch felt like more than mere skin to skin, it felt like his feelings for her made tactile, and she absorbed it all. As an hour slid by with just the devotion of his hands to her body, bringing her pleasure without expectation of return, the feelings that had whirled in her all day threatened to overwhelm her. The intimacy of the act, the tenderness, brought the words almost to her lips. There was so much she wanted to tell him. So much she couldn't say.

Even when his touch changed from massage to caress, there was no fierceness to it, just a sweet tenderness that carried her gently along to a soft wonder of arousal. When he slipped inside her, it was to move slowly, softly, carrying her with him rather than driving her along. When she came, the sudden wash of feeling and emotion left her overwhelmed.

He passed over the brink at the same time, the shudders of his body mirrored in hers, her soft sighs finding their answer in his groans until neither knew where one left off and the other began.

Lost in bliss, she felt him gather her against him to sleep. "Sweet dreams," he murmured, drifting down into sleep.

She floated in languorous pleasure, half asleep herself. "I love you, Cade," she whispered dreamily, the words flowing out before she knew she was saying them. Then anxiety swallowed her whole. "Cade?" she whispered, catching her breath.

He didn't react. A long second crawled by and his breathing deepened.

Muscle by muscle, Ryan relaxed. She brushed her lips over his, then lay back against the pillow. "Sweet dreams," she whispered, breathing a silent sigh of relief and closing her eyes.

And beside her, Cade opened his eyes to stare at the ceiling.

16

WHEN THE FIRST GLOW OF morning hit, he awoke from a restless doze, cradling Ryan's sleeping warmth against him. Slowly, gradually, consciousness kicked in and he worked his way resolutely past a haze of well being to face reality.

She had said she loved him.

It couldn't possibly be true, part of him protested. They'd been involved for less than three weeks. She was just getting carried away by the physical side.

But the rest of him knew he was oversimplifying. He knew his feelings for her were deeper than a mere physical affair would warrant. Love, though? Love was off the radar screen. No matter how much he might care for her, and undeniably he did, he couldn't go there. Even if he thought he might love her, he couldn't trust his feelings to be real.

He thought of his father's string of wives, each one the one true love—at least for a month or so. And each one a failure when the infatuation wore off. He thought of his feelings for Alyssa. He'd thought it was love, truly believed it, but in the end, when the physical obsession had faded, there had been nothing left but emptiness and silence.

He wouldn't go through that again. He wouldn't put Ryan through it. Sure, things felt great now, but that was because the physical part was still hot. Take away the sex, and the rest of the relationship withered.

Liar, a voice in his head whispered as he remembered his feelings from the night before. Oh, but he'd been sure it was deeper with Alyssa, too.

And he'd been wrong.

He wouldn't hurt Ryan like that. Cade rolled his head against the pillow. He should have just stayed on his own, stayed away from the risk of hurting someone he cared about. Now, the only thing left to him was to salvage the situation. He had to extricate himself from the relationship before her feelings could go any deeper, before he damaged her any more than he could avoid. She thought she loved him, but she couldn't really, not this soon. It might cut her some when he ended it, but she'd get over it and be glad of it afterward.

Ryan shifted drowsily and turned against him before falling back into slumber. He pressed a kiss to her forehead and she made a murmurous sound. The thought of giving up her sleepy warmth in the mornings, her soothing companionship in the evenings made his chest constrict. It was best all the way around, though. They'd both be better off for it.

And maybe in time, if he tried hard enough, he could make himself believe it.

Cade glanced at the bedside clock and switched off the alarm before it could chirp. It took him a moment to find his clothes, tossed in a pile on the floor of the bathroom. He leaned over ruefully and picked his wrinkled shirt off the floor. It wasn't like anyone was going to care what he looked like at 6 a.m. anyway, he thought, buttoning his equally wrinkled trousers. He'd have plenty of time to shower and change before going over to pick up Briamante and Littleton.

All he really wanted to do was crawl back into bed and wrap himself around Ryan's warmth, but that was the one thing he couldn't do. The sooner he pulled away the better. For now, he'd leave her a note, then call her over the weekend. With luck, he could break things off amicably. After all, they'd agreed to go until one of them burned out their desire.

Too bad he hadn't even come close.

His clothes were on and he'd sat down to put on his shoes when the door opened and Ryan came in, doe-eyed and sleepy, wrapped in thin red silk. "You're dressed," she said, her throaty morning voice making him tighten involuntarily with desire.

"I've got to get home and clean up before I go get Briamante and his pit bull for the meetings." He kept his voice brisk and started out of the bathroom.

"Cade, wait."

He stopped and turned, steeling himself not to drown in her eyes. "Yep?"

"Last night was wonderful," she said, stepping close for a kiss. "I didn't know it could be like that."

The warmth of her lips worked a magic on him, made him want to forget everything but Ryan, soft and sleepy against him. Why couldn't it last, a voice inside his head asked as he felt the firm spring of her body against him. Who said it had to end?

Who was he *kidding?* Cade broke the kiss and shook his head. Enough. It had to be over. "I'd like nothing better than to climb right back in bed with you, but I've got to go."

Ryan trailed him down the stairs to the front door. "Before I forget, I'm going over to my parents' tonight for dinner." She pushed her hair back out of her eyes. "You're invited too, in case you feel like coming," she said, almost as an afterthought.

He was tempted for a moment, but he knew it would only pull him deeper into the morass, send a message that he was more involved than he really was. Like that was possible, the voice in his head taunted him, but he ignored it. He was doing the best thing he knew how. "I'm sorry, I can't make it. I've got to baby-sit Frank until he's done here."

"Call me later?" she asked.

"I'll try. I'll be playing catch up all weekend, though, so it's going to be crazy."

"That's okay."

The faint surprise in her eyes before she masked it sent regret knifing through him. They'd been together practically 24/7 for the past three weeks. It was natural that he would need time to himself sometime. So why did it feel so wrong?

Cade turned at the bottom of the stairs, unable to resist giving her a real kiss before he headed out the door. He held her for just a moment, eyes closed while he absorbed the feeling. Then he sighed and pulled out of her embrace to drop a soft kiss on her forehead. "Be good."

Ryan watched him go down the stairs, a thread of disquiet stringing through her. Resolutely she pushed it away and turned to climb the stairs, headed for the shower and the start of her day.

THE SCENT OF ROASTING lamb perfumed the air as Ryan walked through the door and into her parents' kitchen.

"Hi Mom," she said, hugging her mother from behind as she mashed potatoes.

"Watch it, you'll wind up getting potatoes everywhere." Sonia put down the masher, wiping her hands on a dish towel. "Hi sweetie. What's new?"

"Oh, life's gotten interesting," Ryan said breezily, crossing to the table to drop a peck on her father's cheek as he read the sports page.

He glanced up from the box scores. "You started that murder mystery yet?"

"Any day, Dad, any day. Red Sox knock the Yankees out of first place yet?"

He made a face. "Any day, Miss Smartie, any day." Ryan grinned as she turned back to the kitchen.

"So how has life gotten interesting?" Sonia asked, pouring juices from the roaster pan into a skillet.

Ryan pulled plates out of the cupboard and began setting the table. "Well," she said nonchalantly, "I've got a beau."

"Really!" Sonia turned in surprise and dropped her wooden spoon.

"I hope it's not that much of a shock," Ryan said lightly, crossing over to pick up the spoon and placing it into the sink.

"Absolutely not, sweetheart, it's just exciting." Sonia hugged her daughter. "I'm so happy for you." She stepped back and took a closer look. "So tell me about him."

Ryan thought of Cade and smiled. "He's the head of a company Beckman Markham's doing some work for. He's wonderful—smart, funny, good-looking, romantic."

Her father put down the paper and tried to look patriarchal. "So should I be asking him his intentions?"

"We've only been seeing each other for three weeks, Dad. I think it's a little early to start the interrogation."

"Okay." Her father started to raise the paper again, then put it back down. "Give it another month and I'll be ready."

Sonia stirred the bubbling gravy in the pan. "Now Phil, no sense in trying to grill her beau before they've even gotten started. Let the poor girl enjoy having a date or two before you start threatening him."

"I'm just trying to be helpful," he protested mildly.

Sonia turned off the gravy and began scooping potatoes into a serving dish. "So do you like this fellow?"

"Oh, well," Ryan started to be casual, but the words wouldn't come. She swallowed. "I think I'm in love with him."

Sonia's hands stilled their busy movements. "Well." She studied her daughter. "That's serious. Have you told him?"

"Yes."

"What did he say?"

Ryan's eyes flicked up to the ceiling. "Um, he wasn't exactly awake at the time."

The corners of Sonia's mouth quirked. "I suppose that's one way to start."

"I didn't mean to tell him. It just sort of came out as I was falling asleep."

"Don't feel ready to try it when he's conscious, yet?"

Ryan pulled on oven mitts and picked a pan of roast asparagus out of the oven. "Well, I don't know how he'll react. It wasn't what we talked about when we got into this. It started out more…casual." Although if she were honest with herself, it had ceased to be casual within the first five minutes. "I can't tell how he feels. Sometimes he's so wonderful it just seems like he's got to feel the same way I do. Other times, I don't know."

Ryan used tongs to lay the asparagus spears alongside the roast on its serving platter and sighed. "I don't understand this boy-girl stuff. Is there some minimum time before you're allowed to say what you really feel? Three weeks seems so soon, and yet I'm sure, Mom." She looked at Sonia levelly. "I'm really sure."

Sonia blew out a breath weakly. "I think I always knew when it happened for you it would be something out of the ordinary. And sometimes three weeks can be enough." She looked across the kitchen to where her husband sat, her eyes softening. "Sometimes you just know."

Ryan sighed. "I didn't hear from him all day. I know he was in meetings, though. I just miss him." She gave a sheepish smile.

"Honey, if you really care for him, you need to tell him.

Maybe not right away, but soon. You can't hide yourself away from him.''

"But what if he doesn't feel the same way? It scares the hell out of me to think about saying something.''

Sonia smiled. "Sometimes you've got to screw up your courage and put yourself out there. I did it with your father.''

"With Dad? Wait a minute, I thought he swept you off your feet.''

"I did,'' her father spoke up from the table. "Flowers, diamond ring, the works.''

Sonia slanted him a look. "Yes indeed, but who said I love you first?''

"Well, I didn't want to hog all the glory,'' he mumbled, folding up his paper.

"Hog all the glory indeed. You were shaking in your boots, just like I was when I told you how I felt.''

He got up from the table and walked over to Sonia. "And I'll never forget the way you looked,'' he said, raising her chin to kiss her softly. "You were an absolute gift. You've been one the whole of my life.''

Misty eyed, Ryan watched them. Their love for each other was an immutable fact in her world. The idea of having that kind of connection herself had always seemed a wonderful impossibility. Now, she wondered if it was perhaps within reach.

The timer went off on the oven and her mother swatted her father on the backside. "Go on, you, or I'll burn dinner.'' She busied herself stirring gravy. "By the way, Ryan, are you aware that your brother leaves for L.A. in less than three weeks? We're having a send-off party for him next weekend.''

"It's not enough that he half broke me with medical school tuition,'' her father moaned, carrying bowls to the table. "Now we're spending a bundle on a fancy party to finish the job."

"Oh hush, you. Your son the doctor finishes his residency and you can't even see your way clear to having a party for him?" Sonia gave a last glance at the table to see that everything was in its place, then sat.

"I suppose he's earned it," Phil allowed, forking up a slice of meat.

"Your Aunt Helen and Uncle Stanley are coming out from Stockbridge," Sonia said, passing the potatoes to Ryan. "Maybe you can bring your gentleman friend."

Ryan considered the idea with a little thrill of nerves. "I don't know, Ma. That's a lot to throw at someone all at once."

"It's a party, it'll be a low-key way for him to meet everyone."

"All right," Ryan said dubiously. "Maybe I'll ask him."

SHE COULDN'T REMEMBER when time had weighed so heavily in her hands. Friday night, she'd hurried back to her apartment to find the answering machine shining steady red, indicating no messages. She'd stayed up a couple of hours reading, hoping, really, that he'd come by or call.

If Friday night had been difficult, Saturday had been excruciating. She'd sat at her computer, trying to force herself to work on the new book while the hours dragged. But the phone and doorbell remained stubbornly silent. There was something unbearably gripping about the silence; she was unable to stop watching and waiting. In a fit of defiance, she went out to do some errands, thinking wryly that of course the minute she walked out the door he'd call. Coming home, she was certain of it, hurrying up the stairs and bursting through her front door.

Only to find the answering machine light solid red.

She didn't want to be clingy, but she'd expected to hear

from Cade at some point. Just a quick hello between tasks.
Just a reminder that he was thinking about her. Played back
in the current context, his behavior Friday morning began
to seem more disconcerting. What if he'd heard her when
she'd told him she loved him? What if he were alarmed,
thrown off by the sudden change in their relationship? She
hadn't intended to say it, but maybe it had scared him off.

Of course, she was just torturing herself with "what if."
The fact was, he'd been dead asleep when the words had
slipped out.

Hadn't he?

Now, Sunday morning, she ran along the Charles, trying
to burn off the nervous tension coiled up in her muscles.
Maybe he just felt that they'd been spending too much time
together. Maybe he had other commitments. Maybe, whispered a voice in her head, he was starting to get burned out.

She headed east on the Cambridge side, trying to ignore
the fact that she'd drawn abreast of Cade's building. She
tried to run past, but her steps slowed and finally stopped.
She gave a quick glance up to what she thought was his
deck, but she couldn't tell if anyone was on it or not. She
stopped and sank down on a bench, staring at the river,
working up her courage.

Her words to her mother played through her head. *Is there
some minimum time before you're allowed to say what you
really feel?* Who said it was too early? Hell, if you added
up the time they'd spent together in the past three weeks, it
probably added up to a couple of months worth of dates for
a normal couple. She knew what she felt, dammit. The more
she thought of it, the more certain she became about her
feelings.

But the love thing was beside the point. Reality said they
were involved. She ought to at least be able to stop by and
say hello without it being a federal case. It was high-

schoolish to be afraid not to. This was the twenty-first century. A woman had a right to drop in on a man.

Quickly, decisively, she rose and hurried across the street before she could change her mind. It was nearly eleven. Even on weekends he was an early riser...certain parts of him in particular, she remembered with a quick tingle of desire. At any rate, whether he'd slept in or not, he'd almost certainly be up by now. She could pop in, then go on her way. Nothing heavy, just a quick visit. Nerves roiled in her stomach as she rode up in the elevator. Then she was standing in front of his front door, ringing the bell.

Cade sat on his deck, staring sightlessly at the Charles. A cool breeze blew off the water, riffling the newspaper that lay on his lap, ignored. Over and over again since Friday morning he'd reached for the phone to call Ryan and stopped himself, if only to demonstrate that he could. Over and over her words echoed in his head, stirring a mix of pleasure and anxiety. However much he might enjoy the thought that she had feelings for him, he couldn't let it continue when he knew she'd wind up hurt.

The bell rang. He frowned, not sure whom or what to expect. He opened the door to find her waiting there.

At first, he felt nothing but a rush of pleasure. The hours since he'd seen her added up to a wasteland of time. He reached for her before he thought to stop himself, closing his eyes to absorb the feel of her in his arms.

Then he made himself let her go.

"Hi," Ryan said brightly, trying not to be disappointed that after two days apart he hadn't even kissed her. Trying not to be alarmed that he'd let her go and backed away. "I was out for a run and wound up in the neighborhood. I thought I'd stop by and say hi."

"Sure, come on in." He stepped back to let her inside. "I was just out on the deck, reading the paper." He led her out onto another deck. The blue waters of the Charles glinted beyond the barrier. The thick bundle of the Sunday paper fluttered on a café table. "Have a seat. You want some orange juice or something?"

"Actually, some water would be great." Water to keep her throat from going completely dry, she thought. She wanted so much to touch him, yet she didn't want to be the one to bridge the gap. She waited until he came back out on the deck carrying her drink. "How've you been?"

"Okay." He dropped into the chair next to her. "Working, mostly, trying to tie up some loose ends that came up during the VC meeting." The breeze caught at Ryan's hair, tossing loose strands around her face and he watched, fascinated.

"It went well, though?"

He nodded. "Yes, it did. They were pretty comfortable when they left, so as long as we keep to our timeline, we're fine." Out of habit, he reached out for her hand. Just in time, he realized what he was about to do and detoured for his orange juice instead. "Thank you again for everything you did. You made a difference."

As he'd made a difference to her, she thought, though perhaps he'd never know. For the first time since they'd become intimate, she felt awkward around him. The ready ease was gone, and stiltedness had taken its place. She took a breath and tried to sound casual. "So, are you having an exciting weekend?"

He moved his shoulders. "As exciting as it gets. I think I left the wild times behind a few years back."

It was an opening and she took it. "Maybe I can help there. My brother Brendan is leaving to work in L.A. in a couple of weeks to start a surgical position at Cedars Sinai. My parents are having a party for him next weekend." She took a sip of her water. "I was wondering if you might want to come."

"To the party, you mean?"

She nodded. "Sure. You can meet my family."

Cade looked away, across to the blue ribbon of the Charles. "I'm not sure that's such a good idea."

Her heart skipped a beat. Ryan stared at him. "Why do you say that?"

"I just don't want people getting the wrong idea." An errant breeze caught at a section of the paper and he concentrated on catching it and folding it back up.

"What do you mean 'the wrong idea'?" she asked carefully.

For the first time, he met her eyes. "We need to be clear about what's going on here."

It was like having ice thrown over her—barrels of it, until she was buried up to her neck, until every part of her was frozen. "And what is going on here?" She forced her voice to stay calm.

"What we agreed on. A physical affair, until one or both of us gets burned out."

"And are you? Burned out, I mean?" She wasn't. She was cold, so cold she didn't think she'd ever be warm again.

He couldn't bear to see the hurt in her eyes. "That's not the point. I think you're getting in too deep."

"What makes you think that?" Ryan wasn't sure she wanted the question answered but she asked it anyway.

He took a long breath and looked at her. "What you said the other night as I was falling asleep."

There was a roaring in her ears. Beats of time went by before she could do anything but stare. "You heard? I thought you were asleep."

"I was…almost. I couldn't be sure whether it was real or a dream."

Unable to keep still, she rose and paced to the rail that ran around the deck. "So you figured you'd just keep quiet and do a disappearing act without saying anything?" She whirled to face him.

"I just thought we needed some distance." He didn't quite look at her. "I thought it was best for both of us. I didn't want to hurt you."

"Really? You seem to be doing an effortless job of it right now," she countered, her voice brittle.

"We agreed not to get involved. To keep it light for as long as it makes sense."

Simmering emotion inside her turned into anger. "News bulletin—we are involved. We've spent the last three weeks together almost nonstop. You can break that off now if you want to, but don't try to pretend it didn't happen."

Just for a moment, he gave into his feelings. "I'm not. It was like nothing that's ever happened to me before."

Was, she thought miserably. As in past tense. "So answer my question. Are you burned out?"

"No, I'm not," he said impatiently. "But it doesn't matter. Like I said, you're getting in too deep and I'm not going to let you go any further."

"You're not going to let me?" Her voice rose. Now it was outrage that fueled her. "How dare you try to decide what's best for me. My feelings are my business."

"No, they're my business too. I don't want to hurt you, and that's just what's going to happen if we don't stop."

"Why? Are you afraid you'll feel guilty? Or are you afraid if this doesn't work out you'll feel like a failure, like your dad?" The barb sank home, she saw, as his eyes focused on hers.

"Don't try to psychoanalyze me," he warned.

"I'm just calling it as I see it."

"I'm not going to hurt you," he said stubbornly.

"Caring is a risk, Cade. If I care about you—and I do, whether you want me to or not—then I'm taking a chance that I'll get hurt. I know that, but it's worth it to me to see where this goes."

"It's not worth it to me."

Anger surged through her. "Why is it that I'm not allowed to care about you?" She burst out at him, her eyes blazing. "If I get hurt, that's my problem. Wanting out, that's one thing, but running away because you think you're doing me some kind of favor, that's a pathetic excuse for bailing." He believed he was saving her from hurt by speaking up now, she thought. He didn't realize that he'd already sliced her to ribbons. "Maybe your parents' marriage made you think that relationships can't last, but you're wrong. You can't base your life on a single event."

"A single event?" Cade snorted in derision. "Hardly. My mother was just the start of it for my father. He's been married and divorced more times than I can count on one hand. Every time, he's sure he's found Ms. Forever. Six months later, it's all over but the divorce. That's what happens when you confuse infatuation and love."

"That's him, that's not you."

"Oh sure," he said bitterly. "I was different. I knew it when I got married. I knew I'd make it last. And then six months after the ceremony I was calling a divorce lawyer." He rolled his head back and stared at the pitiless blue of the sky, then straightened back up to look at Ryan. "My marriage is what happens when you confuse infatuation and love. What we're both feeling right now is infatuation, and I can tell you from personal experience, it doesn't last."

Ryan's eyes drilled into him. "How do you know what I'm feeling? How do you know what's going through me when I look at you?"

"I know how it feels when we're making love. You know yourself that we can't keep our hands off one another. That's infatuation."

Ryan let the anger billow up, let it mask the hurt. "You want to know the first minute I truly fell for you? It wasn't when we were having sex. It was watching you play with Patrick's kids, showing them a beetle. Most guys wouldn't have taken the time. This isn't just about sex, it's about you. Don't you dare trivialize it.''

Her eyes were blazing, her cheeks stained with angry color. She was magnificent. And God, he was pathetic, Cade thought, stuck on her even in the midst of breaking things off. ''Entertaining a couple of kids for five minutes isn't anything. I do it to get them off of Patrick's back.''

''You're lying to yourself,'' she cried out vehemently. ''I was there. I saw you. I saw your face when you watched them walk away. I know that you want what they've got.'' She knew she was going too far, but she was powerless to stop. ''I heard it in your voice when you told me about growing up. You can tell yourself some weak story about your dysfunctional parents all you want. It isn't just about sex and flash for you, what you really want is family. And yet you won't let me in.'' She blinked, her eyes swimming. Now the blind ache was rushing in, too fast for her to stop it.

''I don't want to hurt you.''

''That is such a crock,'' she said, her voice breaking. ''It's you that you're afraid of hurting. You're so afraid that you'll be just like your dad, you're so afraid that you're going to care and be left alone that you won't even look to see what I'm holding out to you. I'm not asking for promises, Cade. I'm not asking for forever. All I'm saying is let's try.''

But forever was what he wanted to give her, even though he knew it would blow up in his face. ''I can't do that,'' he said passionately. ''I won't.''

The silence settled around them, brittle and deafening.

''I guess that's it, then,'' Ryan said, almost too softly to hear. ''You've got what you wanted.'' She turned blindly to go, fumbling to slide open the glass door.

''Ryan, wait.'' He caught up with her in the kitchen.

She turned back to him. "What for? You've already said everything that needed to be said. The sooner we're away from each other, the better." The tears didn't start falling until she walked out the door.

17

RYAN SAT IN HER OFFICE, staring out at the gray drizzle of the morning, which mirrored the bleakness she felt inside. Two days had passed since her debacle with Cade, and nothing had gotten any easier. And it wasn't likely to any time soon, she thought. The void stretched in front of her, a desert of days to get through until the memory began to fade. Days of looking around her office and seeing him there. Days of standing in front of classes, thinking of Cade watching her from the back row. Night upon night of missing him, missing a part of her.

Her phone rang and Helene's name flashed on the caller ID screen. Ryan sighed and reached for the receiver.

"Hello."

"Hey kid." Helene's gravel voice jumped out of the receiver. "How ya doing?"

"Fine," Ryan said colorlessly.

"You don't sound fine. You sound a little tapped out."

"I didn't sleep very well last night." Understatement of the year. She'd tossed and turned until dawn lit the room.

"That guy of yours giving you a workout?"

Ryan closed her eyes. "No. Look, Helene, I'm really busy today. What did you need?"

"Well," Helene said, stretching out the word, "I thought I ought to call you first thing today. I figured you might want a little extra time to write your resignation letter."

"My resignation letter?" Ryan repeated, and then comprehension hit. "You heard from Elaine?"

"She loved it." Helene's voice was triumphant. "She said it's the best stuff you've ever done. The four-book deal is closed. You're a full-time writer, kid."

She should have been thrilled. All she could manage was a sort of dull pleasure. "That's good news."

"Good news? That's all you have to say? I expected you to be shrieking with joy."

Two months ago, she would have. Two months ago, she would have been ecstatic.

Two months ago, she hadn't known Cade Douglas existed.

"What's up, kid?" Helene's voice was puzzled. "I thought you'd be bouncing off the walls. You did it. You can quit now. Your life is your own."

"That's great, Helene." Ryan forced excitement into her voice. "Seriously. It's what I've been waiting for. I couldn't be more pleased."

"You don't sound so pleased. What's going on?" Helene's voice turned suspicious. "This sounds like man trouble. Something going on with Cade?"

"Nothing's going on with Cade."

"I guess that's the problem."

"Helene, stop it. I…" To her horror, she felt sudden tears well up.

"Ryan? Are you okay?" Helene's voice was sharp with concern.

She squeezed her eyes shut and took deep breaths, willing herself to stay in control.

"Ryan?" Helene's voice became more urgent. "Say something. What's going on?"

Ryan blew a breath out. "I'm okay," she managed, striving for calm. "Sorry to worry you. Cade and I aren't seeing each other anymore."

"When did that happen?"

"Sunday."

"You or him?"

"Both of us." She looked bleakly out the window. "If it's not working for him, it can't work for me either, can it?"

"In other words, him." Helene said grimly. "I warned him about hurting you. Just wait until I get ahold of him, I'll make him so sorry—"

"Helene, don't you dare say anything to him." Ryan's voice was energized for the first time in days. "I appreciate the thought, but I'm okay with it, really."

"Yeah, you sound real okay."

"I'm fine. Thanks for the news about the contract. That's great. I've got to go write my resignation letter."

"Not so fast," Helene said. "We've got some other arrangements to discuss. It's time to think about taking things to the next level. There's a publicist here in Manhattan that I've done some work with before. He handles all the marketing, press releases, promotions, everything."

"Why on earth do I need that? I'm not exactly Nora Roberts."

"And you never will be until you start doing some legwork. Now that you're going on multicontract level, we've got to build your name. Perry's the guy to do it." Ryan could hear Helene draw on a cigarette. "He's supposed to be up your way soon. I'll set up a meeting with him and let you know."

"Helene…"

"You need this, kid. This is what happens when the breaks start going your way."

The breaks couldn't be further from going her way, Ryan thought, but she knew Helene well enough to know when it was time to give in. "All right, fine," she sighed. "Let me know when I'm supposed to meet with him and I'll do it."

"Great," Helene said in satisfaction.

"I've really got to go, though. I want to get my notice

in to Barry so I can get this all over with.''

"Enjoy it, kid. You've earned it.''

SHE STOOD IN THE BREAK room the next morning, watching
the coffeemaker brew her a much-needed wake-up. Her discussion with Barry hadn't gone well. He'd been by turns
injured, betrayed, wheedling and bullying. She didn't know
if she was more shocked or affronted at the salary increase
he'd offered in an attempt to keep her; finding out he was
willing to pay her half again as much as her current salary
only told her how much she'd been underpaid.

"Barry, I'll act as a consultant a couple of days a week
until the eTrain project is closed, but that's it,'' she'd said.
He'd mowed over her words obstinately, ignoring the fact
that she'd spoken, very nearly ignoring the fact that she'd
quit. He seemed to think if he acted as though he were still
her boss, he could order her not to leave.

Ryan sighed as she poured herself a cup of coffee, then
headed down the hall to her office. The phone rang as she
dropped into her chair and the caller ID screen lit. Ryan
read the name and caught her breath for an instant, listening
to the ring three times before she made herself pick up the
receiver. "Ryan Donnelly.'' It took work, but she kept her
voice toneless.

"Barry tells me you're leaving.''

There was no hello, no preamble. He took it for granted
that she'd know his voice.

"I gave notice yesterday.'' Why was it that he could
break her heart and still his voice could make her pulse
race? Where was the justice in that?

"I take it your contract came through?''

"Yes. I've told Barry that I'd consult on an as-needed
basis until the eTrain project is done.'' Her voice stayed
toneless. "I should be able to finish taping the basic courses
before I leave, though.''

Cade stared at the phone. The past three days had been
the longest he could remember. He was sure he was doing

the right thing, but he'd never expected it to feel so hollow. And how long was it going to be before he stopped missing her in his life, before he could think of her without a surge of loss? He forced his mind back to the conversation, all too aware that he'd called without really needing to. He'd called just because he couldn't pass up a chance to hear her voice. Pathetic, he thought in irritation, and his words came out clipped. "Do you have a schedule mapped out for the courses that need to be taped? Barry tells me you're only giving two weeks' notice."

"I thought that was sufficient." Pride made her keep her voice calm and impersonal even as loss tore at her. "I can e-mail you the dates for the classes so you can set up the tapings." She paused for just a beat. "I'd take it as a personal favor if you would leave the taping to Pete and me. We have the drill down, now. You don't need to be there."

He bit back a protest. What was wrong with him? She was right, there was no need for him to waste his time. So why did it bother him? And why the hell did he miss her so much? Not her warm body next to his at night, though he missed that too. More the soothing companionship of the evenings, her flashing smile, her throaty laugh. When he'd made the decision to get out of the relationship, he hadn't realized how much doing without her would hit him.

That didn't make his decision wrong, but neither did it make it easy.

"No, I guess you're right." It took work to keep his voice expressionless. "You guys will do fine on your own."

"Good," she said, though the thought gave her no satisfaction.

"How was the rest of your weekend?" He asked in an attempt to make conversation.

"What do you think?" she asked bleakly. Just for a moment the calm slipped to the ocean of anguish below. "Is this conversation done, Cade? Because I have things to do and not a lot of time. Let me know if there's anything critical you need.''

''Okay. And Ryan?''

''Yes?'' Her pulse jumped unsteadily, she couldn't help it.

He hesitated for a moment, just needing to have her on the line a bit longer. ''Good luck.''

The receiver clicked in his ear as she hung up. He wanted to catch her and bring her back, even as he recognized the foolishness of the emotion. Okay, so the new situation took some getting used to. It was still the right thing. It was still the best thing.

But if he was honest with himself, the best thing still felt like hell.

Cade hung up the phone as Patrick came into his office and flopped down into a chair. ''What's up, buddy? You look like someone stole your favorite GI Joe.''

Cade shot him a scathing glance and turned back to his computer.

Patrick gave him a sharp look in return. ''Hey, you really do look like something's going on. What's up?''

He really didn't want to have this conversation, Cade thought. He really didn't want to. ''I just talked with Barry Markham. Their content manager gave notice today.''

''Their content manager?'' Patrick fell silent as the meaning sank home. ''You mean Ryan Donnelly,'' he said flatly. ''As in the woman you're involved with.''

''Was.''

''What?''

''Was involved with.''

''Gee, isn't that a coincidence,'' Patrick said, sarcasm rich in his voice. ''You break things off with her and she gives notice. Any chance it had something to do with you?''

Cade looked at him mutinously.

''Forget it. You don't have to answer that. It's obvious. Any chance you want to tell me why?''

"Things were getting too serious. It was the best thing."

"Getting too..." Patrick stared at him. "Sure. You have an affair with a team member, you break things off, she quits. Sounds like the best thing to me."

"I really don't want to get into this."

Patrick swore, then rose swiftly to shut the office door. "I can't believe you're so goddamned blind."

"Patrick, I told you our personal involvement wouldn't affect the project and it won't." Cade kept his voice calm. "We've got nearly all of her courses on tape, and the rest are scheduled for taping before she leaves. We've got detailed course notes on everything. It's not going to affect us."

"I don't give a damn about the courses," Patrick burst out. "I'm talking about you."

"Me?" Cade looked at him blankly. "What does that have to do with it?"

"It's got everything to do with it! She was a keeper and you never even saw it." Patrick slapped at the corner of the visitor's chair, sending it spinning while he stalked to the windows. "You broke things off because you were getting too close? That's a laugh. You broke things off because you didn't have the balls to stick with it."

Cade's voice rose. "It's none of your goddamn business." Fury surged through him at being lambasted by the usually sedate Patrick. He was not in the mood to take it, not even close.

Patrick rounded on him. "Of course it's my business."

"Oh yeah? Why's that? Because you're freaked about the launch and you feel like yelling at someone?"

"Because I'm your friend, asshole!"

Cade opened his mouth to speak and shut it. All the vitriolic words he'd planned to say deserted him.

Patrick shook his head. "You were happy with her, happy deep down in a way you never were with Alyssa. If you'd said you were fighting or if it was a *Fatal Attraction* kind of thing that would be one thing. But breaking up because it was too good? Because it was getting too close? I never realized you were such a gutless wonder.''

"My father—"

"Just because your father can't keep a relationship going doesn't mean you can't. Give yourself a little credit.''

Cade fought off the guilt, the reproach. "Look, I talked with her about it this weekend and we agreed that it was for the best.''

"And she just happens to quit today?"

"She was planning to quit right along. The timing was just a coincidence.''

Patrick snorted in disgust. "Yeah, right.''

"Yes, right,'' Cade repeated, refusing to back down. "She's been a published writer for years but no one's known about it. She was waiting on a big contract that would let her write full-time. It must have just come through.''

The look Patrick gave him was sly and knowing. "For not wanting to be involved, you sure sound proud of her.''

The observation cut deep. "Give me a break, will you?"

"No, I won't.'' His friend's voice vibrated with frustration. "Why are you so afraid to go after this?"

"Come on, Patrick. You know my history. You know my family's history. I'm not made for this happily-ever-after stuff.'' He tried to keep regret out of his voice.

"You are so wrong,'' Patrick said vehemently. "You're made for it more than anyone I know.''

"Patrick, enough already, okay?" Cade raised his hands up in front of him. "We've got a launch in exactly a week and a half. We don't have time to waste on my personal life right now.''

Unwilling to let it die, Patrick stared at him. "Just ask yourself what you're really doing here. Will you at least do that?"

Cade took a deep breath and let it out slowly. "Yes, okay? Now let's get to work."

"ALL RIGHT, LET'S GO through the final checklist." A week later, Patrick sat at the head of the conference table, his disheveled hair and blue jaw attesting to the all-nighter he'd pulled. The all-nighter all of them had pulled, coming into the launch day.

Cade put a hand to his face, rubbing eyes that felt gritty from lack of sleep. The months of work were coming to fruition now. In minutes, they would be going live.

Patrick glanced at the list in his hand. "Okay, everybody's given the go-ahead." He took a deep breath and locked eyes with Cade. "Ravi, run the build."

There was a strained silence in the room as the servers recompiled the Web site, making what was previously the password-protected beta test version available to the outside world. Minutes ticked by. None of them could help by being in the room watching the computer screen, but none of them could bear to leave.

"It's done," Ravi announced, looking to Patrick for orders.

"Lise, download the first module."

The tomboyish blonde expertly tapped in a URL and made a few clicks on the screen. The cursor in the download bar flowed from side to side as the computer pulled in the data. Finally, it finished, and the screen sat, with the white start button shining in the center.

Patrick cleared his throat. "Okay, everybody, here's where the rubber meets the road. Lise, you want to do the honors?"

She clicked the button, and Ryan appeared on the screen in her magenta suit, looking energetic, approachable and absolutely lovely. Cade's heart twisted, even as a cheer went up around the room, drowning out the sound of her voice.

"Time to celebrate, everyone," shouted Patrick.

"There's champagne in the break room. Come and get it." There was a mass exodus until just Cade sat staring at the monitor, finally able to hear the tones of Ryan's voice.

"Hey, you coming, man?" Ravi stood at the door, his eyebrows raised.

Cade shook his head. "Go ahead. I'll stay here and keep an eye on things."

He wished he could tell Ryan how perfectly it had all worked. How good it was to see her face there. The thought hit him without warning, and he realized the truth of it. Of all the people he knew, she was the one he most wanted to share this success with. She was the one he most wanted to share everything with, the one who made his life complete. Suddenly, abruptly, his whole world shifted on its axis and everything made sense.

Love was the correct term for it. There was no doubt about it, he was in love.

"Hey, bud, you going to stay in here all day or are you going to have a drink with us?" Patrick stood at the door.

"I've got a drink," Cade said, raising the bottle of water he'd opened hours earlier. He didn't take his eyes off of Ryan.

"She's something, isn't she?" Patrick crossed to look over his shoulder at the screen. "You were right. She's got the whole thing down." He stared at Cade. "She's got you, too, doesn't she? You might as well admit it, buddy. You know it's true."

Cade turned to him, shaking his head. "I already figured that one out. The question is, what do I do now? The last time I tried to get ahold of her, she wouldn't take my call."

"Jeez, you are turning into a wuss in your old age. I've never once seen you miss getting something once you've set out to do it."

"Except once." Cade looked at him soberly.

Patrick waved his hand dismissively. "Forget about Alyssa. You and Ryan are made to be together. You fit."

He gave a crooked smile. "Aren't you supposed to be the big negotiator in this group?"

A slow grin spread over Cade's face. "Yeah, I suppose." A crash sounded down in the breakroom. "I think you should go supervise the kids in there before they lose our security deposit for us."

"What, you're not going to help?"

"I wasn't the one who had the big idea of bringing in champagne. I'd say it's your job, partner." Cade reached for the phone. "Besides, I've got other things to take care of."

"HELENE FROST," THE VOICE stated on the phone.

"Helene, it's Cade Douglas."

"Of all the dirty, low-down, rotten, creepy, lowlife things to do." Without pausing for breath, she slipped into a stream of profanity-laced invective that scorched his eardrums.

"All right already, Helene. I probably deserve everything you can say to me, but right now I don't have time."

"Time? Your time means nothing to me, buddy boy, and I intend to do whatever I can to be sure that—"

"Helene!"

The phone line was silent.

"Thank you," Cade said. "Now just hear me out. Yes, I screwed up. I know it, you know it, we all know it. We can make an appointment for you to yell at me next week sometime, but right now I need your help."

Her breath hissed in. "If you think I'm going to lift a finger to he—"

"Yes, I do," he cut her off. "Because it concerns Ryan."

"Don't you even go near her," Helene said venomously.

Cade couldn't quite suppress a grin. "Oh, I intend to do a whole lot more than just go near her—and you're going to help me."

"The hell I am."

"Yes you are, because you know we're right together."

There was a short silence, then he could hear her lighting up. "All right, start talking, but do it quick. And I'm making no promises."

Cade smiled. "At the risk of stating the obvious, I screwed up."

"Screwed up? You crashed and burned."

"Okay, I blew it big time. I didn't know what I was doing. But I do now."

"Oh, really."

"Look, I love Ryan." He was amazed at how easy and right it felt to say it. "I want to be with her for life."

A clapping sound came through the receiver. "Whoopee, let's hear it for Einstein. I could have told you that back in Manhattan."

"Yeah, well, some of us are slow learners."

"And I suppose you've called her to tell her you've seen the light?"

He winced a little. "I've tried. She won't talk to me."

Helene snorted. "I wouldn't either."

"Which is why I need your help."

"Before I do anything, I want to know one thing first." Her voice became intense. "Are you sure you're in love with our girl? Because hurting her once is bad. Hurting her a second time is unforgivable. Make no doubt about it, if you do that I will cut off your family jewels and use them for a key chain. Are you sure about this?"

"I'm more sure of this than of anything in my life."

Her voice brightened. "All right. Tell me what you want me to do. As long as it's good for Ryan, I'll do it. And talk fast."

RYAN DROVE DOWN Massachusetts Avenue looking for her turn, and sighed. The last thing she felt like doing was getting tarted up to meet a publicist who was going to poke her and prod her and trot her out for a populace who couldn't care less. Why couldn't her books succeed on their own merit? Why did she have to brand herself and "develop a publicity plan" and a dozen other things she couldn't care less about right now?

She winced as she pulled up in front of the Copley Plaza Hotel. Of all the places she didn't want to revisit, it was this one, but a meeting was a meeting. Taking a deep breath, she got out of her car and handed the key to the valet. Wishing that Helene hadn't practically ordered her to show up dressed to the nines, she smoothed her dress down and picked her way across the pavement in her heels. Having a chance to see Helene, who was in town for the meeting, was a bonus, but given the way she felt right now, it was a small one at best. It might have been two weeks since Cade had broken things off with her, but that didn't mean the situation was any easier.

The days had crawled by, leaden and gray. She'd thrown herself feverishly into work, developing lesson plans from concepts she'd been carrying around in her head. At each taping, she waited, heart in her throat, for Cade to arrive. In some ways, she'd been relieved that he hadn't shown up, but part of her longed just to see him again. The void he'd left in her life was unimaginably vast.

She stepped into the rotating doors of the hotel, watching her reflection in the glass panes as she pushed the door and stepped out onto the marble tiles of the lobby. And here she was again, back at the Copley Hotel where it had all started. Where her life had changed forever. She got on the escalator and watched the ground floor fall away.

If she had it to do over, would she wipe it all out, knowing she would erase the heartache she felt and go back to her quiet, calm existence? Knowing that she would wipe away all the moments she'd had with Cade, the passion, the frenzy, the uncertainty, the simple joys?

She shook her head to push the thought away. No, she wouldn't lose a moment of it, not even if it meant wiping away the unrelieved misery that she'd lived through for the past two weeks. It had been the love of a lifetime, the love she'd always imagined. Maybe her only love, but the truth, nevertheless.

She stepped off the escalator behind a giant potted fern and took a deep breath before circling around it. Somehow, it all looked the same, as though she had gone back in time. The same piano player was murdering Harry Nilsson. Another collection of conventioneers was drinking in a corner, laughing raucously. A pair of what looked like honeymooners were entwined with each other in a loving embrace that sent a bitter pang through her heart. She didn't see Helene anywhere, though. Ryan gave a sigh and started to turn away toward the bank of house phones.

And then she saw him, sitting on a couch, an empty glass at his elbow. He raised a hand to beckon her.

Cade…

Her knees turned to water.

Walk, dammit, she commanded herself. She was not going to make a fool out of herself by turning into a basket case. She'd go over and say a cordial hello, show him that she could play the game also, that she could act like it had meant nothing to her. Ryan swallowed and crossed the bar toward him. It would all be so much easier if her heart weren't breaking.

He watched her approach and felt emotion surge through him. How could he have been so stupid as to miss all she was to him? How could he have thought for a moment that what he felt was just infatuation? It was so much bigger, so much more than that. He prayed that he hadn't already lost her.

He was still stunningly good-looking, Ryan thought, even when he was sitting in the bar where they'd met, probably looking to pick up a woman just like he'd picked her up. She tried for a smile that failed miserably. ''Hello.'' She settled for the fact that her voice hardly shook.

''Small world.''

"Yes, well, I'm meeting someone, who I expect will be showing up any minute."

"Not here yet, though?" He looked at her inquiringly, then nodded. "In that case, why don't you let me buy you a drink? Maybe a martini? I seem to recall you like them."

Ryan flushed. "No thanks. It didn't wind up working out too well last time."

"Really." His eyes were dark under the slashes of his brows. "I thought it worked out amazingly well. So well I didn't trust myself to believe in it." He reached out for her hand and drew her down to the couch. "So well I got scared and tried to end the best thing that had ever happened to me."

The combination of his words and his touch made her dizzy. "What do you mean?"

He pulled her hand to his mouth and pressed his lips to her palm, the caress made up of equal parts pain, longing, and devotion. He raised his eyes to hers. "I mean I love you. I have for weeks, maybe since the night we met. I was just too paranoid to believe in it."

The breath left her lungs. She heard him through a roaring in her ears.

"You tried to tell me what we were to each other. Patrick tried to tell me, but I just couldn't see it." She looked pale, her eyes huge. He thought about stopping, but he had to get it out. "I couldn't see it until yesterday, when we went live, and everybody in the room was jumping up and down—and the one person I wanted to share it with was you, the person I'd tried to push out of my life. And I realized what I was throwing away." He leaned his forehead against her hands. "I love you so much, Ryan. I miss you, being with you, talking with you, just knowing you're near. And I want to be with you for life. I know I was an idiot, that I hurt you, but I figured it out. Just tell me I figured it out in time."

Ryan felt like she'd been spun around by an amusement park ride, the kind that left you dizzy and giddy and breathless. One moment her world was gray and worn, now it was sparkling with promise. How could everything have turned around to be so utterly right? She saw Cade's eyes on hers, strained and intent, waiting.

Waiting for an answer from her, she realized with a jolt. Okay. The thing to do was to be casual, classy, self-possessed *oh my god* just smile and tell him thank you and *oh my god, he said he loves me*— "Yes!" She laughed, and threw her arms around him, and then their mouths were hungry on one another's, saying in seconds all the words they'd say to each other when they could stand to stop.

Ryan came up for air first, the laughter bubbling up again. "God, we should stop this. I'm supposed to meet Helene and some publicist here. That's all I need is for them to find me making out in the lobby."

He stuck his tongue in his cheek. "I wouldn't worry about that too much. You're not the only one who can spin a yarn."

"What do you…" She stared at him as understanding dawned. "You mean this is all a setup?"

He grinned unrepentantly. "Well, you wouldn't take my calls and I figured I had to find a way to get through to you. I couldn't go another day without you." He pulled her close for a hot, hard kiss. "And I don't intend to do without you one day more."

"What do you want to do, then?"

Cade smiled down at her and pulled her to her feet. "Let's go upstairs and you can tell me a story."

Write what you know, Ryan thought as they crossed to the elevators. The idea of a muse had succeeded beyond Helene's wildest dreams. She knew love, now, she knew romance. And now she knew happy endings too.

HARLEQUIN®
Temptation.

Look for bed, breakfast and more...!

COOPER'S CORNER

*Some of your favorite Temptation authors are
checking in early at Cooper's Corner Bed and Breakfast*

In May 2002:

**#877 *The Baby and the Bachelor*
Kristine Rolofson**

In June 2002:

**#881 *Double Exposure*
Vicki Lewis Thompson**

In July 2002:

**#885 *For the Love of Nick*
Jill Shalvis**

In August 2002 things heat up even more at
Cooper's Corner. There's a whole year of intrigue
and excitement to come—twelve fabulous books
bound to capture your heart and mind!

**Join all your favorite Harlequin authors
in Cooper's Corner!**

HARLEQUIN®
Makes any time special®

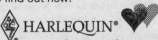

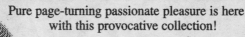